I0820001

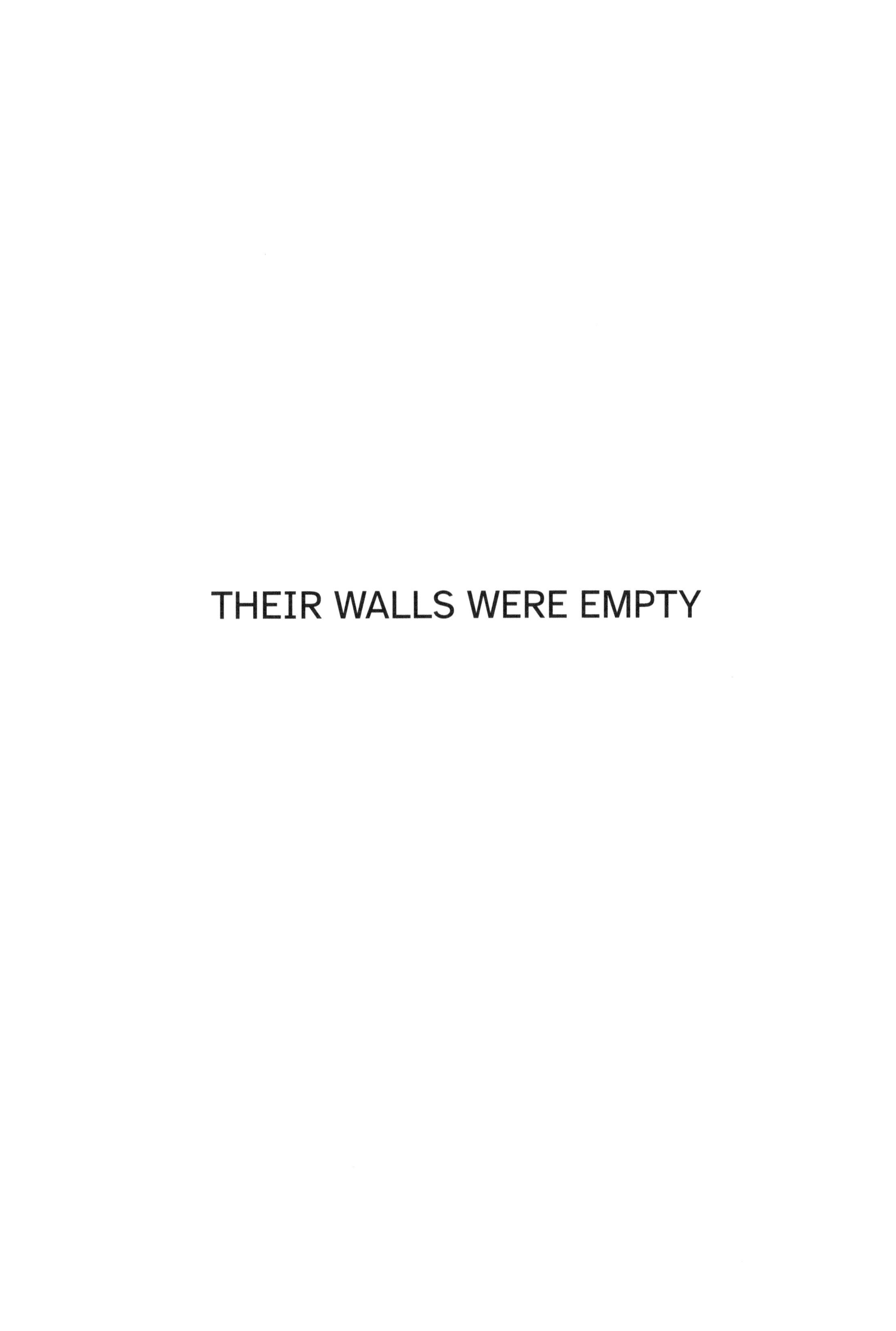

THEIR WALLS WERE EMPTY

ALSO BY P.D. WORKMAN

Zachary Goldman Mysteries

She Wore Mourning

His Hands Were Quiet

She Was Dying Anyway

He Was Walking Alone

They Thought He was Safe

He Was Not There

Her Work Was Everything

She Told a Lie

He Never Forgot

She Was At Risk

He Drowned in Memory

Their Walls Were Empty

They Came for Him (Coming Soon)

Kenzie Kirsch Medical Thrillers

Unlawful Harvest

Doctored Death

Dosed to Death

Gentle Angel

Rushin' Death (Coming Soon)

Posed for Death (Coming Soon)

Death of a Corpse (Coming Soon)

Parks Pat Mysteries

Out with the Sunset

Long Climb to the Top

Dark Water Under the Bridge

Immersed in the View

Skimming Over the Lake

Hazard of the Hills

And more at pdworkman.com

THEIR WALLS WERE EMPTY

ZACHARY GOLDMAN MYSTERIES #12

P.D. Workman

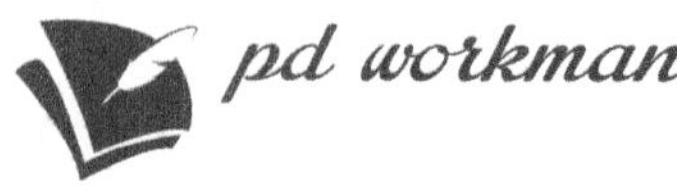

Copyright © 2022 by P.D. Workman

All rights reserved.

No part of this book may be reproduced in any form or by any electronic or mechanical means, including information storage and retrieval systems, without written permission from the author, except for the use of brief quotations in a book review.

ISBN: 9781774682586 (KDP Hardcover)

ISBN: 9781774682579 (KDP Paperback)

ISBN: 9781774682593 (KDP Large Print)

ISBN: 9781774682609 (Lulu Paperback)

ISBN: 9781774682616 (Kindle)

ISBN: 9781774682623 (ePub)

For those who would do anything for family

CHAPTER 1

Zachary sat bolt upright in the bed, gasping for breath. The room was dark and he was disoriented. He felt around him for something that he had lost, desperate to lay hold of whatever it had been. A key? A coin? A baby that had slipped out of his grasp. It was important that he find it before it was lost to him forever. He slid his hands under the covers, under the pillow. He encountered Kenzie beside him, but it was a minute before he knew who it was and that she wasn't the thing he had lost.

"Zachary?" Kenzie's voice was sleepy. "What's wrong? Are you okay?"

"It's... no... I lost it..."

"Lost what, hon'?" Kenzie stirred. She turned over to face him, reaching out to touch him in the dark. A hand on his side, then his chest, which was still heaving from his gasps, his heart pounding so hard and fast he was sure she could feel it right under her fingers. "Hey. It's okay. You had a dream."

"I know, but I needed... I needed to hold on to..." He couldn't even remember what it was, that wisp of a dream that had become concrete in his hands that he had been determined to hold on to this time. Not to let it fall from his grasp and dissolve into nothingness again.

"Shh. It's fine," Kenzie murmured. "Try to go back to sleep."

"No. It's here somewhere. I just have to find it..."

He again slid his fingers under his pillow, looking for it. Frustrated, he reached over to the nightstand and turned on the lamp. Kenzie fell back, covering her eyes with her arm and making an irritated sound.

"Sorry. It's here. It's here somewhere." Zachary lifted up his pillow and looked underneath. He slid out of the bed and pulled back his blankets. There was nothing there. No sign of the precious thing he had lost.

What had it been?

He was anxious. How could he have lost it so quickly? It had been in his hands.

Kenzie lowered her arm slowly and was watching him. “It’s just part of the dream,” she assured him. “It just left you disoriented. That happens sometimes. It might be a side effect of your sleep aid.”

Zachary sat back down on the mattress, feeling bereft. What had he lost?

“I hate this feeling. It can’t just be the dream.”

“Have you had it before? I know sometimes I have part of a dream that sticks with me for a few extra seconds, and it can be a little freaky.”

“Yes.”

“Just take a few minutes to calm down.”

Zachary looked around the room, still sure that he must have missed something. He looked down at the floor to see if something had fallen off of the bed, trying not to let Kenzie see that he was still searching for the lost thing.

"Is everything okay?" he asked her. Though he had woken her up, so she probably didn't know any better than he did. "Did something happen that woke me up? A noise?"

Kenzie appeared to be listening, trying to catch any stray noise that might have startled Zachary awake. A siren in the distance. A tree branch rubbing against the side of the house in the wind. They both listened, but didn't hear anything unusual. Just the usual noises that houses made. Hot air vents. The occasional creaks and pops. Nothing unusual.

Zachary rubbed his eyes.

"Tyrrell," he said suddenly. He turned his head, looking around the room, as if Tyrrell might be there. But he hadn't slept in the same room as his younger brother since he was ten and the house had burned down, and he and Tyrrell had been sent to separate foster families. But Tyrrell was back in his life now, had been back in it for just over a year. And Zachary had brought him home to stay with them while they tried to help him get into a treatment program.

But of course, he wasn't in the bedroom. He was in the guest room, where he had been staying for a few days.

"I have to go see if he's okay."

Kenzie didn't object, just sat there rubbing her eyes. She probably knew better than to argue with him. Knew that when he got into this mood, she couldn't tell him anything. He needed to see Tyrrell, to know that he was okay. To know that he wasn't the thing that Zachary had lost and was still searching for.

Zachary pulled on a pair of pajama pants he had left crumpled on the floor and went to the guest room to make sure that Tyrrell was still there. What if he had left? What if that was what had woken Zachary up, his subconscious brain alert to the fact that if Tyrrell left, he might be in danger. From himself, if not from an outside threat.

He tapped lightly on the guest room door but knew that Tyrrell wouldn't answer it. He would either be gone, or he would be deeply asleep. Not sitting there waiting for Zachary to check in on him and make sure that he was okay. He turned the door handle slowly to try to keep it from squeaking or making any other noise and, when it had turned all the way, pushed it slowly forward.

The room was dark and still. If Tyrrell had gone, he hadn't left a light on behind him to draw attention to the fact that he wasn't there . Zachary tiptoed into the room, trying not to awaken his brother, if he were still there. His eyes had to adjust to the dark again after having turned on the lamp in the master bedroom.

There was a lump on the bed. Tyrrell? Or a couple of pillows and some blankets shaped to look like he was still sleeping in the bed? A juvenile trick, but one that Tyrrell might have used anyway, if he didn't want Zachary to know if he had left.

Zachary reached out and touched the blankets. He expected to feel it all give under his fingers, squashed flat by his touch, but he encountered resistance. Someone was curled up under the blankets. Tyrrell had not snuck out.

Zachary breathed a sigh of relief. For the first time since he had gasped himself awake, his breathing started to slow and settle. More convinced now that no one was in danger, and that the feelings of loss and dread were just that—feelings, artifacts of the dream, as Kenzie had suggested.

"What? Zachary?" Tyrrell turned over in the bed to face him. "What's wrong? What is it?"

"Nothing. Nothing wrong. Sorry. I heard a noise. Wanted to make sure you were okay."

"I'm okay, bro. Just sleeping. Like you should be."

"Yeah. Sorry. I'll go back to bed. You go back to sleep too."

"I plan to," Tyrrell agreed dryly.

Zachary gave his arm a little squeeze, to reassure Tyrrell and himself that everything really was okay, then retraced his steps, closing the guest room door behind him and rejoining Kenzie.

She was dozing even with the bedroom lamp on. Zachary felt bad for waking her up, especially on a work night when she should be able to sleep all the way through and get all of the rest that she needed to be fresh at work.

He sat down on the edge of the bed again, easing down slowly in an effort not to jar her awake again. She made a murmured sound, not really awake, but knowing that he was there.

He probably wouldn't be able to get back to sleep again. And even if he could, he would probably have another nightmare and another waking where he couldn't fully separate himself from the sticky stuff of his dreams. If he stayed in bed, he would probably keep waking Kenzie up again, and she needed her sleep more than he needed his. He was used to operating on just a few hours of sleep.

He turned off the lamp and waited for a moment to see whether that had woken her up again.

“Everything okay?” Kenzie murmured.

“Yeah. It’s fine. Sorry. I didn’t mean to wake you up again.”

“Don’t worry about it. Tyrrell is okay?”

“He’s sleeping. Shouldn’t have woken him up.”

“Mmm.”

Zachary rubbed Kenzie’s shoulder for a minute so that she would think that he was also settling in to go to sleep and would drop off faster. Then, like after putting a baby to sleep, he got back to his feet very slowly so that she wouldn’t be aware of the shift in the mattress and wake back up again. Her breaths continued, long and slow and even.

CHAPTER 2

Zachary adjourned to the living room, which operated as his office and central hub. He sat down, turned on the TV, found a movie to provide some low background noise, then opened his laptop on his mobile desk. He had checked his email before going to bed, so he knew there wouldn't be much more there. Mostly spam. Not a lot of people emailed him overnight.

After glancing over the subject lines, he closed the email inbox and started to go through his project folders, seeing what he could find to keep him occupied for a few hours. There was a backlog due to the amount of time he had spent in the hospital and then searching for Tyrrell. Zachary had only been back at it again for a few days, so there was plenty for him to catch up on.

It was the first year that he had worked with Heather, his older sister, and she had kept things running while he had been in the hospital. She was a remarkably efficient manager. She had conducted skip tracing and done the easier computer work, had sent out bills, collected on some of the delinquent accounts, and generally kept clients happy while Zachary had been unable to tend to his business. He had thought that his PI business would forever be a one-man business, but it was nice to have someone else helping out. He probably wasn't paying Heather enough. He might have to task her with researching how much he should actually be paying her. Her husband was a bookkeeper and probably had sources for that kind of thing. Heather mostly liked having something to do, since she didn't really need the money as much as she did something to fill the empty hours while her husband was at his own job.

The movie playing on the TV helped to cover up any night noises the house was still making but was not interesting enough for Zachary to pay any attention to it as he did some deep research and looked at the insurance investigation files that Heather had opened for him. He didn't really like trying to catch people defrauding their insurance companies. Still, it was, at least, better than chasing after errant husbands. Or wives. He had made a significant shift away from adultery investigations in the past two years, and he was glad of that.

Less surveillance, fewer lives ruined by his pictures, and more time spent on more constructive investigations that might actually make someone happy.

By the time he heard Kenzie up using the shower, the movie had ended. Or maybe two movies; he wasn't sure, since he hadn't actually been watching or listening to any of the action. He got up from the couch, where he had been sitting in the same position for too long, stretched his shoulders and back, and wandered into the kitchen. He put coffee grinds in the hopper, set the carafe under the spout, and started the coffee brewing. He helped himself to a cup once it was finished and went back to his computer, where he checked out his social networks and email again until Kenzie was out of the shower.

She smiled at him, her bright red lipstick looking particularly kissable and dark curls bouncing around her head. "How long have you been up? I didn't hear you get up."

Zachary shrugged. "A few hours."

"You didn't get up after that dream, did you? You got back to sleep for a couple of hours?"

Zachary shrugged and didn't answer to confirm or deny. "There is coffee in the kitchen."

"I can smell it. Thanks."

He followed her into the kitchen, where they worked side by side for a few minutes to prepare their breakfasts. Nothing fancy. A granola bar and yogurt for Zachary and toast with marmalade for Kenzie. And coffee. Then they sat down for their morning visit.

Zachary hadn't realized until they had brought Tyrrell back just how much he valued those quiet breakfast visits. The mornings that Tyrrell woke up early and was prowling around the house and getting his own breakfast or chatting while they were getting theirs, Zachary tended to feel flustered and crowded and just wanted their space back again. But that was selfish. Tyrrell needed them. So Zachary said nothing, but still felt irritated by Tyrrell's presence if he got up for breakfast and much preferred the quiet start with Kenzie when he could get it.

Kenzie watched Zachary open his chocolate chip granola bar in preparation for his breakfast. She smiled, nodding her approval. "So nice to see you eating again. This med cocktail is better for that reason, for sure."

Zachary nodded. It was nice not to be so nauseated in the morning. Much easier to eat if he didn't have to fight his own body to get the food down. And while his appetite still probably wasn't where it should be and he didn't feel hungry most of the time, it was better than it had been with the meds he'd been on the last few years. Which should help him get up to a healthy weight much faster than usual and make his doctors happy.

"It's working okay in other areas too, I think." It was impossible to tell whether it would help him get less depressed before the next Christmas, but that was almost a year away, so he didn't have to worry about it yet. One of the open questions was whether it would help with his obsessive thoughts about

Bridget, his ex-wife, and the compulsions to check in on her or follow her. He knew that he had disappointed Kenzie by giving in to those compulsions again when Bridget had been pregnant, convinced that she could not take care of herself and the twins and that she would need him there, close by. He had been the one to call for help when she had collapsed in the garden the day she had gone into labor, so he hadn't been wrong.

Since getting out of the hospital, he had been able to keep those obsessions reined in. But he had been trying to find Tyrrell, so he'd had something else to occupy his anxious brain. Whether he would be able to keep those thoughts at bay as he got back into the normal routine was still uncertain. He was hopeful that the new cocktail would help. And yet worried that it wouldn't.

CHAPTER 3

Tyrrell was all right when you looked in on him last night?" Kenzie asked.

They had both kept their voices low so as not to wake him up. Like he was the child and they were his parents, and they wanted to have some time together before he got up and started making demands. But Tyrrell wasn't really that demanding. Not really. The first few days had not been easy as he withdrew from alcohol, but he was doing better now.

"Yeah. He was asleep. Said everything was okay."

"He was asleep but told you that everything was okay?"

"I did wake him for a minute. But he went right back to sleep after. Like when I woke you up."

Kenzie nodded, conceding that she had gotten back to sleep again fairly quickly.

"Do you think... that we'll be able to find the right placement for him?" Zachary asked tentatively.

He had thought that it would just be a matter of finding a good treatment center, calling them, and dropping Tyrrell off. He'd never been involved in the administrative end of getting someone into a program like that. But while it sounded like it should be simple, it wasn't. There were a lot of different programs to look at, weighing the pros and cons of each. Of course, one factor to consider was the cost, but Kenzie had said that didn't matter. She would cover it. She had a trust fund and didn't use it very much, so she was happy to cover the expenses of getting Tyrrell clean and sober again.

Maybe with a private program, one that was more expensive, he would get the quality of care that he needed to stay sober long-term. People recovered from addiction. It was possible. But Zachary knew they couldn't force Tyrrell into anything. Even once they found a program that seemed like it was meant to be, they would be faced with the waiting lists. Almost all of the facilities—all of the good, quality programs—had waiting lists. Sometimes waiting lists were months long. Tyrrell needed help now, before he went on another binge.

And when they did find a program that looked promising and was able to take Tyrrell, they would need to talk him into it. If Tyrrell didn't like something about the facility, he didn't have to go. And if he did go, he could just duck out partway through, and Zachary would be left in the position of having to track him down again. Or to let him go.

"I'm waiting for a callback from three different places right now," Kenzie informed Zachary. She told him the name of each of the programs. "If we can get him into any one of those... I think it would be really good. They have good recovery rates in the industry. Good reviews by patients and industry watchdogs."

"And you think that Tyrrell would go into any of them?"

"I hope so. No promises, but he seems like he's willing to try out anything that we think might work."

Zachary turned his head as he heard noises from the guest room. Tyrrell was apparently getting up. Zachary didn't ask anything further about the programs, not wanting Tyrrell to come out of the bedroom and hear them discussing him. He must know that they talked about him, but it still didn't feel right to let him walk in on a discussion about him.

Kenzie took a bite of her toast. "I'm sure we can work something out. It may just take a little longer than we had thought at the start. I naively thought that it would just be a matter of looking up a facility in the yellow pages, giving them a call, and taking him in."

"The yellow pages?" Zachary questioned. "How ancient are you?"

"They still have yellow pages... I think..."

He chuckled. He had no idea whether they still had the big yellow phone books that had been around during his youth. He hadn't seen one in years. Most of his investigative work was in online databases and web searches. Not opening up a book filled of minuscule type.

“Going to be a busy day today?” he asked her.

“Things are always jumping at the office.”

“That’s sort of creepy, knowing you work in the morgue.”

Kenzie laughed, nodding. They both enjoyed a morbid sense of humor about her working in the medical examiner’s office.

“How about you? Feel like you’re getting things under control?”

“It’s a lot easier with Heather helping out. She learned a lot of strategies for ADHD when she was raising her kids, so she has good ideas. I’m not overwhelmed and trying to get everything done at once; I can just work on a certain set of files or tasks... easier to focus on one thing at a time and not be distracted by all the rest.”

"That's good. There's no point in trying to get weeks' worth of jobs all done in a day or two. That would land <u>me</u> in the hospital."

Zachary nodded. "I could use a couple of bigger files. I don't like to just work on small investigations. I like to have one or two that I can dig my teeth into and then work on the smaller ones around the edges. But of course, anything that was big and couldn't wait, someone else took. So it might be a few weeks before I have the balance I like."

"It will come to you."

"Yeah. It will." He found it essential to say 'no' to the cases he didn't want so he would have the time and energy to take on the cases he did. They tended to come to him when he had room for them. He would keep plugging away at the little ones, his bread and butter, until the right cases came along.

Kenzie finished her toast and was licking off her fingers and swigging down the last of her coffee. “Well, I should be getting to it, I guess.”

“You want lunch?”

She hesitated. Zachary had noticed that even though she didn’t like to use the sandwich vending machine at work, she also tended not to take the time to make lunch for herself before work. Then she was forced to either get something from the machine or go out and find something else. “No... I’ll work something out today. We need to go grocery shopping soon. I need to make up a proper list... figure out what I want to make and what I can take to work.”

“If you have a list, I could go pick stuff up.”

“No... I don’t yet.”

And when she did, she probably wouldn’t give it to the most distractible person in the relationship. Zachary was pretty good with lists when he had to physically check items off, just not so good at the kind he had to keep in his head. But Kenzie probably thought he was bad at both.

"If you write one, I'll buy everything on it. I won't only get half of them and forget the rest."

Kenzie eyed him. "Hmm. I might have to test that."

"Good. At least give me a chance to show you I can."

Tyrrell came down the hall and into the kitchen as Kenzie was putting her dishes into the dishwasher. He rubbed his eyes, looking remarkably like the six-year-old Zachary remembered him as, other than the stubble. His dark hair and eyes were similar to Zachary's own; genetic traits inherited from their father. Zachary's hair was kept in a short buzz cut so that he didn't have to worry about taking care of it, and Tyrrell's was a bit longer.

"Morning," he greeted, yawning. He headed for the coffee pot and poured himself a mug.

“How are you doing this morning?” Kenzie asked as she pulled winter clothes from the mudroom just outside the kitchen and prepared to leave.

“Fine, I guess.” Tyrrell gave a half-smile and shrugged.

“We’ll catch up later.” Kenzie gave them both a little wave. Zachary stepped forward to give her a farewell kiss, and then she went through the door to the garage and was gone.

Zachary freshened his cup of coffee with what remained in the pot.

“Did you wake me up last night?” Tyrrell asked, frowning at Zachary.

“Yeah, sorry. I had a dream.”

Tyrrell nodded and didn’t ask anything else about it. He probably assumed that Zachary’s dream had been about the fire. And maybe it had been; Zachary couldn’t remember enough about it to be sure. He still dreamed of the fire frequently, especially when stressed.

And despite what he would have liked to say, having Tyrrell there did make things more stressful. Tyrrell wasn't a child, but Zachary felt like he needed to take care of him anyway. Make sure that he was kept busy, wasn't thinking too much about the past, didn't start thinking too much about his mistakes so that he wouldn't begin binge-drinking again before they managed to get him into detox. Someone needed to be there all the time; he wasn't as free to come and go as he would have liked.

Tyrrell drank his coffee, eyes far away. Zachary wondered if he were thinking of the fire too. Or was he somewhere else? Maybe beating himself up for the ways he had failed his children. Or remembering the things that had happened when they were both children. He had confessed to Zachary that whenever they were together for any length of time, Tyrrell started to remember what things were like at home. The abuses and neglect that they had suffered. Zachary wished that it wasn't true. And that Tyrrell hadn't told him that. He wanted to be with his younger brother and didn't want his nearness to cause Tyrrell distressing memories.

"We should go out today," Tyrrell suggested, maybe picking up on Zachary's itch to leave the house and not just to stay home playing the part of the responsible brother.

"Out where?"

'"I don't know. We can go out and do something. See the sights. Grab a burger. Go to a hockey game."

Zachary didn't know how many tourist places were open during January. And of course, hockey wouldn't be happening until the evening, and he didn't think leaving Kenzie alone while he took Tyrrell to the nearest NHL game was quite what she had in mind when she had suggested Tyrrell could stay at the house until he could get into a detox program.

“Maybe we can go to the grocery store to pick some things up for Kenzie if she puts a list together. But I have other work to do for now. I have to get back to my business.”

Tyrrell sighed loudly and retreated to the guest room with his cup of coffee.

CHAPTER 4

Zachary tried to ignore Tyrrell's presence in the house and focus on his work as if he were the only one there. He wasn't there to babysit Tyrrell, other than keeping him away from any booze if he could. Tyrrell was a grown man and was responsible for himself. If he wanted to shut himself away in the guest room all day because Zachary wouldn't take him out anywhere, he was welcome to do that. Zachary had already taken a week away from his business to find Tyrrell and pull him away from his drunken binge, which meant Zachary was more behind than usual after his Christmas break. He needed to get some work done.

He worked through various items on his list, trying to stick to the stuff Heather had identified as the most important and profitable. Still, he did do some smaller tasks in between because he enjoyed them or they were for a client that he particularly liked.

He wasn't sure what time it was when the doorbell rang. Zachary blinked and looked around, waiting at first to see if anyone else would answer the door. But it was apparently still early enough in the day that Kenzie was not back. Zachary wondered at first whether Tyrrell had ordered pizza or called a friend to come over, but apparently not, because there was no sign that Tyrrell was coming out of the guest room to answer the door.

Which left it to Zachary.

He pushed himself up off of the couch and stretched his back, shoulders, and neck. He knew that hunching over his laptop sitting on the couch was not making his body happy. He should get a proper ergonomic chair, a standing desk, or whatever was the newest ergonomic solution.

On a typical day, he would go out to check a few of the errands on his list off. But he didn't want to leave Tyrrell there by himself and couldn't think of a script that would convince Tyrrell to come with him and be happy about it. He couldn't just tell the other man that he didn't trust him to be home by himself and he couldn't drag him around like a puppy on a leash. Tyrrell had been interested in going out, but to something entertaining and interesting for him, not a supply run or to investigate the victim of an accident to see if they really did have a debilitating back injury.

Zachary squinted through the peephole, which did not give him a very clear image of the person outside the front door. He should probably install one of those doorbell cameras or a proper security camera so that they could see anyone who came to the door properly and not have to worry about opening the door to a stranger or to someone dangerous who had followed Zachary or Kenzie home. Zachary knew only too well how easy it was to follow someone.

The man on the doorstep was dressed in a suit. Zachary couldn't see his face well, but it didn't ring any alarm bells. He didn't look like a hood or cartel member, just like a businessman.

He opened the door and looked at the man's face for a moment before realizing why it was familiar to him. He had, Zachary thought, lost a little weight since the last time he had seen him.

"Walter. Uh... Mr. Kirsch. Kenzie is at work. She isn't home."

"I didn't expect her to be. I was hoping to talk to you about something."

"Oh... okay. Come on in." Zachary stepped back to allow him in.

Kenzie's father was still a stranger to him. They had only met a couple of times, and although Zachary knew that Walter loved his daughter, she had been quite resistant to Zachary meeting him. The last time Walter had come to the house, he had hidden a bug in Kenzie's purse to listen in on her conversations. Not something that inspired confidence. Zachary would have to watch him like a hawk and sweep for bugs again after he was gone.

"How are you feeling?" Walter asked, looking Zachary over.

Zachary wondered whether he was asking because of the viral infection that had landed both Kenzie and Zachary in the hospital following the Halloween ball or whether he knew about Zachary's depression and being in the hospital again over Christmas.

"I'm good," he said, keeping it vague. "They got everything straightened out. Modern medicine is a wonder."

"Good, good. Glad to hear that!"

"Did Kenzie know that you were coming today?" Zachary asked as he sat down on the couch and Walter settled in one of the easy chairs.

Walter waved away the question without answering it. "Kenzie said that you're a private investigator. That you're quite good. I looked into it, and from what I could see from the publicity you've had, she's right."

Zachary shrugged. "I've had some cases that have gone public, so that's good for my reputation." He didn't like to brag about himself, to say how good he was at what he did. He probably couldn't be classified as a great detective. He was dogged. When others had stopped, he continued to look and didn't always take things at face value. Those were good traits for a PI. They helped him turn up clues that the police or other investigators hadn't been able to.

"Modest too," Walter said, shaking his head in amusement. "Well, good for you. I don't really need to ask you if you're good because, as I said, I've already looked you up and checked with some references." He smiled. It made Zachary think of a shark's toothy smile and flat, dead eyes. Walter was a politician, Zachary knew. A lobbyist. Very wealthy, very powerful. Not the kind of man who really needed to go to his daughter's partner for anything.

"How can I help you?" he asked politely. He wasn't sure he would help Walter with anything. The last time he had come calling, it had been to pump Kenzie for information on a case that she was working on and to pressure her to use her influence in the medical examiner's office.

Kenzie had not obliged.

And she had been right about that particular case. The governor hadn't wanted the bad publicity that a rogue virus would have if word got out about it. An outbreak before an election would have been bad for him. He was lucky that Dr. Wiltshire and Kenzie had been able to take action when they had, or the consequences would have been much worse.

“I don't want you to think that this is anything big or political,” Walter cautioned. “If it was, I would hire a bigger firm, one with good optics and a lot more power behind it. And Kenzie didn't want me to involve you in anything relating to my lobbying; I know that. She didn't want me to bring my politics to the table, so to speak.”

Zachary nodded. It sounded like he and Kenzie had already discussed the matter, which helped him relax. He didn't want to do anything behind her back. To be seen as colluding with the enemy. While he was sure Kenzie loved her father, he knew that she didn't get along well with either of her parents and definitely did not trust her father's politics or anything relating to his lobbying.

"In fact, it's so small maybe you won't even want to get involved," Walter said with a shrug. "Maybe it wouldn't be worth your time. It would be a favor to me."

Zachary wrinkled his brow at this. Walter was certainly wealthy enough to pay if Zachary believed Kenzie or the magazines that had profiled Walter.

Walter may have looked into Zachary's reputation, but Zachary had also looked into Walter's. He needed to know what he could about Walter Kirsch and his ex-wife Lisa Cole Kirsch. It wasn't like Kenzie would tell him any more than the bare essentials.

Walter chuckled. "I don't mean that I wouldn't pay you. Of course I will pay your standard—or even premium—rates. I just mean this wouldn't be a highly profitable case for you, and it wouldn't be high-profile."

"I see." So far, everything Walter had to say was as clear as mud. Zachary leaned forward, his elbows on his knees. "Why don't you just tell me about the case, then?"

Walter hesitated. Zachary glanced around the room, waiting to see if he would begin.

"If it's so confidential that you can't even give me the broad strokes..." Zachary started.

"No, no. Of course not. I told you that it wasn't a big deal. I just like to... put all my cards on the table first. And all of yours."

"I don't have anything to put on the table yet. I don't even know what you're here about."

"I suppose not. But what I mean is... I need to tell you that this would be more than just a favor. You know, I guess, that MacKenzie and I have not been close the last few years. I did some things that... she can never forgive me for. Nothing to hurt her, I assure you. Nothing intended to hurt anyone. Just some... choices she didn't believe were ethical." Walter paused as if waiting for Zachary to fill in whether he knew the details. Zachary knew little about the rift between Kenzie and her father, other than that it had something to do with Kenzie's deceased sister and some treatment choices that Walter and Lisa had made.

"Go on," Zachary encouraged.

If he were going to put his cards on the table, then it was time to stop guarding them so carefully.

"I would like to mend fences. I would like to be a bigger part of my daughter's life. I don't think that she would let me do anything for her. She has put her trust fund to use, but that isn't really a gift from me; it is a trust her grandparents set up. I don't think she would take any favors from me."

"Uh-huh." Walter was probably right about that.

"So I can't really do anything for her. She would not accept it. But I can hire you to do what you do professionally and pay you your regular rates. That shows her that... I support her choices..."

Zachary nodded again. He could understand Walter reaching out to Kenzie in this way. The lobbyist was used to exchanging favors in politics, giving to a charity that someone supported rather than to them directly, supporting them on a bill they wanted to get through so that they would later support you on yours, and all sorts of other convoluted bartering scenarios that Zachary was sure he would never be able to follow.

"Okay." Walter spread his hands. "So there it is. I know someone who needs a private investigator. I know that my daughter's partner is a private investigator. I want to give him the business in a way that doesn't compromise any of us but shows my daughter that I value her and her partner."

"So, what is this case?"

CHAPTER 5

You're a man who likes to get down to brass tacks," Walter said.

He sat back, smiling, looking more relaxed now that he'd opened up to Zachary. Though he had probably still held a few cards in reserve, if Zachary was right about the kind of person he was. A politician never put all of his cards on the table. He had made his opening play. It was the beginning of the game, not the end.

"There is a little sports bar near the statehouse. Nothing big and fancy, just a little place that I like to go to occasionally to relax and forget all about the world of politics I live in the rest of the time. The one place that I go to just hang out and be me."

Zachary looked at him speculatively. Walter did not strike him as the sports type. Or the "let it all hang out" kind.

"What sports?"

"Hmm?"

"The bar, you go there to watch football?"

Rugby? Polo? What did high-class lobbyists go to sports bars to watch? He couldn't see Walter getting rowdy and cheering on any sport.

"Like any good Vermonter—baseball in the summer and hockey in the winter."

Zachary would explore that later. "Okay. What does this bar need my services for?"

"You're getting ahead of me. I haven't even told you that they do."

Zachary waited.

"Okay." Walter sighed. "Bypass the sentimental stuff. Yes. The bar was recently the victim of a burglary. A smash-and-grab type job."

“They called the police?”

“Sure. But they ran out of leads and aren’t pursuing it. If the stolen items show up at nearby pawn shops, they’ll follow up. But they don’t really care. It’s just a little job for them, and they have better things to do. More important cases. Which is true, of course. I wouldn’t expect them to turn away from murders, kidnappings, or big heists to chase after this little thing. But that doesn’t help my friends at the bar.”

“What was stolen?”

“Memorabilia. You know that type of place—signed jerseys up on the walls, photographs of the winning team. Pennants. Reminders of the glory days.”

“How valuable?”

“Intrinsically, not a lot. That’s why it’s not a big deal to the police. It isn’t like someone stole Babe Ruth’s rookie card. The stuff may run in the thousands, but we’re not talking millions. And a lot of it is worth a lot less than that. People walk off with stuff. If you have anything really valuable, you have to invest in smash-proof cases, security, stuff like that. For a little business, that's a big investment. They want to surround themselves with happy memories, to provide them to the fans. Make it a comfortable, fun place to hang out. It isn't Fort Knox."

"Do you have a list of the stolen items?"

"Does that mean you're taking the case?"

"I'm still exploring what that would involve."

Walter hesitated. "I should retain you before I show you anything."

"Is the list of stolen items confidential? I thought it was just some mid-range sports memorabilia."

Walter considered this. Eventually, he popped open the slim briefcase he had brought in with him and pulled out a few pieces of paper. He handed them over to Zachary.

He looked down the list. There was a column of dollar values, so he could pick out what the higher-priced bits were and then read the descriptions. But he could not read quickly and he would prefer a few minutes without Walter staring at him to peruse the list.

“There is coffee in the kitchen,” he said. “Why don’t you go help yourself to a cup?”

Walter shifted forward in his seat, his eyes still on the list he had given to Zachary.

“You aren’t going to make any copies of that.”

“No.” Zachary thought this a little paranoid. Walter was clearly used to dealing with paperwork that was a lot more privileged than a list of stolen property. “I just want a minute to review this.”

Walter conceded, getting to his feet and walking into the kitchen. He could still keep an eye on Zachary from there and make sure that he didn't make some kind of copy of the information.

"Uh... the pot is empty. Do you want me to make another?" Walter called back to Zachary when he'd had a chance to look at it.

"Oh, yeah. Can you figure out the machine?"

"I practically live out of hotels. I can probably run any coffee machine on the planet."

"Great. Yeah, go ahead and make another pot."

Zachary probably shouldn't have too much coffee, but he could use at least one more cup to fortify himself while discussing the case with Walter. It would help him to keep his focus.

He shut out everything else to focus on the list of items stolen from the sports bar. He was not a big sports fan, so he didn't know what the various items would go for on the street or in nearby pawn shops, so the column of values was helpful. But he worked a lot with insurance companies investigating possible fraud charges and was immediately suspicious of any list of stolen items that had been prepared for an insurance claim, which he assumed was what he held in his hand. Items could be added and values inflated to reduce the company's losses and how much their premiums would go up once they made a claim. They might have only lost half of the things on the list and planned to sell the other half themselves, getting paid by both the buyer and the insurer.

Nothing jumped out at him as being ridiculously overvalued. It didn't make sense to put things on display that would crater your business if someone walked off with them. As Walter had said, they were more middle-of-the-road memorabilia, not the outrageously expensive collector's pieces.

Walter entered the room to refresh the coffee cup on Zachary's side table, then returned the carafe to the kitchen and resumed his seat in the easy chair. Eventually, Zachary put the list to the side and looked at Walter.

"I don't think it is worth your while to hire me."

Walter frowned, his eyebrows coming together and forming a deep crease on his forehead. "Why do you say that?"

"I will need several days to look into it, mileage to get around, maybe a hotel for a night while doing interviews, and meals. I didn't add it all up, but my bills would eat into the value of anything recovered. Better off just letting insurance pay out."

He knew how much he would have to charge for several full days of work. It wouldn't be quick to track down those stolen items. It wouldn't just be a couple of phone calls.

Walter nodded slowly. Then he shrugged. "That really doesn't matter, though. As I said, they have mostly sentimental value, and you can't put a value on that."

"They might not be willing to pay for recovery for something that only has sentimental value."

"They aren't paying. I am. Out of my own pocket. I want to do this for them. Something you do for friends."

"And you're willing to get nothing back for the money."

"That's why I laid my cards on the table," Walter pointed out. "To show you that I'm doing this for Kenzie. That's what I get out of it. And I get the gratitude of my friends. Maybe a few comped beers the next few times I drink there. It's goodwill, not money."

Zachary was not the type of private investigator who was usually hired to make someone look good. He was hired because someone was grieving. Because there had been an injustice done. Because someone had been betrayed or might be perpetrating a fraud. Trying to wrap his head around the fact that Walter didn't actually want anything concrete from the investigation was difficult.

"So, you're willing to take a loss on this."

"It's like giving to a charity," Walter said. "It gives me a good feeling. It makes me look good. It hopefully makes people like me better. Those are things that have value to me. Maybe you'll be able to recover a few of the items on that list and maybe you won't. Maybe you'll be able to give the police a lead on who was involved in the robbery. Or maybe not. But we will at least have put all of our resources into it, so people feel like everything possible was done."

Zachary considered the list again. He looked back at Walter. "So, do you want a budget and a project outline of what I will be doing?"

"No. Just say that you'll take the case and tell me how much of a deposit you'll need to start. I'll give you all of the details I can and the contact information for the bar owners. They can tell you anything I can't answer. And then... you dive right in."

"I do have other cases that I am working on right now, and my brother is staying with us while he tries to get into—get back on his feet. I can't just leave him with Kenzie to deal with. So it may be a slow start. I'll get the information from you, make some phone calls to the owners, and get as much information as I can from here. Lay the groundwork for the investigation before I go there and start making inquiries."

"That all sounds fine." Walter shrugged. "You know the business the best. I don't. I wouldn't even know where to start."

"I'm not going to have results for you in a couple of days."

"Right. I understand."

Zachary took a deep breath. "Well then... okay. I'll look into it."

CHAPTER 6

Zachary heard the guest room door open and looked up. He hoped that Tyrrell wasn't going to come out in his boxers for what he assumed would be a private discussion, but he didn't know what to say to warn Tyrrell that they were not alone.

Tyrrell was dressed. Zachary blew out his breath. Tyrrell looked at Walter and became flustered.

"Oh, sorry, I didn't know you had someone here. You didn't say you were expecting anyone."

"No, it was unexpected. It's okay. Tyrrell, this is Walter Kirsch, Kenzie's father. Walter, my brother Tyrrell."

The two men nodded at each other but did not get close enough to shake hands.

"Uh, just going to get some more coffee," Tyrrell offered. He looked toward the kitchen but didn't move in that direction.

“Maybe I should head over to Starbucks so that I’m out of your way.”

“No,” Zachary’s answer was sharper than he had intended. “We just made a fresh pot. Help yourself.”

Tyrrell still looked like he would have preferred to go out. But Zachary didn’t want him taking off. There was nothing to stop him from changing his mind and going to the liquor store or bar instead of Starbucks. There were fewer temptations to drink if Tyrrell stayed in the house.

Tyrrell probably read all of this in Zachary’s manner, if he hadn’t figured out already that the reason they wanted him at the house was to keep an eye on him and, if possible, to keep him from going out on his own. He grunted in disgust and turned away into the kitchen. Zachary listened to him pour a coffee cup and go through the cupboards again for something to eat or drink. Eventually, there was the sound of a crinkly wrapper being removed. Maybe a granola bar. It was good that Tyrrell was eating solid food again. But Zachary didn't know how long that would last.

Tyrrell headed back to the guest room, eyeing Zachary as he went through the living room. He was not pleased with his prison, even if there were no bars.

Zachary looked back at Walter, sitting there waiting, watching the little drama with interest. When Zachary looked back at him, he smiled. "How much, then?"

"Hmm?"

"Your retainer. Your deposit. How much to get you started on the case?"

"Oh." Zachary considered and gave Walter what he figured was ten percent of an investigation that took three full man-days.

"Do you want it by check? E-transfer?" Walter asked, obviously not concerned by the amount.

"Sure, e-transfer is good."

He gave Walter his email address and Walter went ahead and made the transfer.

"I'll tell you what I know, but it isn't a lot. Not that there is a lot to tell, it wasn't complicated. The bar is named Barnburners, and I'll send you the contact information for the owners so that you can get any additional details from them. It was a late-night burglary. Window smashed in to get access to the inside lock on the door. Alarms go off. The thieves grab everything they can in two or three minutes and run. By the time the security company and police get there, they're gone."

"Did the police have any leads? Fingerprints? Identity of the thieves? A similar theft in the area?"

"You can ask them, but I don't expect they'll tell you anything. The thieves were wearing gloves, so no fingerprints. They had balaclavas on, obscuring their faces. So pretty hard to make any kind of identification."

"The police probably won't talk to me, but they might tell the owners one or two details, if we're lucky."

"Yeah, you can ask Glen and Janice about it. They'll share whatever they have."

"Were there any security cameras?"

"Yes. But as I say, there was no way to identify the culprits."

Zachary nodded. "If there is video footage, I'd like to see it."

"The police got a copy. The owners have it on a hard drive still. They can show it to you when you get there."

"Or maybe before. They could email it or send me a link to their server."

Walter shrugged. "I don't know all of the technical stuff. You'll have to deal with them on it."

“So how were they informed about the theft? Their security company called them?”

“I think so. Must have been either the security company or the police.”

“Right. Late night or early morning?”

“2 a.m. or something like that. A time when they could be pretty sure that no one would be around.”

“Have there been any similar robberies in the area?”

“Not that anyone has mentioned. I assume that if there were a bunch of similar robberies, they would have made a bigger deal of it. If it’s a gang or a series.”

“You would think so. If they noticed that there was a pattern. Sometimes, you have to look pretty closely to find patterns and start to pull them together.”

"You're welcome to do that. At least internet searches make it easy to search the newspapers going back a few months."

Zachary nodded. "Not like in the old days when you had to look them up on microfiche."

Walter laughed. "Was that a shot?"

"Of course not." Zachary grinned. He was old enough to remember going to the library and playing with the microfiche machines. He'd never used them in his private investigations business, but he could remember them being around.

He was pleased to get the case from Walter, with money already in his pocket and a chance to help to reconcile Kenzie with her father. He didn't expect an immediate turnaround in her attitude. Still, it would certainly help that he had come to Zachary and offered him a legitimate job at a good rate. If he needed an investigation done, then why not retain his daughter's partner to do it when that was his business? Most of the people Zachary knew personally would never have a reason to hire a private investigator. Or, if they had a reason to do it, they wouldn't have the money. Walter had both, and it felt pretty good to get such a nice case when he was just getting back on his feet. It would help to cover his losses from the time he had been in the hospital and investigating Tyrrell's disappearance. It wasn't like he had a lot of expenses when he wasn't working, considering he was now living with Kenzie. But he still had the lease on his old apartment, which he intended to get rid of soon, but hadn't gotten around to yet.

"You have my number if you need anything else from me," Walter said. When Zachary was about to object that he didn't, Walter motioned to Zachary's computer. "It's with the e-transfer. My email and phone number. And I'll send you Glen and Janice's information when I get back to my computer. Set up a time with them and they'll show you around Barnburners. You can see where the thieves broke in, where the items they stole were, watch the security video, all of that. You'll have everything the police do. Only, hopefully, you'll be able to make something of it."

"I'll do my best."

CHAPTER 7

Zachary did what preliminary work he could, creating a project folder to save information to and then checking for any online accounts of the burglary. There were no parallel cases mentioned in the news articles. Of course, that didn't mean that there weren't any, but reporters often picked up on patterns of cases before the police did. He found a few PR articles about Barnburners, probably paid articles that talked about the ambiance and what a great place it was for sports fans to hang out. There were a few pictures of the interior in those articles and in the online reviews that he turned to next. He took note of the pictures and other memorabilia he could see on the walls and tables, looking at the list of stolen items to see if he could tell where the thieves had been concentrating their attention.

Kenzie arrived home from work and, after greeting him briefly, she excused herself to shower and change out of her work clothes. Zachary stretched and massaged the back of his neck and decided that he needed a break from the computer as well.

He went down the hall to the guest room and knocked on the door.

“Come in.”

Zachary opened the door. Tyrrell was lying on the bed with a book, pretty much all that he’d been doing since they had brought him home. Zachary wasn’t sure he was even reading them, but might just be using them as a prop to look like he was busy when he wasn’t. Zachary wanted to ask Tyrrell why he wasn’t busy trying to get into a program, to at least put some effort into helping himself, but he bit back the questions. He already knew that Tyrrell was an addict. Asking an addict why they were addicted and weren’t motivated to do anything else was pointless. Tyrrell might want to stop drinking, but he hadn’t had much success with rehab programs, so Zachary could see how that would be demotivating. Kenzie was looking for something. She would find it.

“What’s up, Zachary?”

"Oh. I thought I would order in so that Kenzie can have a break tonight. Do you want pizza? Thai? Something else?"

"I'm not really hungry, and I don't suppose you'll be ordering drinks with any of those."

"No. What will you eat?"

"Anything. I'm not going to reject anything put in front of me. But I'm not very hungry, so it probably won't be a lot."

Usually, Tyrrell was the one telling Zachary that he needed to eat more. Now he was stuck, not wanting to eat anything as he recovered from his latest binge. His body wanted only one thing, and that was the one thing he couldn't have.

"Okay. I think maybe it will be pizza. You're okay with that?"

"Yeah. Nothing too spicy and no anchovies." Tyrrell thumped his chest. "Been dealing with a lot of heartburn."

"Sure. No problem."

Zachary left Tyrrell to his reading and opened the door to Kenzie's en suite bathroom, full of steam from her shower.

"Kenz, I was going to order pizza. Is that okay with you?"

She let out a little sigh. "Yeah, that would be great. I'm beat and was not looking forward to trying to pull something together for supper. How about Tyrrell? I assume he's good with pizza?"

"He says he's okay with anything and said yes to pizza. Not too spicy and no anchovies."

"Works for me. Half cheese, half veg?"

"Okay."

He started to close the door, then paused when he realized she was speaking again. "Thanks, Zach. I should be out by the time it gets here. But if I'm not..."

Zachary chuckled. It was a good thing she had a big water heater. "I'll come get you. And squeeze the excess water out."

* * *

Kenzie was out of the shower by the time the pizza got there. She was dressed in her warm plaid jammies, and they opened up the pizza in the living room instead of sitting at the table. It was nice to just have a more casual evening. Zachary felt like there was some tension among the two of them due to the added presence of Tyrrell.

Tyrrell helped himself to the first slice of pizza, since Kenzie insisted that he have the first pick as their guest. “Thanks. This looks great.” Tyrrell plopped the large slice onto his plate. “Met your dad today.”

Kenzie held the pizza out to Zachary for him to take a piece, her brows drawing together in a frown that mimicked her father’s.

“What?”

“Your dad,” Tyrrell repeated.

Kenzie was sure to be wondering whether Tyrrell was delusional, or she was.

“Walter came by during the day while you were at work,” Zachary told Kenzie as casually as possible. It was clear that she hadn’t been expecting Walter to stop in, even though he had said that he had first approached her and talked to her about the case. A great detective Zachary was to not even question it.

“Walter. Why did he come here? He knows I work during the day.”

Zachary nodded. He picked the smallest piece of pizza and put it on his paper plate. “He wasn’t looking for you. He was talking to me about a case.”

Kenzie put the pizza box down and looked at Zachary, pulling her feet up onto the couch as she settled in to eat and relax. But her expression told him that she wasn’t relaxed.

“Why would he be talking to you about a case? What case?”

Zachary cleared his throat. “A burglary at a sports bar in Montpelier.”

“What would he have to do with that? That doesn’t make any sense.”

Zachary took a bite of his pizza and glanced over at Tyrrell, nervous about having a conversation with Kenzie about her father in front of Tyrrell. He didn’t want Tyrrell to think that he and Kenzie didn’t get along, didn’t want Kenzie to feel like she had to air her dirty laundry in front of him, and really didn’t want to get into a discussion about fathers at all while Tyrrell was around. Not after Zachary’s recent reunion with their father.

“He asked me if I would look into the case. The police aren’t getting far on it but, of course, it is not a high priority. Not really valuable merchandise, not part of a series of robberies, so it is way down on their list.”

"But what does he have to do with it?"

"I guess it's the bar he likes to hang out at to relax. He knows the owners, and he wanted to do something for them."

And for Kenzie. But he didn't want her to feel like she was being manipulated. Or that Zachary had anything to do with manipulating her.

"He hangs out at a sports bar," Kenzie repeated in a tone of disbelief.

"That's what he said. It's called Barnburners," Zachary added lamely, as if that might make a difference. But he did hope that it would ring a bell with her. Maybe she would remember that he used to go there when he was a kid or that family friends had started it up.

"That's news to me."

"Well… you guys haven't exactly been close the last few years. It could be somewhere that he has just started to frequent recently."

"Of course," Kenzie snapped. "But he hasn't become a completely different person, has he? He doesn't have any interest in sports. He would never hang around somewhere like that."

Zachary shrugged uncomfortably. "People can change. Pick up new hobbies and interests. Maybe he has a… friend who is interested in sports and introduced him to the place."

"A friend?" Kenzie repeated. "Are you saying a girlfriend? You think that he's seeing some woman who has gotten him interested in sports or in this bar? Who owns it?"

"He's going to send me the contact information for the owners. Their first names were Glen and Janice…?" Zachary hoped that she would recognize the names as old family friends and relax. He especially didn't want to discuss whether her father could have a girlfriend and, if he did, how she was influencing him. Men of Walter's age often picked younger women. Not bimbos, necessarily, but younger, more attractive women a couple of decades their juniors. Had Walter recently taken up with a woman Kenzie's age or younger who was interested in sports?

Zachary looked away from Kenzie, trying to find something else in the room to look at other than her accusing gaze.

"I don't know of any Glen and Janice. And if he's got a girlfriend... well, of course he does. It's been years since he and Mother divorced. I wouldn't expect him to go that long without some kind of companionship."

Zachary nodded mutely. In his experience, divorced men usually started looking for companionship very quickly after a divorce. Or before. Walter had probably been through a series of girlfriends, but Kenzie had not been subjected to them because of the rift between her and her father.

Or maybe she knew about some of them and had just not thought to share anything with Zachary. It had been a long time before Kenzie had said anything to Zachary about either of her parents. Kenzie preferred to keep her relationships with her parents separate from her relationship with Zachary. And he respected that. He would never introduce her to his biological parents. He would never see them voluntarily and certainly wouldn't want Kenzie to meet them.

CHAPTER 8

Kenzie took a couple of bites of her pizza, chewing it slowly, but she didn't look like she was enjoying it or even tasting it. Her thoughts were far away.

"What you're telling me," she said eventually, "is that my father has been hanging around some sports bar, which was the target of a burglary, and he wants you to look into it for him."

Zachary nodded.

"As a favor," Kenzie said.

Zachary swallowed. "He is paying me," he countered. "Regular rates."

"But it's still a favor. Right? Because he's my father? He used that to leverage you."

"Well..." Zachary cleared his throat again and looked around for a drink. He didn't know whether it was his meds or the conversation that was making his mouth so dry. He hadn't opened a soft drink to have with the pizza, so he swigged cold coffee from the mug on the side table. “Your name did come up.”

Tyrrell laughed. Kenzie looked at him and smiled grudgingly.

“Okay, so that does sound a little ridiculous,” she admitted. “I wouldn’t expect him to come here and hire Zachary without my name ever being mentioned.”

“You and your dad don’t get along?” Tyrrell guessed.

“Well…” Kenzie grimaced. She took another bite of her pizza, thinking about what to say. “We don’t get along, but we don’t fight. I just… stay as far away from him as possible, and he generally does his own thing.” She looked at Zachary. “Unless he wants something.”

“So it’s good that he’s hiring Zachary for this job, right? It’s a way to reach out to you without disrupting your life.”

Kenzie considered. “Well, it’s a way to get involved in my life without talking to me. Or getting my permission first.” She sent a glare in Zachary’s direction.

Zachary held his hands up. “He sounded like he had talked to you.”

“Did he say that he had?”

Zachary had been thinking about it as they spoke. “I guess not... he said that he had talked to you about me being a private investigator.”

Kenzie snorted. “Maybe in passing. He never discussed this case with me. Certainly, never said anything about this bar he supposedly hangs around at.” She shook her head. “He’s the kind of guy who never buys a drink unless it will get him something. Unless it is for someone else so that he can keep them captive long enough to convince them of whatever it is he wants.”

Tyrrell looked at Zachary and gave a little shrug. He'd done what he could to help Kenzie realize that Zachary had been a victim of Walter's wiles, rather than choosing to do something to aggravate her.

"You've already taken the case," Kenzie said, looking back at Zachary.

"Yes."

"Well, you can un-take it. Tell him that you've reconsidered and you've got too much else on your plate."

"I accepted a retainer."

"So? Give it back. Tell him that you don't want to do it."

"Once I take a retainer, I'm committed. That's my promise that I'll do my best to solve the case."

"But you can tell him that you changed your mind. That you looked into it further and decided that it isn't the kind of thing you want to do."

Zachary ran his thumb over the smooth rim of the paper plate in his hands, considering. "I'd like to see what I can find out. He hasn't done anything wrong by hiring me. I said that I would look into it, so I want to follow through."

It could be hard for Zachary to change direction once he had committed to a course of action. He might jump from one thing to another or follow impulses that weren't always the best decisions, but if he decided to do something, he didn't like to have to change course. And as a professional, he had promised Walter he would find out what he could. His reputation was at stake.

He scratched the back of his neck. "How important is it to you?" he asked finally.

It was a strategy that Dr. Boyle had suggested in couples' therapy. If they had widely varying opinions on something that required a decision to be made, then it was important to know how strongly each of them felt about it. Was it a hill they were willing to die on? Would the wrong decision endanger someone's health or their relationship? Or was it just a preference? Or somewhere in between?

Kenzie frowned, thinking about it. "Well... it's not something I'd risk our relationship over. I want to keep you and my father away from each other to protect you, not because I can't stand him. I don't like you taking a case for him. But if you insist on following through... just be warned that you're dealing with someone without ethics."

"Or without your ethics," Zachary suggested.

"Okay, without my ethics. I'm sure he has his own boundaries that he won't cross, but I don't know what they are. I know that he's been more than willing to cross a lot of the boundaries that I would observe. He's out to get what he wants, and he is very diligent in getting it. He'll run over a lot of people and a lot of… moral codes to get it."

Zachary nodded. He knew from the way she had talked about him in the past that the two of them did not have values that aligned. And he'd seen Walter plant a listening device to eavesdrop on his own daughter when she wouldn't do what he wanted her to. That <u>was</u> someone willing to go to great lengths to get what he wanted.

"But he cares about people, too. He cares about you. And it seems like he cares about your mother."

"But not enough to stay with her. Not enough to make the relationship work. So is that really love? Or is it just self-serving? He cares about people only to the extent that it serves him."

And that was true of a lot of people.

Zachary nodded. He took a bite of his pizza. "Does it help if I say I'll treat him just like any other client? I'm not going to give him any special consideration because he's your dad. And I'm not going to hold you responsible if he does something like... deciding not to pay my bill and calling the cops when I start harassing him for payment."

Kenzie chuckled. "Well, I don't see him doing that. He's usually pretty good about paying his bills, assuming that hasn't changed. It's more likely that he would... tell somebody that you were investigating them, or tell you that I had asked you to get him involved in the case, something like that. Misleading people. Twisting things around or gaslighting you. That's what I'm worried about."

"I've been warned. If he does anything like that, I'm not holding you responsible. In fact, if he does... I'll buy you ice cream and flowers to say, 'you were right.' "

Tyrrell laughed. "You guys are too much. You're so careful of each other! You're like a couple of kids on their first date, trying to decide what movie to go to."

Zachary looked at Tyrrell, irritated. He and Kenzie had broken up once before because he hadn't been willing to talk about his feelings and the boundaries in their relationship. They were working hard with a therapist to build a strong relationship despite Zachary's issues and their vastly different upbringings and personalities.

"It's called being considerate. Thinking about the other person and working things out," he told Tyrrell firmly. Though he would like to have said a lot more. Tyrrell was divorced and his method of dealing with conflict was to run away and disappear for days or weeks at a time. How exactly did he expect to build a happy relationship dealing with problems that way?

Kenzie put her empty pizza plate to the side and put her hand on Zachary's leg. Not to stop him from defending himself against Tyrrell's words, but an unspoken "thank you" for taking her feelings on the matter into account and talking it out.

"Go ahead and take it. Just remember I didn't want you to get hustled by him."

CHAPTER 9

Kenzie was moving around the living room and kitchen, tidying things up. Zachary was aware of her on one level, but blocking her out on another. She wasn't trying to carry on a conversation with him. They'd had breakfast separately because Kenzie had slept in and then had a shower, so it was quite late in the morning by the time she was up and around.

But part of Zachary's brain was aware of what she was doing and starting to wonder why she was cleaning. Had she asked him to help with something? Was someone coming over that he had forgotten about? Was she irritated over the mess that two men made in the house now that Tyrrell was there during the day and not just Zachary? He'd been trying to tidy up after himself and Tyrrell if he saw things that were out of place, but he knew that his awareness of the cleanliness landscape of the house was not good. He would walk around a pile of laundry in the middle of the floor half a dozen times before he really saw it and started to wonder if he were supposed to be doing something about it. He often started a chore and didn't finish it because he got distracted by something else. Maybe an insight into a case that he had to write down or do a quick search on before he forgot about it. Or maybe just a bird flying past the window or a motorcycle buzzing down the street. He could remember more than one foster mom or group-home worker slapping him across the back of the head to try to bring his attention back to the chore or conversation at hand.

Zachary stood up abruptly and looked at Kenzie, as if she'd been the one who had slapped him across the head to get his attention. "What's going on? Do you need help?"

Kenzie raised her eyebrows, looking amused. "Good morning."

"Uh... didn't I say good morning to you yet? Sorry. Hi. Did you have a good sleep?"

"It was nice to be able to laze around. What's going on with you? We did say hello earlier, but why the jack-in-the-box act?"

She gestured to where he had been sitting on the couch, attending to his work.

"Just noticed that you were cleaning up and… thought I should help. Is something going on today? Or is it just… because we're messy?" Zachary gave a little head-tilt in the direction of Tyrrell's room.

"Is he up yet, do you know? I haven't heard him. But I think we should probably get him up before too long…"

Zachary looked at the time on his phone. "He's usually up by now, but maybe he stayed up late watching a movie. Do you need him out of there? Do you want to vacuum?"

"It's like you're a half-trained dog," Kenzie said with a laugh. "You know you should be doing something; you just don't have a clue <u>what</u>."

Zachary nodded, his ears and cheeks burning.

"Alisha and Mason are coming over," Kenzie said in a low, confidential tone. "So... yes, we are having company, but they won't actually care whether things are tidy or not, and I'll probably have to tidy up again after they leave. I'm just full of nervous energy right now, trying to distract myself by doing something physical."

"Alisha and Mason? Does Tyrrell know?" Zachary couldn't fathom how Tyrrell could still be sleeping if he knew that his children were coming over for a visit.

"No, I didn't tell him. That's why I'm wondering if we should get him up. I don't want him to still be in bed when they get here, but I don't want him getting all anxious and stressed out, either."

"When are they coming? In the next hour or two?"

She double-checked the time. "Within the hour."

"Then we'd better get him up."

"Okay... how would you like to do that? He's your brother..."

Zachary laughed at her reluctance, but he didn't really want to be the one to wake Tyrrell up either. He hated waking people up. And Tyrrell wouldn't have any idea why Zachary was interrupting his sleep. "You're the one who invited him to stay over," he reminded her.

"You get in there and wake him up!" Kenzie ordered, miming a slow-motion punch to his shoulder. She knew better than to actually slug him in the shoulder like she'd seen other couples do. He'd been hit too many times by too many different people in his younger years not to react.

"Yes, ma'am."

Zachary marched himself down to the guest room. He knocked on the door and then opened it. Tyrrell was still in bed, in a tangle of sheets, the room still dark with the blind being pulled down.

"Tyrrell! Hey, wake up; we have a surprise for you."

He went over to the window and pushed the blind up to let the bright sunlight stream into the room. He wouldn't shake Tyrrell awake, knowing that he might also have some demons in his past that triggered unexpected violence when someone woke him up abruptly.

"T! Hey, wake up. Guess who's coming over?"

Tyrrell groaned. "What's going on? What are you doing? I was sleeping."

"I know. But it's late, and Kenzie has some guests coming over that you're going to want to see."

Tyrrell moaned. "I barely got any sleep. Leave me alone."

"Alisha and Mason are on their way over. You should probably at least wash your face and comb your hair."

Tyrrell moved around sluggishly, pushing blankets away from his face. "What? What do you mean, Alisha and Mason are on their way over?"

"Kenzie made arrangements, apparently. She didn't tell me either until just now."

At least, Zachary hoped that Kenzie hadn't mentioned it before then, and he'd simply ignored her or forgotten about it.

"Kenzie called Lindsey? And set up a meeting?"

"I guess so. She said they should be here within the hour, so I didn't think you'd want to still be sleeping."

"No." Tyrrell pushed himself up and looked around, blinking groggily. "I'd better... shower and shave."

Zachary nodded his agreement. Alisha and Mason could visit with Tyrrell in the living room and not have to be in the overly warm, sweaty-smelling guest room. But Tyrrell needed to get himself cleaned up and prepared for the visit.

"Okay. I'm up. I'm up."

Zachary didn't leave, waiting for Tyrrell to get on his feet. Even as a little boy, Tyrrell had been difficult to get up in the morning, sometimes crawling back into bed even once he was dressed for school and had his backpack on.

Eventually, Tyrrell got to his feet and lurched toward the door. "Yeah, yeah. I'm up."

Zachary moved to the side and let Tyrrell past him to the main bathroom. "Don't be too long in there."

CHAPTER 10

Tyrrell was out of the bathroom, freshly showered, shaven, and dressed in clean clothes in enough time that Zachary could also take a few minutes to freshen up. Kenzie had the living room tidied as neatly as Zachary had ever seen it. He even stashed his laptop and the rest of his mobile office into the bedroom so that it wouldn't be out when the children arrived.

Tyrrell had been pacing up and down the hallway, waiting for their arrival, but still didn't get to the door fast enough to beat Mason's dash to the doorstep. The doorbell rang, buzzing loudly while he held the button down and completing its two-tone ring when he released it. Kenzie was the first to reach the door, Tyrrell behind her, and Zachary hung back to give them space to get in.

"Hi, Auntie Kenzie!" Mason shouted, then saw Tyrrell and, giving an ear-splitting squeal, tackled him like a linebacker. Tyrrell had difficulty staying on his feet. He reached down and grabbed

Mason, swinging him up into his chest and giving him a tight hug.

“Mason, my man. Look how you’ve grown! I haven’t been away for that long!”

Mason bawled loudly into Tyrrell’s shoulder, answering him in a long wail of words that no one could understand with his face muffled. Tyrrell held him, rocking back and forth and patting him on the back.

“It’s okay, bud. It’s alright. You’re okay. Hey, come on, little man,” he ruffled Mason’s hair. “It’s all okay. Chin up.”

Alisha’s entrance was quieter. She greeted Kenzie, took off her winter boots, and walked up to Tyrrell. She hugged him, putting her arms around both Mason and her father.

“Hi, Alisha. How are you doing, honey?” Tyrrell shifted Mason around to reach Alisha and gave her a kiss on the head. “There, beautiful. It’s so nice to see you guys! How have you been?”

Alisha pulled back, tears in her eyes and escaping in a couple of tracks down her cheeks and chin. She sniffled, trying to keep her emotions under control.

“We’ve been okay,” she told him stoically. “You’re the one who ran away. If you’d stayed home, you could see us whenever you wanted to.”

“Well... there are rules about when I’m allowed to have you for visits,” Tyrrell explained.

“Mom would let you come and see us whenever you wanted,” Alisha informed him firmly.

Tyrrell swallowed and nodded. “Yeah, she probably would,” he admitted. “I’m so sorry, baby. Your daddy... has some problems.”

“You need to stop drinking.”

“I know.”

She nodded. “Then do it.”

There was an answering nod and sobs from Mason. “Please, Daddy, please stop drinking so we can see you at Christmas and not be sad.”

Tyrrell kissed his cheek and then held Mason’s face against his own, looking anguished. “I’m sorry you were sad at Christmas. I really am. I was... it was a really hard time for me, but I know I made a mistake when I started drinking again and didn’t come to visit you.”

Mason pulled back from Tyrrell, so he was sitting on Tyrrell’s encircling arms, face-to-face with him. He put his hands on each side of Tyrrell’s face, holding him still and looking straight into his eyes.

“You just behave,” he ordered. “You’re a big boy now and you can make better choices.”

Clearly, these were words he had heard from his mother or some other authority figure in his life. Zachary felt bad for

Mason, recognizing in him the severe ADHD that had also plagued Zachary as a child, making it impossible for him to make the right choices much of the time or to sit and behave and be a big boy when the adults pleaded with him to. And threatened and meted out punishments when he was unable to control himself.

Tyrrell was looking pretty overwhelmed himself. He pulled his face back from Mason's grasp and bit his lip, not able to come up with a satisfactory reply.

“Let's get your winter clothes off now,” Kenzie invited. “It's cold outside, so you need them, but it's nice and warm in here. I don't want snow puddles all over the house, so let's get these boots off and find a place to hang your coat.”

Tyrrell put Mason down and they helped him get his clothes put away. Alisha followed suit, then they all went into the living room.

“Hi, Uncle Zachary,” Alisha greeted, looking a little shy.

"Hi, Alisha. You're doing a great job," he told her, and put his arm around her shoulders to give her a little squeeze. He didn't need to specify what she was doing good at. Taking care of Mason; being the responsible, mature one; being a listening ear for her mother and a voice of reason to her errant father. She was struggling with a hundred responsibilities that would have been onerous for any grown-up. He wanted to make sure that someone let her know that her efforts were seen.

Alisha smiled and put her arm around his waist to give him a squeeze back. "Thanks."

"We have some games," Kenzie offered. "You remember at the Lodge you guys were playing Clue and some other board games? That was fun, wasn't it?"

Mason looked at the TV, which had been turned off, and glanced around the room for a game controller or other electronic recreation. Then he sighed and nodded. "I guess so."

The children sat down to look through the board games that Kenzie had pulled out for them. Kenzie, Zachary, and Tyrrell sat down. Tyrrell let out a long, slow breath, still looking overwhelmed, but a little more in control of himself.

“If you need a break, then take one,” Zachary told him. “Just say you need a few minutes and go back to your room to decompress for a bit. It’s better than...” He trailed off, not finishing the sentence. Better than having a meltdown? As far as he knew, Tyrrell didn’t do that. Better than running away? He didn’t want to suggest that Tyrrell was going to run away or felt like it. It wasn’t his place to judge or evaluate Tyrrell. He just wanted to support him. “Anyway. I’m not going to stay out here the whole time. I’m going to go get some work done in the bedroom.”

“You don’t have to do that,” Tyrrell protested. “The kids want to see you too.”

"You're the one they need to see. And you don't need me hanging around watching you or making you… think about when we were kids."

"I'll stick around if you need a fourth player," Kenzie said. "But if you don't, I have some errands to run and I'm going to take the opportunity to go while I still have enough energy to manage the crowds. I might pick up some supper, depending on how long it takes."

"Thanks," Tyrrell said appreciatively. "This is really great. I don't know if I could have set something up with how I've been feeling lately. I really didn't want to talk to… you know who."

Alisha looked up from the boxes of games. "We know you mean Mommy," she told him with an impatient shake of her head.

Tyrrell cleared his throat and turned pink.

"Anyway… you guys don't need to run away. I don't want to take over the house on you."

"I've got work to do," Zachary said. He stood up to go to the bedroom. Tyrrell might say that he wanted them to stick around, but Zachary knew that when Tyrrell spent too much time around him, especially with the kids, it brought back Tyrrell's memories of when they were kids, and how Berk had treated them. Which made him both more irritable and impatient with the children and more sensitive to the way he was treating them and all of the ways he was like Berk.

Zachary bent down to rub Mason's head. "I'll be back out later. Don't leave without saying goodbye."

Mason nodded. "Okay."

"And I'm going out unless you need me," Kenzie told Tyrrell again.

Zachary didn't wait around to see if she were staying or going out, and went to the bedroom to work on his computer.

CHAPTER 11

Zachary didn't spend a lot of time in Montpelier. Still, it was the least populous state capital in the United States, so it wasn't hard to find his way around, especially with the GPS on his phone to supplement his knowledge from previous visits.

The owners of Barnburners, Glen and Janice McNichol, had agreed to meet him at the bar, even though it was long before their usual opening time. Zachary found the door unlocked upon his arrival and let himself in.

The couple was sitting at one of the tables with their heads together in discussion, seated where they would be able to see Zachary as soon as he got there. Janice stood up to greet him.

"You must be Zachary Goldman."

"Zachary. Nice to meet you, Mrs. McNichol."

She offered her hand. "Janice is fine. If I'm going to be calling you by your first name, you may as well call me by mine."

Zachary nodded and shook with her. Her skin was cool and dry. No sweaty palms on meeting the investigator. Her handshake was firm, but brief. She motioned to her husband, who hadn't gotten up from the table. "And this is Glen. We were just going over the police reports. I'm not sure what you will want to see."

"Everything you've got. And anything else I can pry out of you." Zachary smiled to reassure her that he was just joking, but of course, he would get everything out of them that he could in their discussion. And probably be back with several more questions as the investigation proceeded.

They were a middle-aged couple, maybe in their mid-forties to early fifties. Still young-looking, but with some fine wrinkles that hadn't been there a decade before and gray creeping into the hair on Glen's temples. No noticeable gray in Janice's hair, but she probably dyed it if there were. They looked like experienced business owners, but maybe put a little off-balance by the burglary.

"Why don't you come sit down? I guess we'll start here with what we've got."

Zachary looked at the papers spread over the table as he sat down with them. "If I could get copies or scans of these documents, that would be great. Then I can review them at my leisure and I don't need to spend all of today's meeting reading."

Janice nodded, though she didn't look pleased that he wasn't going to jump straight into the paperwork.

"I can get a better sense of what happened by talking with you. There will be things that you remember that didn't make it into the official reports. Nuances, feelings, suspicions, all of those things that the police don't really want to hear."

"But you do want to."

"If the cops could solve it based just on the facts you have given them, then they would. How long have they been on the case now? The robbery was a week ago?"

"Last weekend," Glen agreed with a nod. His voice was deeper than Zachary had expected. A warm, resonant baritone.

"That doesn't mean that they won't eventually be able to nail your thieves and recover some of the stolen property, but if their identity was obvious, the police would have made some progress by now. Sometimes, investigations like this can take months before you hear anything back. They work on it as they can, but it isn't a high priority, and it takes time to process evidence and make inquiries."

"What evidence?" Janice demanded. "They didn't even send anyone out to take pictures or fingerprints. They told us to send them a copy of the surveillance video and come in and make our statements. I thought that at the police station, they would at least take the time to discuss it with us. You know how they always sit down with the victim on TV and have coffee and go over everything together. But they were too busy. They just nod and open a file and give you the forms. I tried to talk to one of the police about it when we submitted the forms, the Officer of the Day or whoever was there at the desk. But you could tell he didn't want to hear it. The phones were ringing and other people were waiting and they just pushed us through the process. I doubt the officer we talked to would even remember us the day after we were there. And I'm sure he didn't write anything down. Just filed our reports and said that it would be passed on to the investigators."

"You took some pictures yourselves?" Zachary suggested.

"Sure." Glen got out his phone and tapped it a few times to bring up his photo stream. He handed it to Zachary. Zachary thumbed through the pictures, seeing photos of the broken window glass, of stuff that had been knocked to the floor, and empty shelves and walls where the memorabilia had once been displayed. There were quite a few pictures, and he went through each one slowly, thinking about how they would have felt, walking into the business that they had built from the ground up and lovingly cared for, and seeing the devastation the thieves had left in only a few minutes.

“I’m sorry. It must have been awful to walk in here and see all of that.” Zachary glanced around the bar. The lighting was soft. The McNichols had cleaned everything up so that there was no sign of the destruction. Some of the blank spaces on the walls had been filled with posters, and a few toys, pucks, and baseballs were sprinkled around on the display shelves. Still, there was far less memorabilia than there had been before the theft. “They didn’t take everything. How much of this did they leave behind and how much did you purchase after the burglary?”

Janice looked around and shrugged. “Maybe half and half... we tried to spread stuff out and then purchased some cheaper stuff just to fill the biggest holes. It is going to take a long time to build it back up again if we can’t recover anything that was stolen.”

“Maybe some of your patrons would donate some of their memorabilia. Collectors tend to acquire too much stuff to display everything. They might be proud to have some of their stuff on your walls, even if it was just on loan for a while.”

Janice looked at Glen, who cocked his head to the side and nodded. “Yeah… maybe we could do some kind of donation drive or ask people if they would loan us a few things. We could put up tags to indicate who they were from, so they’d get a bit of publicity.”

“Unless they’re afraid that it would be stolen too,” Janice said. “What if they are worried that we’ll get robbed again?”

Glen sighed and looked at Zachary. “We’re working on getting our security upgraded. But it’s expensive. I don’t suppose you have any recommendations…?”

Zachary took a glance around. “There are some things you can do that are low-tech. Bars and bolts. A guard dog. You have footage of the break-in, so you must already have cameras.”

"It's from neighbors," Glen said, shaking his head. "We haven't invested much in security before now. I guess the burglars knew that."

"Probably," Zachary agreed. "You should at least get front and back door cameras. And maybe something over the bar." He gestured to the ceiling over the bar in the center of the main room. "You want to have some kind of surveillance of the cash registers in case someone holds up your staff or they are skimming from the till."

The couple exchanged looks. Glen moved a couple of papers off of a notebook where he had apparently been making a list of what follow-up actions to take. Zachary nodded.

"If you beef up security and let people know, I don't think they would be as worried about lending you their own memorabilia. You can get anti-theft anchors to make it harder to walk off with artwork. They aren't infallible, but they help in a smash and grab like this. If thieves can't easily pull them off of the hooks and walk away with them, they won't generally take the time to figure out how to detach them."

"We'll look into that."

"I can refer you to a security consultant if you like. Just let them know your budget off the top, so they don't suggest high-priced solutions."

Glen nodded grimly. "That's the problem. We don't have the money to beef up security and replace the stolen items. I'm worried about a drop-off in business if people decide it isn't a safe place to eat and drink and hang out. So far, business has been fine. Everyone wants to come and gawk and to talk about what happened. But once the novelty wears off... are they still going to come here to drink?" He shook his head slowly. "I'm worried that too many of them will go somewhere else instead."

Zachary nodded, but he didn't want to get into a discussion of marketing the bar. That wasn't his area of expertise at all. And if he didn't have anything to offer, he might as well not waste paid investigative time doing it.

CHAPTER 12

Zachary pulled his notepad out of his pocket and opened it up to make some notes. "Why don't you go through what happened the day before the break-in. Was there anything unusual going on that day? Any new customers that you noticed? Any fights or other things that might have distracted your attention?"

"The day before?" Janice shook her head, eyebrows drawing down. "No. How is that going to help you? Like you said, it was a smash and grab. Someone saw an opportunity and just... took it."

"Whoever cased it out was probably in the bar, not just walking by outside and noticing that you didn't have a security camera and that they could smash a window to get access. They probably came in, had a drink, chatted with the staff, walked back to the restrooms and maybe even into the kitchen. Checked out any back exits. Scoped out which memorabilia was worth the most so that they knew what to target."

The couple considered the possibility, looking dismayed. “They were in here?” Glen demanded. “They just walked in here and took a look around so they could come back later and steal everything?”

Zachary nodded. “More than likely.”

Janice scratched her head, frowning and thinking back to the day before the robbery. They had been focusing on that night, on remembering how everything had looked in the early-morning hours when they had been called about the burglary. At that point, it was too late and, if the thieves had been wearing balaclavas and gloves, they had probably not left any physical evidence behind to identify them.

“If they were here to scope the place out, then they wouldn’t cause a disturbance, would they?” she questioned. “They would want to stay quiet, under the radar so that we wouldn’t notice them.”

"Maybe. Or if there was more than one person involved, then one might have had a little look around while the other made a scene to distract you."

"There were more than one," Glen admitted. "That's on the video." He squinted at his wife. "I don't remember anything unusual during the day before the robbery, do you?"

"No... nothing specific," she said. "I mean, sometimes we get people being rowdy. That's pretty normal with a sports bar. Their team is losing or they are being obnoxious about a win. Had too much to drink and they just lose all inhibitions. It's normal to have a disturbance here and there. But I can't think of anything unusual that day."

"Have you had any strange phone calls? Hang-ups? People calling for another business or someone who doesn't work here?"

Both shook their heads, looking mystified.

"Anyone hanging around? Loitering inside or outside? A homeless person, someone who asked for a glass of water and didn't spend anything? Someone asking you questions that are out of the ordinary? Maybe about how long you've been in this location or who does your cleaning?"

"No. Nothing like that. It's pretty cold for the homeless to be hanging around right now," Glen offered. "Most of them have found places in more hospitable parts of town. Near the homeless shelter. We don't really... have anything to do with people like that. They don't come in here, and if they do, we make it clear that this is a paying business, not a place to loiter. Paying customers only."

"Who does your cleaning? Do you hire out?"

"No, we do it ourselves. The staff. We have checklists of procedures to be followed every day. Mopping up at the end of the day, checking the bathrooms, wiping down fixtures, that kind of thing. Anything bigger, we usually do ourselves, or have someone in."

Anticipating Zachary's next question, Janice spoke up. "We don't have a company that we usually go to, just whoever specializes. And we haven't had any contractors in the past few weeks."

Zachary nodded. "I'd like to talk to your staff, see what their recollections are about that day, and if any of them are aware of anything unusual happening in the days before the robbery. What time will they be coming in?"

Janice looked at her watch. "Not for a couple more hours."

"Okay. I should probably look at the video." Zachary started to put his notebook away. "How long have you guys known Walter?"

They both looked at him with blank expressions. Zachary raised his brows, waiting for them to understand.

“The man who is paying me to investigate?” he prompted.

“Oh, Mr. Kirsch. Yeah... I don’t know, how long do you think he’s been coming here, honey?” Glen asked his wife.

“Hard to say. I’m not sure when he started. It’s been a few months, I guess.”

Zachary kept his expression neutral. Only a few months? What had precipitated the change? When Kenzie had said that her father didn’t have any interest in sports, he had assumed that she was wrong. That it was just because she hadn’t been in close contact with him for a number of years that she wasn’t aware of his passion for hockey or baseball or whatever other sport interested him. Hockey and baseball were the ones that he had mentioned, if he remembered right. But if he had only been going to the bar for a few months, even if the McNichols remembered wrong and it was as long as a year, then what had changed?

Had he started dating a puck bunny? Moved to an office building across the street, and just gravitated toward the nearest bar, not caring what their specialty was or how rowdy the customers might get? Was it a childhood interest that had rekindled as he got older and remembered his younger years and tried to recapture that magic?

Nothing felt right. He had believed that Walter knew the owners. He had talked like he did. But considering the fact that they didn't even know his first name, it seemed unlikely that he was good friends with them.

"He must really like the place," Zachary offered. "For him to be willing to lay out this kind of money for the investigation. I mean, you could probably buy a lot of memorabilia with it, if it wasn't earmarked for the investigation."

Glen's eyes widened, as if it were the first time he had thought about such a thing. Maybe they didn't know how expensive it was to hire a private investigator for a few days. But it wasn't pocket change. Zachary was no longer a wet-behind-the-ears investigator. He'd been at it for a lot of years and had worked his way up to the higher rates.

"He must like it," Janice echoed in a faraway voice.

"He's here most nights?" Zachary guessed.

They both shook their heads immediately. They looked at each other, trying to gauge their answer. "Not every night," Janice said. "Maybe... once every couple of weeks?"

"Oh. I had just assumed..."

She shook her head again, more definitely now. "No. He came in here a few times since the summer. But he wasn't what you would call regular."

"Did he only come in when a specific team was playing?" Zachary suggested. "Or for a certain... tournament or cup?" He hoped that his terminology wasn't too far off.

"No. I never saw him pull for any particular team. He didn't wear a jersey or any other team colors. To be honest..." Janice looked at her husband for his corroboration. "I'm not sure he ever watched the TVs. He would just come in for a little while for a drink or an appetizer. And then... he would leave."

Zachary rubbed the bridge of his nose, thinking about that. He tried to picture Walter there, to see him come into the bar, sit down, and have his drink or snack. And then get up and walk back out. It didn't feel right. He couldn't picture Walter in a team jersey, so that part made sense to him, but what didn't make sense was that Walter was spending his time there at all. Not for a specific sport or team.

"Did he come in with someone else? Did he have a friend or a date? Someone he met here? A friend on the staff?"

"No." They both shook their heads together. "I never saw him with someone else. He would chat a bit with the wait staff, just pleasantries, you know. Sometimes Glen or I are on, so he got to know who we were. That we owned the place. But he didn't... ingratiate himself or anything like that. He wasn't expecting special favors for recognizing the owners. I think..." Janice pursed her lips while she thought about it. "I think he was just a lonely old man, that's all. Maybe some night he didn't want to go back home alone. So he came somewhere to be around people for a little while. Even if he didn't know anyone in particular, it's a friendly place. You can come here and feel like you belong to a team or a club. People crack jokes and involve you in a conversation, even if they don't know you. They assume you're pulling for the Habs and talk about their prospects this year. Just... it's a place where you can come and not feel so alone."

"At least, I hope it is," Glen said, turning his palms up. "That's the type of community and atmosphere that we've tried to foster. When you're here, you're family, or however that saying goes."

"Sounds nice," Zachary gave them a warm smile. He could imagine having a place like that to go to. He and Kenzie knew some of the staff at Old Joe's and some of the other local eateries. People recognized you if you were there regularly. And it was nice to be recognized, even if you weren't close friends with them.

"Yeah, it is," Janice agreed. She shrugged. "And obviously Mr. Kirsch thought so too, or he wouldn't have done this." She motioned toward Zachary by way of explanation.

"Yes, he obviously felt comfortable here, and thought highly of you," he agreed.

They looked pleased at his words.

But they were just words. Inside, Zachary was trying to figure out what was going on. Why did Walter care about the robbery if the bar and the people who owned it didn't mean anything to him? He could go and have a drink and a meal anywhere in Montpelier. It didn't have to be the little sports bar.

So why did he care what happened to them?

And even more than that, why did he care about making it right?

CHAPTER 13

Zachary made a few notes in his notepad before putting it away again. He followed Janice to the small office in the back, with a computer and a stack of papers in an overflowing basket that looked like it probably only got cleaned out once a year.

“Sorry for the mess,” she said, waving her fingers to indicate everything in the room.

It wasn’t the messiest office Zachary had ever seen, but it wasn’t the cleanest, either. He remembered fleetingly the feeling he had walking into Isabella Hildebrandt’s office. Widely known as the Happy Artist. Of course, she had not been happy when he had been investigating the death of her son. Isabella’s studio had been a nightmare. Every inch of space was covered with canvases, brushes, paint, or other supplies. Stacked high on shelves in piles that looked like they were going to topple over any minute. The exact opposite of the rest of the house, neatly arranged and maintained by her husband.

"I've seen worse," Zachary told her with a smile.

Janice smiled vaguely in response. He doubted she had even heard what he'd said. Her focus was already on the computer and starting up the video recording they had obtained from one of the neighborhood cameras.

In a few minutes, she turned the monitor partway around so that Zachary could see the black and white video playing on the screen.

It wasn't the horrible, fuzzy images that a lot of the cheaper security cameras captured, but nice, high-resolution pictures with good lighting and contrast. Two figures breaking the window, as Walter had said, and reaching through to unlock the door and let themselves in. There was no sound on the video, but Zachary could tell by the body language of the two thieves that they were aware they had tripped an alarm, whether it was audible or not. Their movements were quick, jerky, with lots of looking around to make sure that the police weren't coming yet. They pushed away anything that was in their way as they grabbed what Zachary assumed were the highest-priced memorabilia, shoving the stuff into duffel bags and what looked like garbage bags. Grab, grab, grab, look around to make sure they weren't yet caught, and then grab, grab, grab again. In a couple of minutes—2:15 according to the timer on the video—one of them grabbed the other by the arm, and they hustled out.

"The security company arrived a few minutes later," Janice said. "Never caught sight of them. And then the police after that. And as you can see, they were wearing masks and gloves, so… there isn't much to go on."

"No," Zachary agreed, looking at the screen where the video had now ended and was sitting waiting to be replayed. "Can you play it through one more time?"

"I'll send you a copy and you can watch it as many times as you want, but I don't think you're going to be able to get anything from it. Unless you can perform some magic on it that the police can't. But I know all that stuff they do on TV with magnifying images ten times and bringing stuff up in reflections is mostly made up. And even if it wasn't, the cops aren't going to be spending much time looking at the video. It isn't a high-priority case. They just need to confirm to the insurers that it was a burglary, watch for any of our stuff to show up in the pawnshops, and maybe keep their ears to the ground in case there is a series of similar burglaries or someone starts talking about it."

"Just play it one more time," Zachary urged. "I'll watch it on my own computer too, but I just want to see it one more time while I'm here. In case there is anything that I have to look at while I'm on the scene."

Janice shrugged. "Fine." She clicked the video again and they watched the same sequence play through. Zachary watched the whole screen, not just focusing on the thieves, but trying to impress it all on his memory. When the video had finished playing a second time, Janice swiveled in her chair and looked at him. "Okay? Anything else?"

"And you've checked with anyone else who might have had a camera in the vicinity? To see if anyone caught the getaway vehicle or its license plates? What direction they went after the burglary?"

"I don't know. I can ask the police if they did that. We didn't go door to door; we just asked the businesses nearby to check their videos to see if they caught the break-in. This one came from the restaurant across the street. I thought it was pretty good. It's just disappointing that it doesn't give us anything we can use."

"Yeah. Well, I'll look at it a few more times. It might turn out that there is something I can use on it." Zachary looked at the time on his phone. "We've still got some time before your employees come in. Could you walk me through the bar and show me where each of the stolen items on the list was to start with?"

Janice rolled her eyes. She didn't think that it would do anyone any good. The police had already told her that the whole investigation was a waste of time. They might be grateful to Walter for hiring someone privately to look into the burglary, but she didn't really think that it was going to come to anything. Zachary would tell them the same thing as the police. That he had no clue who had committed the break-in and theft and they would just have to replace what they could.

"Let me just print off the list again," Janice said with a deep sigh. So much work for something that was hopeless.

Zachary looked around the little office as she tracked down the document on her computer and sent it to the ancient HP printer across the desk. It was a nice little office. Crowded, admittedly, and Janice was definitely behind in her paperwork. Still, Zachary could picture himself retreating to this room after a busy night in the main room of the bar, shutting the door against the music and noise and stink of the crowd and taking a breather. There wasn't any memorabilia in the office, which seemed a little strange. If they were collectors and the items that had been stolen had a lot of sentimental value, then why hadn't they decorated the office as well? Maybe kept an item or two with special significance to them there in the back where they could enjoy them and they wouldn't be a temptation to patrons or burglars casing out the place?

"Here we go, then," Janice rattled the printout of the stolen items. She led the way back out to the main room and started to work her way down the list.

They were mostly arranged on the list by placement. Everything on one wall in a grouping, then moving to the next segment of shelves or the pieces that had been displayed on the tables or the display at the back of the bar. A couple of times, Janice had to consult with Glen, and they discussed which position an item had been displayed in, but mostly they agreed and didn't have any problem telling Zachary where each thing belonged. He didn't write them all down, but concentrated hard as she worked through the list, trying to memorize as many of the displays as possible. He could refer back to the social media and review site photos as well, actually see what was missing with his own eyes rather than having to imagine it.

The door banged open as the employees started to arrive, each bringing with them a rush of cold air from outside.

CHAPTER 14

They must have to keep the heater cranked pretty high during the winter, as people came and went all night. Although body heat would help keep the room warm as well.

As the employees shed their outerwear and looked curiously at Zachary, Janice and Glen introduced him and told him who the employees were and the positions they held.

"You hired a detective?" demanded Stacy, a woman with short, bleach blonde hair and numerous piercings.

"We didn't hire him. One of the customers did."

Stacy frowned and shook her head. "Who?"

"He's this guy who comes every now and then. Sits over there," Janice gestured to a table in the corner that was not in a good position to view the TVs and was a little more private than some of the other seats, away from the kitchen and bathroom doors. “His name is Kirsch. Uh…” She looked at Zachary for help. “Mr. Kirsch…?”

“Walter Kirsch,” Zachary supplied. He smiled at Stacy. “He has very generously covered my fees so that I can see if I can recover any of the stolen property or figure out who the thieves were.”

She frowned, shaking her head. “Walter Kirsch? Who is that? Is he some sports bigwig?”

“No. Just someone who enjoys coming in here now and then and wanted to help out.”

“The suit?”

She looked at the other employees, and they all looked back at Janice. She nodded.

“Yes, the suit who sits over there sometimes.”

“Weirdo,” Stacy muttered.

"Did he ever hit on you? Say something offensive?" Zachary asked, studying her for any clue in her expression or body language.

"No. He was just a weirdo. Why would you come in here if you weren't even interested in sports? Why not go to a bar or a private club for people like that? He comes in here, eats, chats up the staff, touches the memorabilia, but doesn't know a thing about sports. Any sports. Why would anyone do that?"

"Touches the memorabilia?" Zachary repeated.

"Yeah. Fiddles, I guess. Or stares at it. I don't know. Maybe he's thinking of becoming a collector. But it wasn't like there was anything that expensive here. Nothing that he would want to buy and display in his fancy-schmancy house." Stacy made a gesture to the limited memorabilia now displayed on the walls and shelves. "It isn't like this is the high-end stuff, the stuff that goes for hundreds of thousands of dollars, or even millions. It's just mid-range, sentimental stuff."

"Maybe he's remembering something from his childhood. Maybe his dad was a sports guy and they used to go to games together, or he went to his dad's sports bar with him, or they had a bunch of memorabilia like that around their home." From what Kenzie had said, Zachary knew that Walter's father had been a wealthy, politically inclined man, much like Walter. But that didn't mean that he couldn't have a hobby. Something that he liked to go out and do to unwind. He wasn't likely to have thrown around a baseball with his son, but maybe they had watched games when they went into the city. "Was there any particular team that he seemed to lean toward?"

Stacy stood with her hands on her hips, looking at him. "So you really are a PI? A private eye? And you care about the stuff that was stolen? I've never met a PI in real life before."

"Yes, I am." Zachary stepped toward her, drawing a business card out of his pocket and reaching out to hand it to her.

She looked him over. "Where is your gun?"

"I don't have a gun. That's a TV thing. In real life, private investigators do a lot of computer work and phone calls. And coming to a scene like this to see if we can find any other evidence when a crime has been committed, or there is something else you want investigated. We're not Magnum or the Equalizer having shoot-outs in parking lots or from speeding cars."

She smiled, chuckling at this. Picturing Zachary in one of those situations, he assumed. And he certainly did not measure up to Tom Selleck on any level.

"So," Zachary ventured, "did you notice that there was any one particular team that he followed or seemed fond of?"

"He didn't watch the games."

"No, that's what Janice said. I just wondered, when you said that he touched the memorabilia, <u>which</u> memorabilia it was. Was there a particular team?"

“No, I don’t think so…” Stacy thought about it, her voice fading out. “I just remember him playing with the die-cast car that was on that table.”

Zachary raised his brows. There had been several die-cast collector’s items on the list of stolen items. Those limited-edition reproductions that he used to see on TV or in magazines, that were probably now all over the shopping channel and other paid advertising.

“It was a little station wagon. You know, the wood-grain panels on the sides and team logos on it. The Habs.”

Zachary pulled his notepad out to make a note of it. “The Habs?” he repeated, trying to recall a local team this might refer to.

Janice giggled. “You’re worse than he is. The Habs? The Montreal hockey team.”

"I thought they were..." Zachary frowned, reaching for the name. "The Montreal Canadiens."

"Yeah. The Habs."

He tried to figure out how a team called the Canadiens ended up with a nickname of the Habs, but shrugged it off. It didn't matter why they were known by that name; he needed to stay focused on his line of inquiry.

"Why do you even care?" Stacy asked. "I mean, if he's the one who hired you, then it isn't exactly as if he is a suspect. Mr. Fancy-Pants would never get involved in a smash-and-grab like that anyway. If he was going to steal something, it would be all super-secret and involve a corporate takeover or insider trading or something like that."

"No. You're right. I don't think he had anything to do with it; I just want to know everything about him that I can, especially as it relates to this bar. It could be relevant. He could have an emotional attachment that explains why he was so concerned about the theft and catching the thieves and getting the mementos back. And if he has an emotional attachment, then someone else might too... Or there could be something that was <u>very</u> valuable to a Habs fan that wouldn't have been to a..." He trailed off.

"A Bruins fan," Janice supplied.

Zachary shrugged with one shoulder. "To a Bruins fan."

"There wasn't anything that valuable, even to a big fan," Janice said. "I mean, we had game pucks and signed jerseys and things like that. But so does everyone who is a fan or collector. I don't think he had any particular connection with the Habs." Janice looked at the staff members who had assembled so far. "I don't think... did anyone notice anything?"

There were head shakes and murmurs. They looked at each other, but no one jumped in with any insight into why Walter might have cared about the stolen memorabilia, for the Habs or any other team.

CHAPTER 15

Well, apparently, that's not important," Zachary said, closing the topic. "Sorry. A lot of being a private investigator is just following rabbit trails. They don't always lead anywhere. I'd like to talk to each employee separately, if I could. It won't be long. No torture or sweating you out under a bare light bulb," he joked. "Just fifteen minutes to talk about anything that happened the day of the robbery and what you remember about the weeks before. I'm just looking for any patterns or the possibility that the bar was cased out ahead of time. We could start with you...?" He addressed this to Stacy.

"Actually, if I could go first," offered Nate, the tall Black barman. "I need to get set up for the evening and can't be interrupted later."

Zachary nodded. "Sure, of course." He looked at Janice. "Should we use your office? Or is there another room? Or just one of the tables here?"

Janice rubbed the creases across her forehead. “I need to get some office work done. We don’t really have anywhere else, other than the kitchen or supply room, so if you could just take a table that’s out of the way...” She motioned to the booth in the corner. “Why don’t you take Mr. Kirsch’s table? Maybe that will be good luck.”

Zachary nodded. It would be far enough away from the other employees that they could talk quietly and not be overheard. He preferred not to have one employee’s comments taint another’s recollections. Always best to interview witnesses independently. “Sure, let’s go over there,” he told Nate.

The man strolled over, his long legs eating up the gap before Zachary was halfway across the room, even though he only appeared to be walking at half the speed Zachary was. Zachary nodded when the other man did not offer to shake hands, assuming that he preferred not to make physical contact. They sat down.

"Thanks for volunteering to go first," he said. "You always need someone to break the ice, and it can be hard in something like this. People are nervous about talking to an investigator, even if it's just a private citizen like me. They're afraid that they're going to get in trouble somehow."

Nate nodded politely. "Sure. No problem. What do you need to know?"

"Were you on the evening before the robbery?"

"Sure, yeah. I'm usually here every night. We have other people who can cover the bar when I'm not able to, but I'm the one who is usually there."

"Do you remember anything unusual happening that night?"

"No. Just a regular night. Nothing stands out."

"I know that sometimes sports fans can get pretty rowdy."

"That wouldn't be out of the ordinary."

"Do you remember any fights or disruptions that night?"

"No. I don't think there were. Maybe some arguments or raised voices, but that doesn't qualify as anything unusual. Just boys being boys." He smiled. "Though we have more and more female fans, and they aren't any quieter than the men. In fact, some of them can be quite vocal."

"I imagine so. Any women making noise that night?" Zachary prompted. Nate's mention of women might have been triggered by a memory about the night of the burglary. Something he wasn't even consciously aware of.

"Women..." Nate thought about it, closing his eyes briefly. "Probably, but I don't remember anything. It was just a regular night. Nothing unusual."

"Did anyone get kicked out? Was there any reason to call the police or get a bouncer involved?"

"No."

"Anyone who... ditched without paying?"

He shook his head again. "What about the kitchen? Anyone snooping around the back? Someone who said that they were just looking for a bathroom or going out for a smoke in the alley?"

"That kind of thing happens all the time."

"No one that night?"

"Nothing I recall."

"What about in the weeks before the robbery. Was there anything unusual or concerning? Any phone hang-ups or threats? Someone who expressed anger toward Janice or Glen?"

"No. It's a quiet place. I mean, it's noisy when a game is on, but it isn't the kind of place that the mob or drug dealers hang out. It's quiet that way. There's no one making book at the bar or running illegal games or selling drugs out of the back. It's all aboveboard. Maybe it's not family entertainment because of the alcohol, but if it wasn't for that... it's just people getting together to watch a game and cheer for their favorite team. To get together with other fans and have a good time together."

"Anyone loitering around the sidewalk out front, or coming inside just for a look around and not for something to eat or drink or to watch a game? Someone homeless or a stranger? Someone like Walter who really didn't belong?"

"I can't think of anyone recently. The homeless population kind of disappears when it gets too cold. They go somewhere else for help. And the suit... he's the only one I can think of who was really out of place. Maybe the occasional businessperson, but they usually show at least some interest in who is playing."

"Did you ever see Walter—Mr. Kirsch—meet here with anyone? Chat with anyone aside from the wait staff?"

"No, I don't think so. But I'm usually quite busy at the bar; I don't spend any time watching the tables."

"Is there anyone on the staff who is having financial trouble?"

Nate raised an eyebrow, looking at him. "Why?"

Zachary knew that Nate had a pretty good idea already. "In case there is an inside connection. Is there anyone who might be struggling who would see the memorabilia as a possible way to dig themselves out?"

"Nah," Nate shook his head. He frowned, brows drawing down. "Nah, no one would do that. We're like family here. And what is all of that stuff going to get? There isn't anything worth more than a couple of thousand dollars, if that. And you're not going to get that at a pawnshop."

"No," Zachary agreed. "But sometimes a person is desperate, even for just a few hundred dollars. Everything that was taken from here, they'd get at least that."

Nate scratched his head. "Really, no. I don't think so. I don't know anyone's financial affairs. But I mean... there isn't anyone sleeping on the street or talking about getting evicted or going bankrupt. People whine about their problems sometimes, but nothing like that."

"Okay. Well, that's all you can say. You can't know anyone else's business if they haven't been talking about it. Unless maybe their clothes are wrinkled from sleeping in the car, or they're talking about not being able to pay all of the bills."

"I'm telling you, there's no one living like that here."

"If you think of anything that might help me—anything 'off' that happened the night of the robbery or in the weeks before—would you give me a call?" Zachary slid one of his business cards across the table.

Nate looked around before picking it up, as if he were worried about someone seeing him taking it. He tucked it into his shirt pocket. "I don't know anything. I'm not going to think of anything."

"Understood. But if you do think of anything, or see or hear anything, just let me know...?"

CHAPTER 16

Two of the waitresses came over to the table after Zachary had finished talking to Nate.

"If you could come one at a time..." Zachary suggested.

"I can't," the younger girl suggested, clutching at the arm of the older one. "I'm too nervous!" She looked at the other woman, making sure that she wasn't going to abandon her to Zachary.

Zachary raised his brows and waited, seeing if the young woman would screw up her courage and sit down with him when she saw that he wasn't a big, foul-mouthed, rough-and-ready private eye like she might have seen on TV. Just a guy, short and slight, non-threatening, asking her a few questions while in a familiar, safe place. But the woman shook her head again.

"I don't want to do this," she reasserted. "I'm sure not doing it by myself."

Zachary wondered how she had the courage to serve people she'd never met before drinks in a noisy bar. Maybe she'd needed the other woman at her side for the first few days there, too, until she'd gotten to know the regular patrons and knew that she wasn't going to screw everything up when she worked by herself.

The older woman finally sat down. "Come on, Martha. It's no big deal."

Neither was very old. Young, cute waitresses were apparently what was expected in a sports bar. Martha was perhaps nineteen and the other woman in her early to mid-twenties.

"I'm Jennifer," the older one introduced herself.

Martha sat down beside Jennifer, both of them across the table from Zachary.

"Nice to meet you, Jennifer, Martha," Zachary greeted, giving them both a warm smile, hoping that Martha would be able to relax a little once she saw that Zachary was no one to be afraid of. “How long have you worked here?”

Hopefully, with some bland, easy questions to start, Martha would let down her guard.

“I’ve been here a couple of years,” Jennifer offered.

Martha had her mouth behind her hand as if she were hiding from Zachary. “Not long,” she said, “just a few months.”

“How do you like it here?”

“It’s good,” Jennifer contributed. “Good, steady paycheck. As many hours as you need. Tips are good. It’s not like the places where they’re allowed to grope you.”

“The owners seem nice. Glen and Janice.”

Jennifer’s eyes flickered toward Glen, who was talking at the bar with Nate. “Yeah. They’re good. Never had any trouble with either of them.”

Zachary looked at Martha. “What do you think? Is this your first job?”

“I’ve worked at… like… Subway. But not at a bar before.”

“How has it been? Big culture shock?”

“It was a bit to get used to. But Jenn’s right… it hasn’t been too bad.”

“I’ve worked a lot worse places,” Jennifer asserted. “You’re lucky to be starting out somewhere they support your rights and don’t just expect you to put up with being manhandled or catcalled.”

Martha nodded, looking anxious at the idea.

“Were either of you on the day before the burglary?” Zachary asked.

“I was,” Jennifer offered, nodding. “Helped to close.”

"I was on earlier in the afternoon," Martha said, squaring her shoulders. "But I wasn't on until close."

"How was it?"

"How was it?" Jennifer repeated, shaking her head slightly. "What do you mean?"

"Well, some shifts are good, and some days... it's a full moon or something and everyone is acting crazy or out of sorts... or you didn't get enough sleep and you're dropping everything or forgetting orders..." He shrugged. "Just... how was it?"

"Normal, I guess. Nothing out of the ordinary. What about you?" Jennifer looked at Martha.

"Yeah, I guess. It wasn't a bad day. Not a holiday or a cup day or anything. No full moon, I guess."

Zachary nodded. "You have any customers who gave you a hard time or acted strangely?"

"No." Both women shook their heads together.

"Anyone hanging out where they shouldn't? In the kitchen or back hallway?"

"No."

"Can you remember who was here? Who are your regulars?"

Jennifer and Martha looked at each other. Jennifer offered a couple of patrons that she was familiar with, but shook her head at Zachary. "I don't know how that's going to help you. And I really don't know... who else was around."

"I didn't see anyone casing it out," Martha said, finally offering something on her own. "I would think I would have noticed if someone was acting suspiciously."

"Have you ever been worried about security? Walking back to your car at the end of a shift?"

Jennifer shook her head. Martha shrugged. "I take the bus?" Her voice curled up, like it was a question she was asking him.

"So I'm always a little nervous? Kind of paranoid about anyone following me, you know?"

Zachary nodded understandingly.

"When you see in the paper about women getting killed," Martha offered, "Knifed by a stranger or pulled behind the bushes and assaulted, they always say it was one o'clock in the morning and she was going home from work, you know? So... I'm always watching... being aware of my surroundings. Don't wear earphones or anything like that." She looked proud of herself. Like she had prevented an assault just by doing that.

Little did she know how hard it was to fight off an ambush or gang attack in the middle of the night when the streets were dark and lonely. Zachary gripped the edge of the table and tried not to let his brain drift back to when he had been attacked by a group of skinheads leaving a bar after asking questions on a case. He forced a weak smile.

“That’s good,” he told Martha. “I’m glad that you’re being careful and trying to protect yourself. You never know what to expect out there.”

“I’ve told her taking transit that late at night is not a good idea,” Jennifer said, “she should get someone to pick her up or get herself a car for a couple hundred bucks. It’s not worth getting jumped on your way home.”

Funny that scared little Martha hadn’t heeded these words. But maybe she just didn’t have the means. No one who would pick her up, no savings to put into a car. She might be able to buy a car for a couple hundred bucks, but who knew where a junker like that might leave her stranded. It might be somewhere much worse than a well-trafficked sidewalk between the bar and the bus stop.

“Have you ever had a patron that you’ve had to report to management? Because he was giving you the wrong kind of attention? Someone you had a bad feeling about, even if you didn't report him?"

"Sure," Jennifer admitted. "But nothing recently."

Martha shook her head wordlessly, her eyes wide. Zachary could see that he would not be able to pursue that line of questioning. Not unless he wanted to cost the bar a waitress.

CHAPTER 17

The next couple of interviews had similar results. No one had noticed anything unusual in the day before or weeks ahead of the robbery. If someone had cased the bar out ahead of time, they had done so quietly and without drawing attention to themselves. Zachary didn't think it would have taken more than a few minutes inside to sort out the security concerns. Watching from outside would give anyone the information they needed about when shifts started and ended. It wasn't a bank heist. Any nonprofessional could have pulled it off at least as well as the two who had broken in and made off with the loot.

Stacy seemed to be avoiding an interview but, eventually, Zachary managed to get her pinned down, getting Glen to lean on her, telling her that she could take a break from her prep duties to talk to Zachary. She couldn't give any more excuses, and finally gave in. To begin with, she just stood beside the table, looking as though she might run at any minute.

She was older than he had thought at first. Looking at her close up, he could see the wrinkles around her mouth. Lines running down from her nose that had been camouflaged with makeup. Her hands were dry and wrinkled, yellowed around the tips. No age spots, but she was definitely not in her twenties as he had initially thought.

“This is going to take a bit,” Zachary told her. “You might as well get off of your feet while you can.”

She just looked at him, her hip cocked, making it clear that she didn’t want to talk to him.

“You must get sore feet by the end of the day,” Zachary commented, pulling out his notepad to browse through the notes he had made, giving her some time to think about that without any scrutiny. Eventually, she sighed and sat down across from him.

“This is a waste of time. I’m telling you that at the start. You’re just wasting your time talking to me and the rest of the employees. None of us know anything about what happened. We've already talked it over, you know? And none of us have been able to come up with anything. No suspects. Nothing suspicious. It was just chance. Bad luck. Someone was walking by outside and saw the memorabilia through the window, and decided it was something they wanted."

"You don't think it was a customer or someone who had ever been in here. Just completely random."

"Exactly. Random. A stranger. Someone who had never even been here before. Well, obviously, because if they'd been here before, they would have done it then. Nobody is going to set up some big plan to rob a little place like this. It isn't like the McNichols have any enemies. They're not into drugs or something like that. It's a little mom-and-pop shop. Who rips off someone like that?"

Anyone who wanted to, apparently.

"Little mom-and-pop places get ripped off regularly," Zachary pointed out. "They're easy targets. But they are <u>not</u> very profitable targets. Somewhere like this, with all of the memorabilia around, maybe they make a little more, but it isn't likely to have been set up by some kingpin. Someone who needed a fix or couldn't pay the rent this month. Someone desperate for a little cash."

"Yeah, I guess." Stacy twisted her fingers together. She shook her head at him. "I really can't think of how anyone would do something like this. I mean, why target Barnburners? Or the McNichols?"

"It was someone who didn't care about Glen and Janice. Maybe didn't even know who they were. It's easier to rip off a nameless business than it is someone you know, who has been kind to you."

She nodded slowly. "I suppose so. Easier if they aren't anyone you know." She paused. "They really are nice people. Don't think they're involved in anything shady, because they aren't. I know a lot of businesspeople operate another, less legitimate business to stay afloat, but Janice and Glen aren't like that. They have the bar. They love what they do. They put all of their energy into it."

"They seem like nice folks," Zachary agreed. And they did seem to be very into what they did. He liked to see people engaged in what they were really passionate about. With a business like Barnburners, it could be the difference between a business that failed and a business that succeeded. "I'm sure you and the other employees wouldn't want to see them go under because of something like this."

"Why would they go under because of this?" Stacy furrowed her brow at him. It made the piercings above her eye wiggle in a distracting way. "It's not that big of a loss, and they can claim it on insurance."

"It might increase their rates too much to be worth it. When you take into account whatever the deductible is, what percentage of the actual value they will get to replace the stolen items, and how much their insurance rates will go up after a claim, then it's sometimes cheaper to just take the loss."

"Really?" Her piercings wiggled some more. "I would have thought that a small claim… it wouldn't affect their rates that much."

"Small claims are rarely worth it. Better to save it for the time something big happens. A real disaster."

"Like getting burned to the ground?" Stacy challenged.

Zachary tried to keep his expression flat. But he couldn't help a grimace at the mention of a fire. Having survived the burning inferno of a house fire when he was ten, the mention of a house or building on fire could still send him back there in a flashback. He was doing better, but it was still a struggle to remain grounded and stay focused on the conversation instead of letting himself be sucked into the flashback that threatened at the edge of his vision.

"What?" Stacy asked, apparently seeing something in his expression. "Oh, you mean because it's called Barnburners?" She shrugged. "It's not literal, you know. It just refers to a high-scoring game. Lots of goals. It's called a barnburner."

Zachary nodded politely. He had wondered at the name and what it had to do with sports, and now he knew. "That makes sense. I didn't know where it came from."

"I like it. I think it's more unique than Top Shelf or The Puck Stops Here or some of the other sports bar names that you see over and over again in different cities. Everyone thinks they had the idea first and don't realize that it's been used a dozen times before."

CHAPTER 18

The other thing that I wondered about," Zachary continued with the investigation, not wanting to get sidetracked, "is whether anyone who works here is having financial trouble. Have you heard anything..."

"Financial trouble? Who isn't? What does that have to do with the theft?"

"Sometimes, someone on the inside is involved. Maybe just bribed to provide a key piece of information or make a phone call. Just a little thing, in exchange for part of the take. I'm not saying that anyone did. I'm just saying that it happens. It's something that I need to consider in my investigation."

"No. No one here would ever do anything to hurt the McNichols."

"They might have thought, like you, that Glen and Janice wouldn't really lose anything because of insurance. Or maybe didn't realize the sentimental value of the things that were stolen, and that they can't just be replaced."

"No. No one here would have helped the thieves."

"You can't think of anyone who might be in financial trouble and be tempted to take a few things to pay the bills? Get them out of a sticky situation?"

She shook her head firmly. "No, of course not."

Zachary nodded. "Okay, well, if you think of anything..." He again slid a business card across the table as he had to each of the other employees. "If you could give me a call. That would be great."

"No." She pushed the card back toward him. "No, really. I'm not going to call you. I've got nothing."

"You might think of something. Or overhear something from one of the others. Or even from a customer or someone hanging out having a smoke at the same time as you."

She looked down at her fingers, tips stained yellow with nicotine. She curled them into fists to hide them from him.

"I don't know anything, and I'm not going to magically overhear anything," she asserted. "Sorry, I just can't help you."

"You don't want to help Janice and Glen? I thought you said they were good people."

"They are. And I appreciate the job here. But I don't work with cops. I just want to be left alone."

"I'm not a cop. I'm just a private consultant, making some inquiries. I'm not turning anybody over to the police. The police have already given up on this case. So whatever you're worried about, it's not going to happen."

"I'm not worried about anything. I just don't want to be involved. Now I've answered your questions. I've told you everything I can remember. It just isn't anything helpful, so I'm sorry. These guys, whoever they were, were just random thieves picking a random target. Okay?" Her voice had risen, causing the other employees to look in her direction while they pretended to be doing other things.

“Okay.”

Stacy looked at him. She was prepared to argue. To have a fit, throwing a chair over and stomping off in a tantrum. She wasn’t ready for his simple acquiescence. She stared at him.

“Okay?” she repeated.

Zachary nodded and waited.

“So I can go?” She made a motion away from the table, still waiting for him to object or grab her by the arm, to try to force her to do something.

Zachary nodded. “Have a nice day.”

She stood up, still watching for him to make his move. Then she marched away from him resolutely and went into the back rooms without a backward look.

Glen was nearby. He watched Stacy go and turned to look back at Zachary. He didn't get closer to the table, but was already close enough to have heard what was said in raised voices, if not when they had been speaking quietly.

"Sorry about that," he said. "Maybe I should have warned you; Stacy is a bit temperamental."

"That's okay."

"You handled her pretty well. She tends to... provoke people. Get into arguments with her even when they didn't have a beef to start with. Like she's always looking for a fight. Even though she's..." Glen frowned, reaching for the words. "She's small and sort of fragile."

Zachary nodded. He'd seen that sort of behavior before. He knew what it was like to feel that way. Himself against the whole world. Ready to fight everyone who got close to him, whether there was any chance of his winning it or not. Because no one was safe and everybody was out to get him. He might as well start the fight on his own terms and have a chance of controlling some part of it, even if only the beginning. It wasn't easy, fighting the whole world.

"I get it," he said. "I've been there myself."

Glen looked at him for a minute. Zachary knew what he saw. A skinny, short man who clearly wasn't up to facing off against any high school or college jocks. Unless he had unseen ninja skills like in a B movie.

"Yeah? Well, like I say, you managed her okay. I was expecting broken dishes."

There weren't even any dishes out on the table. Zachary didn't know if that meant she would have retreated to the kitchen and thrown them around in a rage there, or if he only meant it figuratively. He smiled slightly and shrugged again.

"You have employees who aren't here tonight?"

"A couple. Not a lot. We run a pretty tight ship here."

"If I could get their contact information, I'll get ahold of them by phone or email and run through the process with them too."

Glen pulled out a leather case from his pocket with index cards held by corner tabs. He started to jot the information down. "You don't really expect to find anything, though, do you?"

"Well… I might. I'm going to work my hardest to. And I'm pretty dogged. I've broken other cases that the police had given up on. Because I don't really like to let things go. I like to put a file to bed knowing that I did everything I was hired to do."

"That's admirable. But not possible in all cases, I would guess."

"No."

Glen looked at the information he had written down, reviewing it to see if he should add anything. He had, Zachary noticed, not needed to look up the phone numbers or email addresses. He pulled out the index card he had written on and handed it to

Zachary. “I’ll give them a heads-up that you are going to be contacting them.”

“That would be great, thanks.” It always made it easier if employees knew that their employer was onside with the investigation and they weren’t expected to hide anything or protect him. Though there were always those who didn’t want to do their bosses any favors and would be more resistant if warned ahead of time. But those guys were in the minority. Odds were that neither of the final two employees would cause him any trouble.

CHAPTER 19

Zachary had hoped to get some more investigating done the first day, but there had been more to do than he had anticipated. He couldn't fit everything into one day, but he had known he had several days' work ahead of him. He needed to rest and recharge, or he would crash before he had the case solved.

"Things went well?" Kenzie asked, curious about her father's case despite her objection to Zachary taking it in the first place. She sat down at the other end of the couch, sitting along it, perpendicular to him.

"A good first day," Zachary confirmed. "Had a look around, talked to the owners, most of the employees. Saw the video of the burglary and them snatching what they could and then taking off before the cops arrived."

"Professionals?" she asked.

"Hmm." Zachary had been wondering about that himself. "They looked pretty competent, and they got out of there before the security company was there to investigate the alarm being set off. They got away with a good amount of loot, considering the time they spent there. But I still got the feeling that... there was something wrong." He shook his head, unable to put his finger on precisely what had bothered him about the video. "I watched it a couple of times, and they said they would email it to me so I can watch it again until I figure out what the problem is."

"So you think that they're not professionals? Just somebody who thought there was a hole in their security that they could take advantage of?"

"Maybe. I can't say at this point. It was pulled off nice and cleanly, good planning and execution. But something still didn't feel right." He replayed the video in his head, thinking about it. Jerky, birdlike movements, keeping a close eye on the door to make sure they could get back to their vehicle before someone arrived to put a stop to the looting. The quick, efficient way they had cleared everything out in the allotted time. He tried to slow everything down in his head, but he lost focus. He needed to watch the video again. Probably a few more times. Eventually, he would identify what it was that was bothering him.

Kenzie shrugged. She put her bare feet on his leg, curling her toes against him, then pulled one of the throw blankets over her. She tended to get cold feet during the winter evenings, but didn't like to wear socks or slippers to keep them warm. She smiled at him and wiggled her toes again against his leg, taking advantage of his body heat.

"So... anyone have anything to say about my dad? Why he's so interested in this case? Does he own a partnership share in the bar? Owe them a favor for saving his life one day? Been bewitched or hypnotized to serve them?"

"I don't think so." Zachary pulled one of her feet onto his lap and massaged it.

Kenzie sighed.

“Nobody there really seemed to know him very well,” Zachary told her. “They recognized who he was when I described him or the owners pointed out where he would sit when he went in. But no one was friends with him, not even the owners. He knew their names from when they waited on him. That’s all.”

“So... he’s just this mysterious benefactor that decided to hire someone to investigate the burglary of their establishment.”

“Yup.”

“That makes no sense.”

“I know. But that’s all I’ve got so far. They called him ‘the suit’ or Mr. Kirsch. Didn’t even know his first name. Said he didn’t wear team colors or talk to anyone about the games that were playing. A friendly guy who came in every couple of weeks or so, had a drink or a snack, and then left again.”

“He must have been meeting with someone there.”

Zachary shook his head. “They say not. Said that he was only ever there by himself.”

“Walter. At a sports bar.” Kenzie closed her eyes. “That still makes no sense to me.”

“Do you think he used to go to sports with his father? Anything that might make him nostalgic? Any particular team that he might have been interested in once? Even if it was just a passing mention.”

“No. He’s never been interested in anything like that, thinks it’s a waste of time. And as far as I know, his parents were the same way. His dad was high finance, not the type to ever take a day off or relax with a beer and a game at the end of the day.”

“Did you ever play sports in school?”

“No.” Kenzie pulled her foot out of Zachary’s hand and replaced it with the other one. He massaged the arch and the ball of her foot. “To be honest, we were too wrapped up in Amanda’s illness by the time I was old enough to join any school sports teams. Amanda was all our family was focused on. Taking care of her, keeping her healthy, finding a way to help her." She shook her head, her eyes shiny with tears. "I was just counting the days until I was old enough to donate a kidney. My parents wouldn't give permission while I was a minor."

"Why not?"

"They said it was major surgery, that they didn't want to endanger my health. What if my remaining kidney failed down the line? They said they would find a non-related donor. That she was okay on dialysis until then. They wouldn't let the doctors bring it up around me. But I didn't need the doctors to tell me anything. I could figure it out on my own."

"They protected you. Didn't want to save one child at the risk of the other."

"Yeah. I think it was pretty presumptuous of them, actually. I wanted so much to help Amanda. I would have given her my kidney a couple of years earlier if they'd let me."

Zachary nodded slowly. Bit by bit, he was finding out more about Kenzie and the rift between her and her parents. It was nothing like his split from his biological parents. She was still in contact with them. But it was hard for her to talk about it. And about what had happened to Amanda.

CHAPTER 20

Do you want to see the video?"

Kenzie blinked at him. "Sure. You're okay with sharing it?"

He usually limited the information he shared with her to generalities or medical stuff that he needed her advice on. He tried to keep anything that might be confidential to himself. But the burglary wasn't exactly confidential. He'd already told her about it. And the video hadn't even been taped by them, but had come from a neighborhood camera. The video might not exactly be public, but it wasn't something that the McNichols could quash, even if they wanted to. And they hadn't had any problem sharing it.

Zachary reached for his computer table and pulled it over to himself. It only took a minute to open the clamshell, find a link to the video in his email, and bring it up on the screen. Kenzie changed position to lean on his shoulder, and they watched it together.

"Wow." Kenzie pushed the button to watch it again. "I wasn't expecting it to be so... violent. I mean, there's no violence against any people, but the way that they rip through there, throwing things down and grabbing whatever they can. It's very visceral, isn't it?"

Zachary nodded, though visceral wasn't a word that he would have come up with. He understood what Kenzie meant by it being violent. Even if no one was hurt, they had shown a certain level of anger and disregard for personal property that was disturbing.

He watched the scene play out again in front of him. The broken glass, the door being opened, the two people moving through the restaurant, grabbing what memorabilia they wanted and letting other items crash to the floor, along with chairs and tables they swept out of their way, not even bothering to walk around the furniture.

Kenzie watched closely. She touched the tip of her fingernail to the screen. “That one is a woman.”

Zachary paid closer attention, examining the masked figure. It was swathed in bulky winter outerwear, making it difficult to see its shape underneath. “Are you sure?”

“I couldn’t swear to it in court, no. But the way she moves—her gait, the way she positions her body—I’m pretty sure.”

“She is shorter than the other.”

“And he moves like a man. Maybe they are a couple.”

“That would make sense. If they need money for household bills or drugs, they could easily team up to do something like this. Get each other worked up over it. Keep talking about it until it becomes normalized instead of seeming like something they wouldn’t consider doing.”

They continued to watch the video, replaying it several times. Kenzie shrugged. “I don’t have anything else to contribute. You can’t really see much, can you?”

“No. But there’s still something more that keeps niggling at the back of my brain.”

“Sleep on it. Maybe it will occur to you in the morning.”

Zachary nodded. He watched it one more time for good measure, but was still left with the feeling that he was missing something, like an itch that was just out of his reach.

* * *

Kenzie’s advice to sleep on it was good. Still, Zachary couldn’t help thinking about the video as he was trying to go to sleep, replaying it in his head over and over again, which was not conducive to settling down to sleep. He knew from experience that doing certain activities before bed would keep him from being able to fall asleep, and he tried to shut off his computer and phone at least an hour before retiring so that he had time to unwind and let his brain slow down before sleep. He should have known better than to think about the video before bed. But once he did, he couldn't stop.

It took a long time to get to sleep, and he wasn't sure when he had actually crossed the barrier between his waking review of the video and then dreaming about it after he had dropped off. He kept dreaming it, analyzing it in his sleep. But as dreams do, it changed. Different people took on the role of the thieves in the dream. Kenzie, Tyrrell, Mr. Peterson, Walter Kirsch. Other masked figures who were bigger and carried weapons. He found himself running into the bar in his dream, trying to save some nameless person who was in the path of the destruction. But how could he defend anyone against the monsters with guns? How could he reach the person he needed to save and get them out of the bar before the inevitable happened? And then the inevitable did happen and Barnburners went up in flames. Zachary's anxiety morphed into panic as he screamed for everyone to get out. The person he had been protecting. The thieves. Walter, Kenzie, Tyrrell.

“T!” Zachary shouted, his voice constricted by the smoke and his own panic. “T, get out! Get out; there’s a fire!”

“It’s okay. It’s okay, Zachary. Shh. Wake up.” There were gentle hands on him, nudging him, urging him to escape the nightmare.

“T. We’ve got to get them out,” Zachary croaked.

“Everyone is safe. Everyone got out of the fire,” Kenzie assured him. “The firemen got everyone out safe.”

He turned toward her and held her against him, his heart thumping wildly. Kenzie snuggled into him, repeating the reassurances. Letting him know that the nightmare was over and he was no longer a ten-year-old trapped in the burning house, screaming at his siblings to get out.

"It was the bar," he told her, trying to get the words out into the open. "This time, it was the bar that was on fire, not the house."

"Well, that didn't happen. The bar was fine. Just a burglary. They'll recover from that."

"And Tyrrell wasn't there."

"No."

"Not you. Not anyone."

"No. No one was there. Everyone you know is safe."

He breathed slowly for a few minutes, paying attention to each breath in and out. When he had been in the fire, his airways had been swollen and painful. It had been hard to breathe, even when they put an oxygen mask over his face. But lying there in bed with Kenzie, his breathing was normal. Cool air flowed through his throat and into his lungs and didn't hurt. He was okay. There hadn't been a fire at the bar; it had just been a dream.

He sat up slowly, trying not to disturb Kenzie, but she reached out and touched him. “Stay here. Go back to sleep.”

“Can’t right now. I’ll get up for a while and see if I can get tired again.”

She groaned. “You won’t go back to sleep if you get up now.”

“It’s okay. You can go back to sleep. You need to work tomorrow.”

He got out of bed. Kenzie didn’t try to stop him. He pulled on pajama pants and a t-shirt and went out to the living room, where he started to go through his notes and review his emails, studiously ignoring the video file.

CHAPTER 21

Even though Zachary's brain desperately wanted to watch the video again, stuck in the rut of replaying it in his memory, Zachary resisted. He pushed it as far from his thoughts as he could and let his subconscious mind work on it. That was the part of his brain that knew something was wrong. If he refused to acknowledge it, sooner or later, his brain would be forced to process it and push it back to his conscious mind.

He looked through the "before" pictures that he had downloaded from social media and reviews, along with the "after" pictures that he had taken at the bar. Pulling out the list of stolen property, he tried to match each item on the list to its image in the pictures. Of course, not all of them would have been captured on social media, and they probably changed and were added to from time to time as the McNichols acquired new pieces. But they had walked him through where each one had been displayed, and he worked from his memory and the photos to identify each one he could.

When he had finished, he looked at the after pictures. Not everything had been stolen, of course. Just what the thieves had been able to grab in the two minutes they had been inside the bar. Items not itemized in the list should all still be on the walls, display shelves, and tables.

When Kenzie got up in the morning, Zachary's eyes were gritty, and he knew he had been staring at the computer screen for too long. It was time to blink, put some eye drops in, and have coffee and breakfast with Kenzie.

"Morning," Kenzie greeted, rubbing her eyes. "How are you doing?"

She didn't point out that she had been right about him not getting tired and returning to the bedroom. But of course, both of them had known that she was right at the time. That didn't matter. Zachary had known that he wouldn't go back to sleep if he stayed in bed, either. If he tossed and turned and got frustrated lying there, he would just keep her awake, and she needed to get her sleep in order to function at work. Zachary could always take a break during the day for a nap. Though, of course, that never happened. He didn't sleep during the day unless he was sick or traumatized.

"Good, good," he assured her. "How was your sleep?"

"Great. I went back to sleep. Which it doesn't look like you did."

There were times when he could stretch out on the couch to snooze or had fallen asleep working on his computer, but those occasions were pretty rare.

"No. But I got some work done. Billable hours." He smiled. "For your dad."

"Well, that's good. If the case is going to keep you awake, you may as well bill him for it."

Zachary pressed his lids closed for a few seconds, trying to work up some tears to irrigate them. "How did you know the case was keeping me awake?"

"You said you dreamed about a fire at the bar."

"Oh, yeah. That's right."

"Did you find anything interesting?"

"In fact... I did."

* * *

Zachary's next step was a review of social media. Most of the employees at the bar were young, and young people were on social media all the time. He could look at each employee's social networks and construct a timeline. See who had been where at what time. Who was friends with whom. Who might have had reasons to make a very bad choice.

It wasn't hard. In a society that chose to be on camera 24/7, Zachary had no need for warrants for video footage or the police to put the suspects under surveillance. He could find everything he needed right there on their feeds.

There was no need for Big Brother. They had Little Brother, held right there in the palms of their hands and on selfie sticks. Monitoring themselves without any need for an overlord to interfere in their private lives.

Zachary went through each popular social network methodically. It was still going to be a guess, but he wanted it to be an educated guess. He wanted to be pretty dang sure before he started making accusations.

Once he was sure, he would go back to Montpelier.

* * *

Zachary scouted out the first address on his list. He was about eighty percent confident that he knew who the culprit was. He walked down the street in front of the building and then down the alley behind it. The garbage bins had been set out for collection, which was a lucky break that he hadn't expected. After glancing up and down the alley to make sure there were no backyard mechanics watching him, he lifted the lid on the bin behind the house and started pulling out the garbage bags.

It was a fourplex, so there was only a one in four chance that any one bag belonged to his target, but he might get lucky. He ripped each open on the ground, spreading the contents out for inspection, then balling them back up in the ripped bag to return to the bin afterward.

He was down to the last bag, not having found anything worth mentioning, when he hit pay dirt. Two black balaclavas and medical gloves like the thieves had been wearing in the security footage. Zachary's heart raced as he looked down at them. He glanced up and down the lane again, making sure that he was not being watched.

After putting everything else back in the bin, he dialed his phone.

"Emergency services. Can I get your name and location, please?"

Zachary dutifully went through his information as he answered each question in turn, waiting for the opportunity to tell what he had called for. It was a good thing that someone wasn't in immediate danger. But then, if the operator could hear a fracas in the background, maybe she would have gotten to the crux faster than she did.

"What is the problem?" the dispatcher finally asked.

"I have evidence that the residents here were involved in a burglary and theft at a bar a week ago. I need someone from the police department to secure the evidence and hopefully to make an arrest."

"What makes you think that they were involved in this theft?" She sounded bored. How many times a day did she have to listen to muddled stories and sort out the real complaints from the nonsense people called in?

"I've watched the security video of the burglary and theft several times and identified them as the most likely suspects.

I've just looked through their trash and found the masks and gloves they were wearing during the burglary."

"I see. Where was this burglary and was it reported to the police?"

"Yes, it was. The bar is called Barnburners." He gave the address and Glen and Janice McNichols's names.

"Do you know who the detective assigned to the case was?"

"I don't have his name, no. I haven't been in contact with him."

"Can you hold, please?" she said with a sigh.

She was gone before Zachary had a chance to answer. He held the phone to his ear, looking around again. Before long, someone was going to notice his presence there and want to know what was going on. People could get nasty quickly if they thought someone was up to no good, casing them out or rummaging through the garbage...

CHAPTER 22

He was also getting cold and had left his car on the street back around the front of the house. He didn't want to let the gloves and masks out of his sight, but he wanted to leave them there where he had found them. Even if the detective on the case decided it was worth his while to come out to the house and take a look at the "evidence" that a civilian had turned up, it would be at least twenty minutes to half an hour before he made it there.

Zachary should have worn heavier gloves. He'd already spent a good length of time out in the wintry air going through the garbage bags.

He started to pace up and down the back lane, still within sight of the evidence but trying to keep his toes from freezing while he stood there. He tucked one hand under his armpit while using the other to hold the phone to his ear, then switched hands to try to warm up the other.

Winter was not a good time to be doing outdoor investigating in Vermont. It was at least fifteen minutes before the dispatcher finally returned to the call, maybe closer to half an hour. Zachary's ears were hurting, even though he had his hat pulled down to cover them.

"Mr. Goldman, thank you for holding."

"Hi." Zachary was finding himself a little breathless from the cold. "So, are you sending someone out here?"

"The detective on the case isn't available right now, and we don't have any available units. I'm afraid we can't get anyone over to you right now."

"You can't spare anyone to collect evidence that breaks a case? There isn't anyone free?"

"I'm sorry. Everyone is tied up at the moment. We don't have a large police force. We'll send someone over as soon as we can, but it probably won't be for a few hours."

"I can't stay here that long. I'm already frozen."

"We're not asking you to, sir. I'll note your issue and make sure that the detective gets it. And as soon as I have a spare unit, I'll send it over. That's the best I can do."

"So I'm supposed to just... leave the evidence out here and hope that it's still there when someone comes over? It would make more sense for me to collect it... I can swear an affidavit about where I found it..."

"Just leave everything as it is, sir."

"Seriously?"

"Yes, sir. We appreciate your cooperation."

"You really don't want to solve this case, do you?"

Her voice grew testy. "I told you that I just don't have anyone available at the moment, sir. That doesn't mean that we don't want to solve the case. It means we're operating under the restrictions that we have. You wouldn't expect an officer to drop an emergency he's on now, putting lives in danger, to collect your evidence."

"No. I would expect that you would have enough staff to take care of calls as they come in."

"I would too," she sighed. "But that's just not reality. We have to prioritize cases. Someone will follow up as soon as possible. But in the meantime, you don't need to stay there. I have taken down all of your details."

"And I should just leave the evidence here."

"Yes."

Zachary couldn't think of anything else to say. It wasn't like he would be able to talk her into having more police units available. They had to play the hand they were dealt. Shaking his head, Zachary lowered his hand and took off his glove to operate the freezing cold phone. He was lucky that it hadn't turned off in the time that he'd been waiting on the 9-1-1 dispatcher. He'd had that issue before when phones shut off due to the temperature. Working as quickly as he could, he tapped the screen with numb fingers to take a few pictures of the hats and gloves, the garbage bin, and the number on the fence. He looked around for anything else that they might need to put the pictures into context and, as he walked away down the lane, he snapped a few more shots of the alley.

Back in his car with the engine running, he waited for his fingers and toes to start warming up. It hadn't seemed that bitterly cold to begin with, but he had been outside long enough that the cold had really gotten down into his joints. He remembered being on the street a couple of times as a child or teen. Never for very long. He found he didn't like roughing it. Especially not during the winter. Too easy to get hypothermia.

He started to shiver as he warmed up and realized that he had pushed it a bit too far. He'd obviously been colder than he had thought. He'd thought he'd kept his core temperature up to where it needed to be. But with his weight being so low, he didn't have the insulation needed to keep him warm.

Once his fingers thawed out and he stopped shivering, he paged through the photos on the phone, looking them over and deciding whether he needed to take any more. The front of the house? The side? If he were lucky and they were away from home—and so far, he had been lucky on the case—then he might be able to see something incriminating through the windows. Who knew how long it would be before the police got there and whether they would bother to get a warrant based on what he had said on the phone. More than likely, they would wait until they had seen the evidence with their own eyes, and then take time to process what it meant for the case and if they had enough to arrest the couple for their part in the theft.

Once he was feeling pretty toasty again, Zachary got out of the car and took a couple of pictures of the front of the fourplex. There still didn't appear to be anyone around. He walked to the side and took pictures of the door and mailbox. A few envelopes were sticking out of the mailbox, and he pulled them partway out to check the full names of the recipients and the senders. One of the mail pieces was from an auction house.

Zachary swore under his breath. He held the envelope overhead against the sunlight and tried to make out any words on the letter inside. But it was folded in thirds and he couldn't see any words.

If they were dealing with an auction house, then the memorabilia they had stolen could already be on the block. It would be risky to sell them again so quickly, but criminals were not known for making good decisions. Criminal masterminds tended to be something from TV, not reality.

He walked around the building, aware that he was leaving footprints in the snow. It would be obvious to the residents that someone had walked the house's perimeter looking in all of the windows.

When he returned to the couple's door, his luck ran out. A woman in a tattered coat stood there, smoking a cigarette, watching him like a hawk. She was tall and round, and she looked tough, like she might have wrestled or done some kind of hand-to-hand combat in the past.

"Who are you?" she demanded. "What are you doing skulking around here?"

CHAPTER 23

Zachary's brain raced on ahead, trying to come up with the most plausible approach. Of course, the best thing to do would just be to retreat. Walk back to his car. If she called the police, she wouldn't be able to get them there before Zachary got away from the scene. What if she did get his license plate? The local police were clearly too overworked to stay on top of cases that were not considered priority.

But that would mean abandoning what he had already found out and any chance he had of advancing the case further. The masks and gloves would be gone by the time the police got there. There would be nothing but Zachary's guesses to connect the couple with the robbery. They were good guesses, obviously. But they wouldn't be enough for the police to investigate. Not once the masks and gloves were removed from the scene.

"Oh, thank goodness you're here!" Zachary told the large woman fervently. "Do you have the key? She said someone would be here with the key, and I've rung all of the bells, but there is no one around and I thought... I thought something had happened."

"What key?" the woman asked, frowning.

"To unit C," Zachary gestured to the door. "I'm supposed to feed the cat!"

"What cat? There are no pets allowed in the building."

"Oh... no, I didn't mean that. I meant... they wanted me to check in and make sure that everything was okay while they were gone."

"They've got a cat?" The woman chuckled. "I've got a chihuahua myself. Not easy to keep it from the landlord if he comes around without notice. One water leak could blow us all."

"She didn't want anything to happen to it while she's gone," Zachary confessed. Despite the cold, his face was sweating. A bead of sweat ran down his back as well. "The cat has diabetes, and it's supposed to have insulin shots and be fed at the same time every day. If it doesn't get its shots, it could die." Zachary nodded to emphasize this. "It could; she said so."

The woman puffed on her cigarette and rubbed her forehead, thinking about it. "I didn't know they had a cat. But then, why would they tell me? Everybody has their secrets."

"So... does that mean you don't have a key?" Zachary looked around. "Someone was supposed to be here to give me a key."

The neighbor looked around, but there was no one nearby paying them any attention. Whoever was supposed to have given Zachary the keys to feed the poor diabetic cat had obviously fallen down on the job.

"Maybe they were in an accident," Zachary said. "Man, I hope that nothing happened! If they broke a leg or something and can't get here, then how am I going to get in?" He looked at the house and shuddered. "I couldn't break a window. Someone would kill me. Besides, then the cat would be able to get out."

The woman considered, still looking around for someone to materialize. She scratched her neck.

"The landlord keyed all of the doors the same," she said finally. "He's a lazy so-and-so and doesn't want to have to carry around more than one set of keys and figure out which one it is. We're not supposed to know, but of course, we figured it out a long time ago."

"Does that mean your key would work on this door?" Zachary pointed to unit C hopefully. It would be great if someone would let him into the suite. He didn't plan on getting caught, but if he did, things would be far more likely to go in his direction if he'd been let in by someone with a key.

"Yes," the woman admitted. "But you have to promise me that you're legit. You're really here to feed the cat?"

"Yes. Of course. I don't randomly go around breaking into people's houses."

She nodded, chuckling. Eventually, she leaned toward the door and produced her own keys to unlock the door. She turned the handle and pushed it open. Zachary stepped forward, catching the door quickly so that it only opened a crack. “You don’t want it to get out!” he warned. Making himself as small as possible, he slid through the door, pulling it shut behind him.

He had a feeling that the woman wasn’t going to stay there. She would come in after him to make sure that there really was a cat and he was there to feed it rather than getting into mischief.

He hurried through the entryway, cut through the living room, and entered the kitchen. It still smelled of whatever they had fried up for breakfast. The suite was warm and comfortable. Zachary went through the cupboards, quickly gathering what he would need.

He was right about the neighbor not being able to stay outside. She had to enter and make sure that he was not telling her a story.

“Well?” she demanded, looking around, “Where is the cat?”

“Fido?” Zachary called loudly and made kissing noises. “Snowball?”

They both stood there and listened for answering footsteps or bells.

“Hiding somewhere,” Zachary said, shaking his head. “She said they’re pretty shy. I might have to stick around for a while to find them and get their trust.”

“It’s two cats now?” She demanded. “Or a cat and a dog?”

“Well...” Zachary did his best to appear sheepish and wiped sweat from his forehead. “I’m really not supposed to say. If it is a no-pet building...”

He ran water into a bowl and set it down on the floor while the woman watched. She looked at the brown, pasty glop in the other bowl. “Don’t you think that’s too much?”

“For two cats?” Zachary looked down at it. “I didn’t measure it, but she said to give them enough. You can always throw out what they don’t eat, but if the cat doesn’t get enough to eat during the day, it could go into shock or something. They have to have enough to eat, and I have to give it the insulin...” Zachary went to the fridge and started pushing things around as if looking for the vials of insulin. He looked over the door at the woman. “Was there anything else? I don’t think I’m supposed to let anyone else in here.”

The woman raised her hands. “Okay, fine. I’ll go. Looks like you’ve got everything under control here.”

She turned and went back out. Zachary listened until he heard the outside door open and close again, then waited a few more seconds to make sure that she was really gone and it wasn't just a trick.

"Fido?" he called again. "Snowball?"

Not waiting for the imaginary pets to show their faces, he pulled the can of refried beans back out of the sink and looked at it. "Thank goodness they like Mexican." He put the remainder of the can into the garbage, burying it under what was already there. As the trash was nearly full, he hoped that they would be taking it out to the bin soon and would not notice the smell of the refried beans. He would clean up the "cat" bowls before he left, but left them where they were in the meantime, just in case the neighbor came back.

It was time to check out the rest of the unit before the suspects returned. He did not want to get caught there. Coming up with an explanation for his presence would be a lot more difficult than fooling the neighbor had been.

CHAPTER 24

Zachary left the kitchen, looked briefly around the living room, and then walked through to the bedrooms and bathroom in the back of the unit. The first bedroom looked pretty normal. A queen bed, low to the floor, and a couple of side tables with lamps, clothes closet, items of clothing messily strewn here and there. Lived in. Not tidied up for company. They didn't expect anyone else to be in there. He didn't spend any time searching it. There wasn't space under the bed for storage and a glance at the open closet assured him that there would be nothing to find there. Not unless they had another storage space hidden behind a false wall.

He went to the other bedroom. The couple didn't have any children; he knew that from their social media. The second bedroom should be a guest room, storage, or home office. But as far as he could tell, they didn't have a home business, both of them working outside the home.

At first glance, a storage room. Several stacks of moving boxes that had probably been there since they had moved in together. A few items of smaller furniture or decor that they did not have the space for in the suite. But there were stacks of boxes to his right, lined up along the wall beside the doorway. Bending down to look at them, he saw that shipping labels were affixed to them. Zachary moved the boxes in order to examine each label. Not all addressed to individuals. There were two that were addressed to auction companies. He took out his keys and opened the pen knife on his keychain. He slit the packing tape down the middle of the two flaps and snapped them open.

And there it was. Sports memorabilia taken from Barnburners. He reached automatically for his phone, then paused. There was no point in calling the police; he'd already been told that the detective on the case was unavailable and so was anyone else in the department. There was not even a car available to come and secure the evidence from the garbage bins. There was no point in calling them and having the same discussion again.

He took pictures of the boxes and the contents of the one that he had opened. He stepped back and took several shots of the room, then walked around the suite, snapping photos of the other rooms as proof that he had been there and hadn't just staged the boxes somewhere else. Was there anything else to do? He could send the pictures to the police, and they could arrange for a warrant when it reached the top of their priorities list and come by and pick up the boxes. Then the thieves could be arrested and the case closed.

But that didn't sit well with Zachary.

He could wait and let the police do it right. That was, ninety-nine percent of the time, the right choice. But there was always that last percent or fraction of a percent.

The thieves had already disposed of the evidence that they had been involved in the burglary. That evidence would probably be gone by the time the police got there. The mask and gloves would be taken or cleaned up by someone walking down the alley. Or the couple themselves would see that someone had been into the garbage and would see the evidence of their wrongdoing there on display for all the world to see.

And the rest of the evidence was packaged up and ready to go. The couple had been quick to find buyers for some of the products and an auction house to deal with the rest. It was probably not the first time they had done something like this. They were not likely to leave the packed and labeled boxes in the storage room. They would get home from work and one of them would take them to the nearest shipper and send them on their way. And then all evidence of what they had done would be gone. Zachary would be unable to prove anything to the police. He had the pictures, but that would probably not be enough to convict them. And they might not be able to get back the items that had been sold to third parties.

He went back and looked at the packaged and labeled boxes, running scenarios through his brain. With things as they currently stood, he saw more opportunities for things to go sideways and the memorabilia to be permanently out of their reach than he did for them to line up properly, with the police getting all of the evidence they needed and the stolen memorabilia going back to Glen and Janice.

Zachary pressed his lips together grimly, deciding what to do next.

In a couple of minutes, he had carried the first couple of boxes out to his car, popped them into the trunk, and was heading back inside for another load.

The nosy but ultimately helpful neighbor again stood by the door, her eyes sharp, ready with another barrage of questions. Zachary looked at her, raising one eyebrow.

“Thanks for your help,” he told her crisply. “I just have a few more things to take care of here.”

“What are you doing?”

“Taking some deliveries to the post office.” He stared at her. “I don’t see how that’s any of your business.”

She didn’t stop him from going back into the suite, but she was still there when he came out with the next set of boxes. She leaned in to look at them as he walked by. Taller than he was, it wasn’t hard for her to see the address label on the top box. She could see that everything was properly packaged and labeled for delivery.

“You didn’t say you were picking up any parcels,” she pointed out.

“I didn’t think I was required to tell you everything I was doing here.”

“All you said was that you needed to feed the cat.”

Zachary shifted his grip on the heavy boxes and kept walking. “The cat was what I was most worried about. The boxes could wait if I couldn't get into the house. But a cat with diabetes? It couldn't wait, not even a few hours. It could be dead by the time I got in if it didn't get its food and insulin at the right times."

He kept walking to his car and settled the next set of boxes into the trunk. He closed the trunk lid to prevent the neighbor from taking pictures or pulling a box or two out for further examination. One more trip should do it.

He grabbed the last couple of boxes and set them down outside the door. Turning, he took the time to lock the door before closing it again. He was done there. It would be obvious to the thieves that someone had been there, but they couldn't exactly go to the police about it.

The neighbor watched as he trudged back to his car with the last couple of boxes and slid them into the back seat.

"Thanks again for your help," he told her, forcing a smile. "Have a great day!"

She probably wouldn't. Not once the thieves realized what had happened and looked into how someone had gotten into their suite.

CHAPTER 25

Zachary made sure he was out of sight of the house and that there was no one around to observe him before tapping the Bluetooth button on his steering wheel and placing an outgoing call to Janice. The call went almost immediately to voicemail. Zachary hung up and tried Glen. His phone also went to voicemail right away. He hung up, then frowned and thought about that for a few minutes.

They were somewhere that they could not answer their phones. Maybe a theater or a business meeting that could not be disturbed. Or maybe they turned off their phones for some quiet time together during the day. That wasn't the usual behavior for a dedicated smartphone user, and Zachary had seen both of them using their phones regularly while performing various tasks. But of course, they could be an exception. One of those few couples who actually implemented the Do Not Disturb or Focus features of their phones.

More likely, they were somewhere phones were not allowed. That worried him, but he couldn't do anything about it. He called Janice once more, hoping that it was just a phone network issue and that it would be answered this time, but again it rang directly through to voicemail. Zachary waited for her outgoing message to finish, then left a brief voicemail.

"Hi Janice, it's Zachary Goldman. I've made some progress on the case and would be grateful if you would give me a call. Thanks." He left his number again, even though she would be able to see it on her screen.

Hopefully, it wouldn't be too long before she called back. Zachary decided to stop and have lunch while he waited. Kenzie would be impressed.

He selected a drive-through so that he wouldn't have to leave the loot alone in the car, and sat in the warm cabin eating slowly while he scrolled through the email and social networks on his phone, waiting for it to ring with a call back from Janice.

But the call did not come. Zachary had waited for an hour and a half and couldn't stand sitting in the car any longer without something constructive to do. There was only so much work he could do on his phone. There was no call from the police to say that they were on their way to pick up the evidence. No call from Janice or Glen, apologizing for being out of reach. He couldn't just sit around waiting for them to get back to him all afternoon.

Eventually, he turned around and headed for home. The memorabilia would keep. It would be safe at Kenzie's house until he could get it to Janice and Glen.

* * *

He apologized immediately to Kenzie when she came home and saw the boxes in her living room. "Just let me know where you want me to put this stuff. It should only be a day. I didn't know if you wanted them in the garage or in the office… I just didn't want to leave it in the car because of security…"

Kenzie looked at the stack of boxes and shook her head. "This is everything that was stolen from the sports bar?"

"Well, I haven't itemized it yet. But it looks like it. I wanted to leave as much of it as possible intact for the police. There might be fingerprints on the packing tape, hairs, other forensic evidence..."

"They're really not going to be doing a bunch of forensic testing on a few boxes of recovered memorabilia," she pointed out with a chuckle.

"I know..." Zachary was always disappointed when the real-life police did not imitate those he saw on TV who were always intent on finding and analyzing every last bit of forensic evidence in even the smallest, least significant cases. Because you never knew what might be a clue to a bigger crime, an organized syndicate or serial killer. But of course, Kenzie was right. They would ask Glen and Janice if that was all their stolen property, then close the file. He would be lucky if they went on to arrest the culprits, considering the fact that Zachary had removed evidence from the scene. “But they could.”

“They could,” Kenzie conceded. “Why don’t you put them in the office for now? Just stack them against the wall.”

He had thought she would prefer having them stored in the garage, so it was a good thing he had asked. She probably didn’t want to risk his bumping a hand cart full of boxes into her “baby,” Kenzie’s red convertible.

“I’ll get them out of here,” Zachary agreed.

Kenzie probably wouldn’t react violently to things being out of place or somewhere other than where she wanted them to be as Bridget would have. Still, he didn’t want the presence of the boxes to irritate her, especially if they reminded her of her father and how Zachary had gone ahead and taken Walter’s case when she didn’t want him to.

He grabbed a couple of boxes, carried them down the hall to the office, put them down to open the door, and then set them against the wall. The room was small and didn't boast a lot of extra space, so it would feel cramped once he had all of the boxes in place. But at least they would be out of sight. Kenzie didn't use her office very often. Zachary was sure that he would be able to talk to Glen and Janice before then and take the boxes to them.

He made a couple more trips out to the living room and back and had the boxes all neatly stacked out of sight in the office in a few minutes. Kenzie was rummaging around in the kitchen, starting to get dinner ready. They hadn't discussed what they were having, but Kenzie obviously had something in mind, so he didn't make any suggestions and started setting the table. Whatever they were eating, they were going to need plates, cups, and cutlery.

Kenzie filled a pot with water, put it on the burner, then turned to face Zachary, leaning against the calendar.

"I've got a program for Tyrrell."

"You do? That's great. Where is it?"

Kenzie started to fill him in on the details. "They're going to want him right away, which is good, because I think he's waited long enough. If we have to keep waiting..."

Zachary nodded. "He's going to have a setback sooner or later. Once he's in the program, it will be easier."

"He's done really well, but I don't want to tempt fate."

Zachary was relieved that it was a longer program. It had been hard to find one that was longer than 30 days or six weeks. If they could keep Tyrrell in a longer-term program, with some good transition services, he would have a better chance of really integrating the change. Zachary didn't believe in God, but felt like he should send a prayer out to the universe somehow that this time, sobriety would "take" and Tyrrell wouldn't keep relapsing.

"One day at a time," Kenzie advised, meeting his eyes.

Zachary nodded. He took a deep breath and let it out. “Yeah. Take things as they come.” Dr. B had given him several strategies to avoid getting overly anxious about things that hadn’t happened yet. There was no point in assuming that things would go wrong, or that they would go right, for that matter. It was best to just take each day as it came and be flexible with it.

Flexibility was not something that came easily to him. But Dr. B said it was something he could work on and get better at. He took a couple more deep breaths, looking ahead just one or two days, as Tyrrell was admitted into the facility.

“He should see Mason and Alisha before he goes in. Do they allow visitors during the program?”

Kenzie nodded. “Not for the first few weeks. It’s closed until then, just the patients working with the professionals and group. No distractions. No one who might try to pull them away from the program. It would be good if they could see him one more time before he goes in. Maybe talk to him about that?"

"Have you told him about the program?"

She nodded. "I called Tyrrell to make sure it was okay and gave him the main points. I think he's eager to get to it."

"I'll go talk to him, then."

CHAPTER 26

He left Kenzie to work on the dinner and went down the hall to the guest room. He hadn't seen Tyrrell since he had arrived home with the boxes, but assumed that he was cocooned in the guest room as usual. He tapped lightly on the door and, after waiting a few seconds, opened it a crack.

"Hey, T?"

Tyrrell was stretched out on the bed, listening to something on his phone, earbuds in his ears. He heard Zachary or saw the movement of the door and turned his head, then sat up and took the earbuds out, tapping the phone to pause whatever was playing.

"Hey, Zach. How's it going?"

"Good. How about you?"

"Fine. Dinnertime?"

"No, Kenzie's just working on it now." Zachary walked into the room and stood a few feet away from Tyrrell, folding his arms and trying to affect a casual stance, not hovering over Tyrrell or giving off any anxiety. "She just told me about the program that she's got you into."

Tyrrell nodded, smiling at that. "Yeah, she's really a gem, Zachary. You really got a winner in her."

"I know. She's amazing." He didn't give Kenzie enough credit. It was too easy to get used to someone, to get used to being around her and her doing things for him, not realizing how much it really was. Kenzie put up with a lot with Zachary's quirks and issues and never yelled and berated him the way Bridget had. Kenzie got impatient sometimes, was curt or said something she later regretted but, as far as Zachary was concerned, she was pretty close to perfect.

"Yeah. You're lucky." Tyrrell's voice was a little wistful. Undoubtedly thinking about his own lack of a partner. How things had not turned out for him and Lindsey the way they had for Zachary and Kenzie. And probably blaming himself for the fact that things had fallen apart, the marriage too stressed by Tyrrell's drinking, two children, one of them with behavioral issues, and Tyrrell's absences whenever things got to be too difficult.

"I was just thinking," Zachary said, trying to move quickly away from morose thoughts about the failure of Tyrrell's marriage. "The kids aren't going to be able to see you for a few weeks, the first little while you're in this program. So you should see if you can visit with them one more time before you go in."

Tyrrell scratched his chin. He hadn't shaven that day. Maybe for a few days. "I don't know. I don't like to ask Lindsey for something like that. It's not on the visitation schedule."

"It isn't yet. But she'll understand that you can't visit with them while you're in a closed program. You don't think she would try to make it work?"

"I don't think I should ask. I've asked too much of her already."

"All she can do is say no."

"She can say a lot more than <u>that</u>!" Tyrrell said with a laugh, then looked embarrassed that he had said it. "It's just... I know the kids have school and after-school activities, and Lindsey has work. It's not a good time to be asking for an extra visit. Maybe if it was the weekend, but..."

Zachary stood there, trying to figure out what to do. Was it a hard "no," or was Tyrrell just reluctant to call? If he pushed back, would Tyrrell give in and agree, or resist and be angry with Zachary for interfering with his family relationships?

"What if I called her?" he asked eventually. "If the request is coming from someone other than you, would that be better?"

Tyrrell nodded, looking relieved. It probably wasn't good for Zachary to be enabling Tyrrell backing out of his responsibilities. It was clearly Tyrrell's job to make the call and see if he could visit his kids for a few more hours before going into the program. But they could worry about building responsibility after Tyrrell was out of the program. Before, it was probably best to help out where he could and not put more stress on Tyrrell before then.

The last thing they needed was Tyrrell disappearing again before entering the program. Zachary had already spent a week tracking him down. He knew where to look now, but if Tyrrell really wanted to avoid being found, he could find another bar to hide out in. He could go anywhere in the state. Anywhere that he could get to with the gas already in his tank. Farther if he happened to have a working credit card.

"Okay. I'll give Lindsey a call."

"Thanks, bro. I really appreciate it."

Zachary hesitated for a moment, trying to decide between calling Lindsey on speakerphone with Tyrrell in the room, so he could hear her and respond to any questions she might have, or leaving the room so that Tyrrell didn't have to participate at all.

He decided that keeping Tyrrell calm and relaxed was probably best and walked out of the guest room while he tapped the contact on his phone to get a hold of Lindsey.

* * *

Contrary to what Tyrrell had thought, Lindsey had been very accommodating about getting one more visit in with the kids before entering the program. She promised to see what she could do about changing her schedule and would pull the kids from whatever their usual after-school activities were to get them some time together.

“It’s really tough dealing with them after they get back from a visit,” Lindsey confessed to Zachary. “They get depressed, act up, don’t want to do anything I tell them to... I know Alisha worries about whether that’s the last time she’ll ever see him. Mason probably feels the same way but doesn’t realize it. It makes me question sometimes whether it is worth setting up visitations.”

Zachary tried to think of what to say to counter this. He knew Lindsey wasn't really asking his position, but he didn't want to support the idea of keeping the kids apart from Tyrrell.

"But I know it's the right thing," Lindsey went on before Zachary could say anything. "Even if they are stressed and crabby afterward... at least they get to see him. To know that he's okay and have a bit of a chance to build their relationship."

"Yeah," Zachary agreed, glad that he didn't have to say anything to convince her about it being worth it. He could have argued that the court would force visitation if she didn't allow it, but that would be confrontational and might not even be true. With the right expert witnesses on her side, she probably could convince a judge that Tyrrell's disappearances and temper when he was drinking were detrimental to the children and they shouldn't be forced to see him when it was just doing them more emotional harm.

"I'll get them over there tomorrow, one way or another," Lindsey said. "That will work, right? He'll at least take a day before he checks into this program?"

"I'm sure we can take a day to pack and get ready for it. He said he wanted to see them but wasn't sure he would be able to before the weekend."

"I'll make it work."

"Okay. If you want to just give me a call or shoot me a text when you've worked it out, I'll let him know what time."

"Thanks, Zachary. And... thanks for acting as a buffer between us. It makes it easier for me."

"Oh... you're welcome." He had thought that she would prefer to deal with Tyrrell directly, so he was a little surprised at her comment. Maybe both of them needed an intermediary for a little while. Until they both felt up to talking to each other directly again. He might bring it up to Dr. Boyle during their couple's therapy session and see if she had any advice on the matter. Couple's therapy wasn't really the time to be discussing someone else's relationship issues. Still, he thought he could find a way to make it more relevant to his and Kenzie's relationship. A hypothetical situation, maybe. Or just a question on when it was okay to involve an intermediary when a discussion was difficult.

CHAPTER 27

As Zachary was helping to clean up after dinner, his phone started to vibrate, and he looked at it, hoping that it would be Janice or Glen. Dreading that it would be the police and he would have to explain what he had done and why. But instead, it was Walter. Zachary looked at it for a moment as it rang, trying to decide on a course of action.

"I'd better take this," he said eventually, and walked out of the room before answering. "Zachary here."

"Zachary." Walter's voice was ebullient; rich and cheery. "I was just hoping for an update on how the case is going. I know you'll let me know when there is something to report, but..."

"Oh. Actually, yeah, I do have news. I was hoping to reach Glen and Janice first, but they've been out of touch all day." He worried that thought over in his mind for a few seconds, a knot of dread in his stomach. Had something happened to them? Why had they just disappeared from view so suddenly?

It was sure to be something minor. Just a problem with their phone carrier, or a lunch date at the restaurant, after which they had forgotten to take their phones out of Do Not Disturb mode. Nothing had happened to them.

“Well, that’s great,” Walter exclaimed, apparently unconcerned by the couple’s unavailability. “Tell me about it.”

“I should start at the beginning. Are you at your computer? Can I do a screen share with you to show you what I discovered?”

“Sure. Send me an invitation and I’ll meet you.”

In a few minutes, they had switched from the phone call to a web conference, with Zachary sharing his screen with his client.

“You’ve seen the video, right?” Zachary asked. “Footage of the break-in?”

“No, I haven’t seen it.”

“Oh, okay. Let me just play that first, then.”

Zachary brought up the video and played it full screen. As Kenzie had noted, it was startling in its violence. Zachary was getting used to it, but he tried to see it as Walter would be seeing it for the first time. With no preconceived notions. Not something that he had watched a hundred times before and broken down and analyzed in detail. He let his vision blur and just watched the shapes moving on the screen. Angry or anxious, jerky, watching for the cops, knocking stuff over and grabbing whatever they could of the sports memorabilia.

Walter swore. “That’s brutal,” he said. “I had no idea of the... ferocity. I just pictured... like you see on TV, on a heist movie. A quiet break-in, moving carefully from room to room to avoid setting off any security alarms... targeting the one thing in the room that they came for. This is far more... feral.”

“Kenzie noticed that too,” Zachary acknowledged. Maybe mentioning his daughter would help Walter feel like he was getting his money’s worth out of this case. An unconscious confirmation that he was getting what he wanted.

"You showed it to Kenzie?"

"Uh... yes. I didn't think it was confidential."

"No. No, of course not. So... there was something on that video that you could use?"

"At first, I was just looking at it for the general stuff—how did they get in, what were they looking for, was there anything to identify who the burglars were..."

"Right. And you found something?"

"Kenzie thought that this burglar," Zachary moved a spotlight cursor over one of the figures in the frozen video, "is a woman."

"Oh. Well... I suppose it's possible. She is smaller than the other one."

"And she moves differently. Kenzie thought she moved more like a woman."

"I'll take her word for it," Walter chuckled.

Zachary knew that he could often tell whether a person he saw on a surveillance job was a man or a woman based on how they moved, without seeing their body shape and without gendered clothing styles. He wasn't sure he would have Kenzie's confidence with it and had not noticed that the person in the video was a woman. Still, he often subconsciously absorbed much more about a person than he realized.

"So, this looks pretty much like you expected it to," Zachary said, moving his spotlight over the walls in the video. "The way that the bar looks, not the robbery itself."

"Sure. I'd recognize that as Barnburners. It's obvious."

"I have some other photos." Zachary opened his file folder and opened up several pictures to look at. "These are mostly from social media and reviews. People who have taken pictures while they were there."

“Right,” Walter agreed, but his voice held a note of hesitation. Wondering where Zachary was going with his narrative.

“Compare this photo,” Zachary brought it to the right of the video, now reduced on the screen.

They weren’t the same angle but showed the same wall and a corner of the bar.

“Are you saying that isn’t Barnburners?” Walter asked, confused.

“No, I’m sure it is. But just look at the two pictures. Do you see the differences?”

There was a brief silence as Walter looked at the two photos. It apparently didn’t take him long to see what Zachary had. “The amount of memorabilia on the wall. At this point in the video, they’ve already taken most of the pictures and display items.”

"Right," Zachary agreed. He pulled the dot on the video timeline all the way to the left, rewinding the video back to the beginning. "Now watch again and look for that wall."

The opening sequence of the video played again. The two burglars breaking into the bar. Starting to remove the valuable items and putting them into their bags. He froze the video when it reached the same point again.

"Notice anything?"

"They haven't touched anything on that wall yet. They've been across the room."

"Yeah."

"But..." Walter tried to reconcile these facts. "The items on that wall were gone <u>before</u> the burglary."

Zachary nodded. "Exactly."

"How could that be?"

"There was too much loot to be grabbed in two minutes by only two people, even with the speed they were blasting through there. This video was staged to distract everyone from when the real thefts actually took place."

"Before that."

"Yeah."

"How much before?" Walter took a sharp intake of breath. "It was an inside job."

"It was an inside job," Zachary confirmed.

"Nicely done, Zachary! Wow. So, the next job is to figure out who did it. Not Janice and Glen, I hope..."

"If you look at the height discrepancy between the two thieves in the video, you can see that it is not Janice and Glen."

"Thank goodness for that. So how are you going to figure it out? It's helpful to eliminate the McNichols, but how do you nail down who it is? There are another half dozen employees, and they aren't all couples, so you can't use the height thing to sort them all out."

"You asked when the actual theft took place. It would have to be between the close of business and the smash and grab."

"Because the McNichols and the staff would have noticed if there was a bunch of stuff missing from the walls during the day."

"Right. So that gives us a pretty narrow window to find alibis for."

"How are you going to do that? Get them to give you proof of where they were? And what about the ones who don't have any alibi?"

Zachary opened another folder and brought up the images it contained on the screen. Each image was labeled with the name of an employee and a time. "These are social media pictures and posts that establish where the different employees were and at what time."

"All of the employees?" Walter asked.

"No, not quite all. But the employees tend to be young people who post regularly on social media which establishes where they were."

"But not everyone posted."

"There were only a couple of employees who didn't post anything on social media during the evening and up until the time of the burglary. But those people still have social media accounts. They just aren't posting as actively as the others or were not posting that night. So there are still social media posts that show them with their best friend or partner."

Zachary brought up a couple more pictures for Walter to see. He didn't say anything at first.

"But only one couple matches the body types on the video," Walter eventually saw.

"Right. This is Jennifer Brown and her boyfriend, Michael Martin. It's not definitive proof, but it's pretty good evidence. It could be someone else with a similar body size who posted fake posts on their social media to cover their tracks, but I really don't think that our thieves would have thought to do something like that. The smash and grab was to cover the actual theft. They wouldn't have thought they needed another alibi on top of that or that she was the only employee not posting to social media during that period."

"Have you contacted the police with this? You've done a fantastic job, Zachary. With all of this, the police might be able to recover the stolen property, or at least some of it."

Zachary considered how much to tell Walter about what had gone down at the fourplex. He probably shouldn't admit to getting into Brown's residence and removing the stolen property. Even though he felt like it had been the right thing and the only way to recover the stolen property with the police being unavailable, it was probably best to keep the details of the recovery vague.

"As it turns out," he said slowly, "I did manage to recover the stolen property. I haven't yet been able to talk to the detective on the case, so he is probably not going to be too happy that I went ahead without him, but I do have the memorabilia here, safe and sound."

"All of it?" Walter demanded.

"I haven't itemized it, but yes, I suspect everything is here. It looks like a professional operation. They already had auction accounts and buyers. They may not have pulled off an operation just like this before, but they're clearly used to selling valuables quickly."

"That's amazing. I assume you've already called Glen and Janice? Have they made arrangements to pick up the stolen property?"

"No. I haven't been able to get ahold of them today. I'm not sure where they are or if something is wrong with their phone service provider. And I should probably talk to the detective before I turn anything over to anyone. He probably won't actually want it. From the way they have been handling this case, I'm not sure he'll even want to look at it. But I should talk to him before handing anything over to the McNichols."

"You just have a box of stolen goods sitting there at Kenzie's house—your house—for pickup?"

"Several boxes. They had already packaged everything up to send to the buyers and auction house. It's out of the way and is fine to stay here until I get everything sorted out with the police."

"That's great news, Zachary. You've certainly been worth your fee. Be sure to get me an invoice for the rest of your time and I'll transfer you the money right away."

Zachary smiled, pleased. At the back end, when all of the work was done, clients sometimes balked at paying the rest of his fees, thinking that since they got what they wanted, it was time to renegotiate the cost so that they didn't have to spend as much.

"I'll be sure to get it to you," he agreed.

CHAPTER 28

Zachary slept pretty well that night. His shortened sleep the night before, the action of the day, and the satisfaction of having cracked the case all combined, and he fell asleep soon after his head hit the pillow. There was no need to be replaying the video in his head this time. He had a little bit of anxiety from thinking about exactly how he would explain it all to the police detective when he finally got around to calling Zachary back. Still, he could suppress this worry enough that it didn't keep him awake.

He still awoke before Kenzie, but without nightmares or other sleep disturbances. He rose quietly and moved out to the living room so that he wouldn't wake her, and started in on his inbox and the other work awaiting him. He had more than just the Barnburners file to work on, and now that the burglary case was solved, he knew he needed to get back to the rest.

There were still no calls or messages from the McNichols. Maybe they didn't think he would find anything, so they didn't see the need to call him back immediately. Or maybe their phones were still down and they had no idea that he'd been trying to reach them. Either way, the property was safe for the moment. It would wait until they got back to him.

* * *

The arrival of Mason and Alisha in the late afternoon was not nearly as dramatic as the previous visit had been. Zachary was glad to see that things were more normal. The children and Tyrrell were happy to see each other, and the children were reassured that their father was going to get some help for his drinking problem. They probably knew by now that Tyrrell going into a new program wasn't any guarantee of success, but it was at least positive. He was trying.

The weather wasn't too bad, and Mason had seen kids sledding down a nearby hill as they had arrived, so he harassed and cajoled Tyrrell into taking the two of them to the sledding hill. They didn't have sleds with them, but Kenzie equipped them with a couple of flat pieces of cardboard from filing boxes and some large garbage bags, and they would probably also be able to make friends with the kids already out on the hill and get turns on their sleds and toboggans. That was the way things worked on community sledding hills.

“We’ll make some hot chocolate for when they get back,” Kenzie said, watching Tyrrell and the children traipsing off for the hill.

“I’m sure they’ll be ready for it,” Zachary agreed. The thought of sledding and coming home to hot chocolate was enough to make him want to chase after Tyrrell and join in on the fun. The last time he had gone sledding with Tyrrell would have been the winter of the fire, with Zachary ten and Tyrrell six. They’d never had sleds of their own and had made do with whatever cardboard, plastic sheeting, or garbage can lids they could put their hands on. He remembered the neighborhood park as idyllic, somewhere the Goldman kids spent a lot of time hanging out and playing tag and made-up games without having to worry about their parents and the unfair rules of the grown-up world. It was probably nothing like he remembered it. Just a broken-down, worn-out little park in a low-rent neighborhood. But for them, it had been paradise.

“Zachary?”

Zachary tore his eyes from the window and looked at Kenzie.

“Do you want to go?” Kenzie nodded toward the distant figures.

“No. I’ve got work to do, and Tyrrell should have some time with them to himself.”

“All right. I’ll call you when the hot chocolate is ready, then.”

Zachary returned to the bedroom where he had stowed his computer and went back to work. He found it hard to concentrate, his mind repeatedly returning to the children at the park and his own childhood memories. It was strange that they should come back so clearly just from being around Alisha and Mason.

And that made him remember how Tyrrell had said that being around Zachary made him remember home. Not just the good times that they had enjoyed together in the park, but their abusive parents and the violence and neglect that the children had endured before the dissolution of the family. Being with Zachary and then being with his children was a bad combination for Tyrrell, making him think he was a bad parent when he got frustrated or impatient with them. Zachary chewed on the inside of his cheek while he typed, hoping that everything would be okay and that Tyrrell and the children would be able to have a good visit together.

They were gone for about an hour. Zachary heard them return to the house, the door banging, thumps as they removed their winter boots, loud voices rising. Zachary cocked his head, listening, trying to decide whether the children were just excited or whether they were arguing about something.

Kenzie tapped on the bedroom door and opened it. “Come on out for hot chocolate. There are marshmallows!”

"Okay. Everything all right out there?" Zachary was still anxious about a fight, despite the lightness in Kenzie's tone.

"The kids are a bit hyper. That's all."

Zachary nodded. He saved the document he was working on, but left his work out on the bed, intending to return to it after the hot chocolate break. He followed Kenzie out to the kitchen. Mason and Alisha were getting their hot chocolate prepared, adding milk to cool it down and dropping marshmallows on top. Mason was making bombing noises as he dropped the marshmallows in.

"Stop it," Alisha complained. "You're bothering me."

Mason continued to bomb his hot chocolate with marshmallows, splashing hot chocolate on the table.

"Now, look!" Alisha got after him. "I told you to stop!"

"I can do it if I want to!" Mason told her. "You can't stop me!"

“Mason,” Tyrrell told him sharply. “Stop bugging your sister.”

“I don’t have to!” Mason shot back. “I’m not doing anything wrong! If it’s bothering her, then she can go somewhere else!”

“Mason, you’re a visitor in someone else’s home. You should be on your best behavior. We’re all going to have hot chocolate, so you need to be considerate of others. Alisha shouldn’t have to miss out on hot chocolate because you’re intentionally annoying her.”

“I’m not intentionally annoying her! She’s just being annoyed!”

“Mason!” Tyrrell snapped.

“It’s not fair!” Mason shouted, pushing a handful of marshmallows into his cup so violently that the hot chocolate splashed up over the rim of the cup, soaked the front of his shirt, and spread in a puddle across the table. Mason howled. “Now, look what you made me do!”

“Come here,” Tyrrell grabbed Mason by the arm and pulled him back from the table. “I can’t believe that you’re behaving like this. You need to—”

“You made me wreck my shirt. I want my hot chocolate!” Mason protested as Tyrrell pulled him away and he realized he wasn’t going to get his treat. “Daddy! I want my drink!”

“Look at me!” Tyrrell shook Mason by the shoulders, glaring at him. “You need a time out. Go down the hall and sit on my bed. And stay there until I come get you. This is...” Tyrrell shook his head angrily. “This is not acceptable behavior.”

Mason wrenched himself away from Tyrrell and stormed off down the hall. He slammed the door and set up wailing about not having any fun or having his drink when he was so thirsty and how Daddy was so mean and unfair.

CHAPTER 29

Everyone in the kitchen just stood there for a minute, taking a collective breath and trying to figure out what to do. Zachary felt like running into the master bedroom and shutting the door. He hated confrontations and he hated seeing Tyrrell angry at his children and Mason so distressed. Zachary had been a kid like Mason. While he understood how annoying it was to deal with Mason's hyperactivity and impulsiveness, he also understood how unfair it felt to Mason to be attacked just for having a little harmless fun with the marshmallows.

Kenzie grabbed a dishcloth from the sink and started to mop up the hot chocolate that was spreading across the table, trying to move everything else out of the way before they came in contact with the chocolatey pool of milk.

"I'm sorry, Daddy." Alisha started to weep. "I'm sorry, I didn't mean to cause a fight. Mason can put marshmallows in his hot chocolate. I don't care."

"You didn't do anything wrong," Tyrrell told her. "You just asked him to stop making the noise and being too wild." He took a deep breath, obviously trying to calm himself down. He hated it when he lost his temper with Mason.

"But he was just having fun, and I know he has a hard time stopping when he's playing a game..."

"You didn't do anything wrong," Tyrrell repeated. "It's okay. Grab your hot chocolate and sit down. We'll all have our hot chocolate now."

Sniffling, Alisha picked up her mug and sat down on one of the chairs, holding it close to her chest. Tears still streamed down her cheeks. Kenzie squeezed out the dishcloth, rinsed it, squeezed it out again, and mopped down the table once more. The spilled hot chocolate was taken care of. "Don't cry over spilled milk," they always said. But Alisha was still crying, Mason was weeping sporadically in the guest room, and Zachary just wanted to withdraw and be by himself before their emotions became too much for him too.

Kenzie firmly put a mug in front of Tyrrell and gestured for him to doctor it to his liking. She looked at Zachary, still standing in the doorway between the living room and the kitchen. Instead of telling him to come in and get his ready as well, she put the final two mugs in front of herself and filled them both. She added marshmallows to one and pushed it across the table in Zachary's direction. Zachary stepped into the kitchen and picked it up, but he didn't immediately drink it. Kenzie picked hers up and sat beside Alisha, starting a "girlfriend" type conversation about school and what Alisha and her friends had been up to recently.

Tyrrell picked up his mug and took several hard swallows without first cooling it down with milk. Zachary stared down at his hot chocolate. The marshmallows were dissolving around the edges and making a foam over the surface of the liquid.

“Have fun sledding?” he asked Tyrrell, unsure what else to say.

“The kids had fun. I went down a few times, but there weren’t a lot of other parents participating, so...”

Maybe Zachary should have gone with them so that Tyrrell would have had someone to enjoy the sledding with. If they were both going down together, Tyrrell wouldn’t have had to feel awkward at being the only dad who was acting like a little kid.

He should have gone.

Zachary continued to stare down at his hot chocolate. He couldn’t drink it. Not with the big knot in his stomach caused by the fight.

Which was silly. A little childish behavior did not put him in danger and should not be anything to worry about. Zachary wasn’t unsafe and neither was Mason. Tyrrell hadn’t been physically or verbally abusive to Mason, had just told him to stop, and then had told him to go to his room when things got out of hand. A perfectly valid parental response. Mason's sobs had already chugged to a stop. He was, Zachary assumed, waiting on Tyrrell's bed for his father to come talk to him and then invite him back out to finish his hot chocolate. Zachary didn't think Tyrrell would take the treat away altogether.

But Zachary still felt like things might explode around him, and there was no way he could force his hot chocolate down.

Kenzie was watching him but didn't say anything. She probably understood perfectly well why Zachary wasn't drinking. She was trying to just calm things down and make them nice for Alisha and Tyrrell. The sooner everyone could get back to normal, the sooner Mason could return and they could get on with the visit. No one wanted it to be ruined by a little spat. Tyrrell wasn't going to see his children for several weeks and wouldn't want the visit to end on a sour note.

As everyone started to relax and Alisha chattered with Kenzie, Zachary went over to the sink. He discreetly lowered the mug into the sink out of sight before dumping the hot chocolate down the drain. The marshmallows were not completely dissolved and they stuck in the strainer. He swallowed and turned back to the others.

“I guess I’d better get back to work. That was really nice, Kenzie, thank you.” He looked at Tyrrell. “Did you want me to tell Mason he can come out now?”

Tyrrell took a deep breath in and blew it out. “Yes. If he’s calmed down, he can come out and drink his hot chocolate.” Tyrrell looked at the half-mug of hot chocolate that had survived the marshmallow bombing. “Though it is probably cold chocolate now.”

“We can heat it up in the microwave,” Kenzie said. “But... maybe it’s best if I don’t.”

“Just leave it like it is,” Tyrrell said firmly. “He can deal with it.”

Zachary slipped out of the kitchen and went down the hall to the guest bedroom. He tapped on the door and opened it, then looked around, confused. There was no sign of Mason. Zachary looked in the closet and under the bed, then left the bedroom, puzzled. He had heard Mason stomp down the hall and slam the door. Mason hadn't come out, or he would have walked past the kitchen.

Kenzie's office.

Zachary took a few steps down the hall to the next door and opened it. Mason startled and looked up at Zachary, his eyes wide and guilty. Sports memorabilia was scattered in a circle around him, and he had the Montreal Canadiens die-cast car in his hand, running it along the carpet as he made motor noises.

"Mason." Zachary looked at the boxes and saw that they had all been opened, even the ones he had left sealed closed with packing tape. Mason had rummaged through them all, pulling out the bits that interested him the most. "These are not yours. They were closed. You shouldn't have gotten into them."

"I thought... they were toys. So, I could play with them."

"They aren't yours. They belong to a client of mine, and they shouldn't have been touched. That's why most of the boxes were still sealed shut."

"Oh… I'm sorry." Mason started to pick them up and shove them haphazardly into boxes, not taking any care to sort them or pack them properly. He held the Canadiens car up for Zachary to see. "This is really cool. Did you know that the doors really open—"

"Put it away with the others," Zachary interrupted. "It's not to play with."

"Can I show you, though—"

"No."

Mason frowned. He scrubbed at his eyes with his fists, maybe remembering the hot chocolate now and that he was supposed to be upset about something. That was one of the positive aspects of ADHD for Zachary—the ability to be distracted by something interesting and forget all about what he had been upset about.

Except for those times when the obsessive part of Zachary's brain refused to let something go or be distracted by anything else. Anxiety and hyperfocus could overwhelm the distractibility and keep him preoccupied. Like not being able to forget about the video until he had identified what was wrong with it. Or fantasizing about returning to Bridget when he loved Kenzie and wanted to be with her.

"Go on out to the kitchen and have your hot chocolate," he told Mason. "Your daddy is waiting for you."

CHAPTER 30

As Zachary worked through the tasks in his email and task list, his phone vibrated. It was off to the side and he was busy with other things, so he didn't look at it at first, planning to just let it go to voicemail. But it occurred to him that he was waiting for more than one person to call him back, so he pried himself away from the page he was looking at to see if it was a call he had to answer.

Janice McNichol.

Zachary grabbed the phone and swiped to answer the call. "Janice. Hey, I've been trying to reach you. But I guess... you've been having phone trouble?"

"I wish that's all it was." Janice's sigh carried down the line. "It's been a pretty rough couple of days."

"What happened?"

"That police detective who is in charge of the burglary case? He contacted us. Yesterday, I guess. It's all running together. I can't keep the days straight."

"Oh, that's good. I was waiting for a call from him too. What did he have to say?"

"What didn't he say? The guy was like a bulldog. He's determined that it was an inside job, so it must have been me and Glen. Or we at least knew something about it or colluded with whoever actually pulled it off, because we weren't anywhere near the bar at the time. He just… wouldn't give it up. He had… phone records from the bar to known fences. He actually called them that. Fences. I thought that was just TV jargon. He said that he didn't believe the video footage was real. He thought it was staged, so we must have done it. We can't alibi each other and we can't prove that we were somewhere other than at home, because that's where we were. We weren't out burgling our own bar. Believe me, at the end of a long day at Barnburners, I don't want to do anything other than go home and go to bed. And that's what we did. We didn't know about the burglary until the alarm company called us."

"It was an inside job," Zachary agreed. "But I know it wasn't you."

"What do you mean? It wasn't an inside job. No one we work with would do something like that to us."

"Your waitress, Jennifer Brown. She and her boyfriend."

"Jenn? That doesn't make any sense. Jenn has worked there for two years. I've never had a lick of trouble with her."

"Well, maybe she was influenced by the boyfriend. Or maybe they got into debt and they needed to make some quick cash. But from what I could tell, they've done this before. Or he has, anyway. He had accounts with auction companies. Had buyers lined up for some of the stolen merchandise."

"No! Jenn would never do that."

"Maybe she was coerced. I don't know."

"You can't tell that detective that she did it."

"I'm going to need to tell him something. He'll want to know how I got the stolen articles back."

There was a gasp from Janice. "You got them back? Really? How did you get them back?"

"I went over to Jennifer's house. They were all boxed up, ready to be shipped."

Janice swore, wonder in her voice. "How could she do that to me? I don't understand why or how she would do that."

"I'll show you the video if you're at your computer, and some other photos, and you can clearly see what happened..."

"No. I'm not at my computer and probably won't be for a few more days."

Zachary was surprised. “Where are you?”

“I’m at the hospital.”

“Oh, I’m sorry. I didn’t know. Did you have an accident? What happened?”

It was no wonder she hadn’t answered his phone calls. She’d had her phone switched off at the hospital.

“It isn’t me; it’s Glen. All of this stuff...” Janice groaned. “You don’t know how stressful it’s been. I wake up in the morning and I just want to hear that it was all a bad dream. I don’t want to deal with it, and it seems like the pressure keeps getting to be more and more, not less.”

It sounded as if Glen had had a breakdown of some kind. Janice sounded at the end of her rope herself.

“Has he been admitted? Is there anything I can do?”

“There’s nothing. The hospital is doing everything they can and I’m just keeping him company. They’re going to do surgery tomorrow. The one where they thread the balloon in through your veins...?"

Zachary blinked, trying to understand what she was saying. He shook his head. "Sorry, what happened? What procedure is he having? I thought you meant he'd had a... that he was under too much stress. What actually happened?"

"He had a heart attack," Janice said, in an annoyed tone that suggested Zachary should have known that.

"Oh, dear."

"Right when we were in the middle of talking to the detective. He's badgering us and insisting that it had to be an inside job and that we must know all about it, that we're just trying to defraud the insurance company or something. Glen is getting paler and paler, and then he just... collapses. Facedown on the table, all gray, it scared me to death."

"I'll bet." Zachary could see it in his mind's eye. All of the pressure from the police, insisting that they must be in on it or know something about it, making threats about what would happen to them, encouraging them to cooperate if they wanted to stay out of prison. And then Glen grabbing his chest and toppling over onto the table, skin gray, eyes lifeless. The detective jumping up and calling for an ambulance. Maybe performing CPR to keep him alive until the paramedics could get there. Police were trained in CPR, weren't they? The police station probably even had one of those mobile defibrillators so that they could shock him and bring him back to life.

"I'm so sorry that happened to him," Zachary said.

No wonder they hadn't bothered to call him back. Being interrogated by the police, then a heart attack and racing to the hospital to try to keep Glen alive and figure out what to do with him. Janice had probably sat by his bed the last twenty-four hours, waiting for some word.

Now the rest of what Janice had said was starting to make sense. Glen was having a procedure the next day to clear out the arteries to his heart. So neither of them was likely to be available for a few days. They had enough to worry about without recovering the stolen goods. Those could stay in Kenzie's home office until the McNichols were able to get their lives back on track. Poor Glen.

"Is there anything I can do? Do you guys need anything?"

"No, we're okay here. But we're not going to be able to deal with this... I guess we'll have to call Detective Shelly back. Explain that we know what happened now. That should make him happier."

"Do you want me to call him? It sounds like you've got a lot on your plate right now."

"Yeah, I would? That would be really good?" Janice's voice went up at the ends of her sentences as if she were asking a question. And maybe she was. Would he call the detective? Would he handle it all so that she didn't have to face him again? Zachary could only imagine how she must feel toward the detective now, after watching him bully her husband into having a heart attack. That probably wasn't fair. Glen probably would have had a heart attack sooner or later anyway if his arteries were in bad shape. But it still must have been very traumatic to watch, and Zachary was sure she would blame what had happened on the police detective.

"If you would give me his contact information, I'll give him a call today," Zachary agreed. "Then you won't have to think about it."

"Thank you! You don't know how much of a load off of my mind this is. Getting the stolen memorabilia back, knowing what happened, getting the detective off of our case, that will be such a relief for both of us."

She sounded so strained, it was a wonder she hadn't had a heart attack too.

"I'll take care of it."

CHAPTER 31

Of course, telling Janice that he would take care of it and actually taking care of it were two different things. Zachary didn't relish the thought of facing off against the "bulldog" of a detective. It was going to be hard enough to explain how he had discovered that Jennifer Brown and her boyfriend were the thieves and how he had come to possess the stolen items. It would be that much harder if the detective was a bully. Zachary did not enjoy talking to bullies.

He sat there on the bed for a while, trying to sort out in his mind what he was going to say to the cop that wouldn't sound too suspicious or defensive. It was not going to be easy. He didn't feel like he was getting any closer to a script that would work, so he decided to scrap that idea and just wing it.

When nothing was going to work, it was better to just jump in and get it over with than to spend the day being anxious about it.

He dialed the number that Janice had given him, which wasn't the one that he had been using to contact the police department. Hopefully, the detective's direct line or cell phone. Something that the cop would answer, while ignoring all of the pink message slips that the phone operator had left on his desk. Or maybe they were sent to him as email messages that were languishing in his inbox.

"Shelly!" The voice that answered the phone on the second ring had a snap that made Zachary jump. He was glad that they were on the phone and not face to face.

"Uh, Detective Shelly. I'm glad I got through to you. My name is Zachary Goldman, and I'm a private investigator—"

"I don't deal with private investigators. Talk to our public affairs liaison."

"I was hired to work on one of the cases that you have been dealing with—"

"Don't deal with PI's. I have nothing to say to you. Get your information somewhere else."

"I'm not calling to get information from you. I have information to give you. About your case."

There was a pause while Shelly considered this. Then he sighed, a deep grumble that told Zachary it had been a long day and he really didn't want to deal with a pesky PI, even one who claimed to have information.

"It's about the Barnburners burglary," Zachary explained, hoping to get some momentum going. "I managed to sort out what happened. I can give you the names of the perpetrators and I have the recovered stolen property here."

Shelly coughed explosively. Zachary winced and pulled the phone away from his ear, waiting for the detective to stop coughing. He put it back to his ear.

"Oh, you have the loot, do you?" Shelly demanded. He made a noise that might have been a laugh or another cough. "Well, that's very convenient, isn't it? How much are the McNichols paying you to smooth this all out for them? They have some gall, setting you on me the day after he has his so-called heart attack. They could at least make it look like it took a while to recover the merchandise."

"This is not a set-up by Janice and Glen. They are still at the hospital. Glen has a procedure tomorrow, one of those angio-whatevers. Janice has been by his side the whole time. They didn't know that I had broken the case until today."

"I'm sure. Funny how they didn't even mention hiring you when we were talking yesterday."

"They weren't the ones who hired me. But they knew about it and I had talked to them and interviewed their employees. They didn't know that I had made any progress on the case, so they wouldn't have had anything to tell you. I doubt you asked them if they had a private investigator on the case."

“Of course not,” Shelly agreed. “I don’t deal with private investigators.” But there was a wry note of amusement in his voice this time, maybe acknowledging to himself that he was, in fact, dealing with a private investigator.

“Do you want me to go through the progress on the case with you or just give you the names of the thieves?”

“Are you the one who called and left me messages about evidence in the garbage at Michael Martin’s home?”

“Yeah, that was me.” At least he’d gotten the messages. Zachary wasn’t sure until then that he knew anything about it.

“Well, that was a wild goose chase. I went by there today and there was nothing. Not only that, but it looks like they have cleared out. I don’t have enough evidence to get a warrant to get inside, but by all appearances, their suite is empty.”

“Sorry, I tried to get you as soon as I found anything. The dispatcher I talked to wasn’t able to get any police officers over there to gather the evidence, and I couldn't stay there and sit on it all night."

"If you hadn't interfered, then it would still be there and maybe we could prosecute him, but since you've royally screwed everything up, chances are, we will never find him, let alone be able to charge him with anything."

Zachary set his teeth and did his best not to react to the accusations. "Sorry to hear that he's run. I did my best."

"And how is he related to the bar? I don't believe that this was just a random theft. Everything points toward it being an inside job."

"Yeah. Martin's girlfriend is Jennifer Brown, one of the waitresses at the bar."

"The McNichols spent all day yesterday swearing up and down that it couldn't have been an inside job."

"I'm not surprised. They're quite close to their employees. They didn't have anything to do with it, and I'm sure they would never have suspected Jennifer or any of the other employees of being mixed up in it. They're trusting people."

"You think they didn't have anything to do with it?" Shelly snorted. "I think you should look again. They're the ones who would benefit the most by making an insurance claim for the 'stolen' items. Sell them off and claim insurance on them. Get twice the money. They told me yesterday how they're going to hold a fundraiser to replace some of the stolen stuff. So they get triple-compensated. Not a bad deal."

"Did they say they were making an insurance claim? I didn't think it would be worth it."

"Maybe not if you were only looking at what they would get out of it and the bump up in insurance premiums. But multiply the value of the stolen goods by three, and it's a different story."

He did have a point there. But Zachary hadn't seen any sign that Janice and Glen were involved in the theft.

"Do you want the stolen goods, or should I just return them to the McNichols? I wasn't sure how you would want to handle it."

"I can't drop everything I'm doing to come out there and collect stuff. Are you able to bring it here?"

"I'm not in town, so it can't be today. I'll try to get it to you in the next day or two."

"Where are you located?"

"Roxboro." Zachary gave Shelly the address. Despite what Shelly said, it sounded like he planned to pick it up. "Should I wait, then?" he asked uncertainly.

"Maybe. Hold off for now. I may be able to get a cop from Roxboro out there to pick it up."

And, Zachary supposed, to have a little look around to see what kind of a character Zachary was and whether there was any sign that he or the McNichols had been involved in the theft.

"Okay. I won't touch anything unless I hear from you," he promised. But there was a knot in his stomach as he remembered that Mason had already opened all of the boxes, touched and played with the toys, and repacked them differently.

He'd have to explain that later. He didn't need to do it over the phone with Shelly. Maybe the cop who came to pick up the stolen property would be easier to talk to. He wouldn't be coming into the case assuming that the McNichols were guilty. Unless Shelly told him they were.

Zachary suppressed a sigh.

"I'll have more questions for you," Shelly said. "Give me your contact details and I'll follow up with you when I'm not in the middle of my supper."

“Oh, sure. Sorry about that. I just got a call from Janice, so I called you back right away.”

Shelly grunted, which Zachary suspected was the closest he was going to get to an acknowledgment that this had been the right thing to do, even if it was at an inconvenient time for Shelly.

He gave Shelly his contact details. Shelly thanked him and terminated the call.

CHAPTER 32

Driving Tyrrell to the treatment facility and getting him checked in had been a little rough. Kenzie and Tyrrell had both told Zachary that he could stay home if he felt like he wasn't up to it. Kenzie wanted to be involved since she was a medical professional. She wanted a chance to see the facilities in person and to talk to the doctors and therapists.

So Tyrrell had a ride and someone who knew what they were doing to check him in. But Zachary felt like Tyrrell needed family there too. Someone who really cared about Tyrrell, deep down in his bones. Kenzie was friendly to Tyrrell and had willingly accepted him as part of her extended family. But she couldn't feel the same way about him as Zachary. They had the same DNA, the same background, the same fierce and protective love for each other.

Kenzie separated from them to take her tour of the facilities, giving Zachary and Tyrrell a small measure of privacy as they said their goodbyes.

They both remained as stoic as possible in the reception area of the treatment facility, where Tyrrell would go on and Zachary would not. Tight hugs and manly slaps on the back. Both of them with determined smiles that were grimaces of pain and sorrow rather than pleasure.

“It won’t be long,” Zachary assured Tyrrell. “You can’t have visitors the first few weeks, but once they say that you can, you’re not going to be able to keep me away.”

“I figured that,” Tyrrell agreed, pretending to be annoyed. He punched Zachary lightly in the shoulder. “I have work to do here, you know. Can’t have too many distractions.”

Zachary gave him one final hug, holding just a little too tightly and a little too long, until Tyrrell squirmed away.

"It will be fine, bro," Tyrrell assured Zachary, his Adam's apple bobbing up and down as he tried to swallow his own emotion. "Tell Kenzie thanks again for helping me to get into this place."

"I will."

Zachary separated from Tyrrell and walked back out to the car, taking slow, deliberate steps, refusing to allow himself to look back over his shoulder. Tyrrell was right. He had hard work to do. He would need to be strong, and Zachary needed to show that he was too, so Tyrrell wouldn't worry about him.

In the car, he sat down and immersed himself in his social networks, email, and, eventually, cat videos to distract himself from his anxiety over the separation from Tyrrell and whether the rehabilitation program would be more successful than the programs Tyrrell had completed in the past.

Eventually, Kenzie finished her tour and returned to the car. She put her hand on Zachary's knee for a minute before starting the engine.

“How are you doing?”

“Fine.”

She waited. Zachary looked up at her. One of the cardinal rules they had established in couples therapy was that they were not allowed to say they were “fine.” No covering up real emotion with something fake and more socially acceptable. They could talk about how they really felt or decline to answer, but “fine” was not an option.

Zachary sighed. “It sucks,” he acknowledged. “I know that this is where he needs to be and that they’ll be able to help him more than anything I could ever do. I’m really glad that you found this program, and so is he. But I’m afraid and… upset that I won’t be able to see him for a while… and just… really emotional. I don’t think I can label everything I’m feeling.”

Kenzie squeezed his knee again and started the car. She pulled out of the parking lot and headed for home in silence. Zachary turned on the radio and found a station that they would hopefully both enjoy. Not that he cared what he listened to. He just wanted to drown out the thoughts that grew in the silence.

"Are you sure you want to be home alone?" Kenzie asked. "I could ask Dr. Wiltshire for the rest of the day off if you need someone around. Or you could go out somewhere that you won't be alone. Run errands or go see Heather... go for a walk in the park."

"Too cold for a walk."

"You would be fine if you bundled up."

"It's okay. I don't mind being by myself. If I get antsy, I'll go out somewhere. But you don't need to miss a whole day of work."

"Well... give me a call if you need to talk. Or just to take a break from your work. I'm still reachable. I don't have an autopsy scheduled; I'll be at my desk."

"Sure," Zachary agreed. "I'll call if I need to."

She didn't push him any further, just drove him the rest of the way home and dropped him in front of the house.

"Don't forget to disarm the burglar alarm."

Zachary nodded. "Thanks."

While it irritated him to be reminded, her comment was timely. If there were a day that he would walk into the house, forget to punch his code, and be utterly oblivious to the warning beep of the alarm, this would be that day. He couldn't criticize her for reminding him to do something he had forgotten once before—ending up in handcuffs because his name hadn't been on her security company's file. It was now, but he would prefer not to be surprised by the siren of the burglar alarm, having to remember his passphrase while off-balance to give to the security company before the police were alerted.

Once in the door, he carefully punched his code into the alarm system, and stopped and waited for the red light to turn green. He even stood there a moment longer to make sure that the warning beep didn't come on. He closed the door, still watching the alarm panel. The little screen flashed FRONT DOOR CLOSED and then returned to STANDBY. Zachary headed to his computer and got to work on some routine skip tracing. Normally, he had Heather do that now, but he wanted to do something that didn't take a lot of attention, and he could just lose himself in the process.

CHAPTER 33

Zachary was working at his computer when he started to get an uneasy feeling. The first few seconds, he tried to push it aside, assuming that it was just anxiety over Tyrrell going into detox. He wanted Tyrrell to detox, so he could just push that feeling away. But it didn't work. His sense of disquiet grew, getting more and more ominous. He looked away from his computer, glancing around the room first but, of course, he was home alone and there was nothing else in the room that should cause him to be anxious.

He turned and looked out the big living room window and, for just an instant, saw movement, off to the side, close to the house, too close for him to get a good view line. He leaned forward into the window, trying to look all the way along the front of the house. Kenzie had the sense not to grow bushes around the windows and entryways where they could obscure a burglar, but the way that the front steps jutted out, he was blocked from seeing anything past it.

But he had seen a movement.

Not a cat or a squirrel. A person. And that person had gotten closer to the house but had not rung the doorbell. If it were a delivery person, then he should have rung the doorbell or at least tossed the package up onto the doorstep by that time and be heading back to his truck. But there was no Amazon Prime truck at the curb, no unfamiliar cars that could be private couriers.

Maybe it was the cop that Detective Shelly had sent by to get the memorabilia, and he thought he'd have a quick look around the house before going in. That was the kind of thing that a cop might do. See what he could find out about the subject before ringing the doorbell. As a PI, that was what Zachary often did.

He stood up from the couch and headed toward the front door, planning to peek out and see if he could catch the cop at it.

But as he rounded the corner to the front door, he discovered his mistake. The cop hadn't gone around the house to scope out the backyard.

And it wasn't a cop.

And the reason that he hadn't rung the doorbell was that he was already inside and didn't want Zachary to be forewarned.

There were two of them.

Zachary turned to make a break for it out the door to the garage. His movements seemed incredibly slow to him, like the slo-mo shot of sprinters bursting through the tape at the finish line of a race. He was only too aware of how long it was taking him to pivot, how many strides it would take to get to the door, his brain already ahead of him, anticipating the need to unlock and turn the doorknob when he reached the door, to jump down the three steps to the garage floor level, and to hit the button that would raise the big garage door, even knowing how grindingly slow it was. How else would he get out?

Could he slide or roll under the garage door as it opened a crack, like in a Star Trek action sequence? Get out of there before the intruders could?

But it all seemed hopeless. Unlike he, the intruders had anticipated his being there and had been ready for his appearance, even if they were trying to take him unaware. They were coiled for action and Zachary was not.

He reached the door between the kitchen and the garage, but he didn't manage to turn the lock and get it open. Even if he had succeeded in doing that, there was no way the big garage door would have opened quickly enough for him to escape.

Strong, hard hands grabbed him from behind, not being careful, not caring whether they injured him. Zachary fought to free himself, flailing, using his elbows, trying to kick out.

But he was no kung fu fighter. Watching Jackie Chan movies a hundred times would not turn him into an expert in hand-to-hand combat or any of the martial arts. He was still Zachary

Goldman: small, too thin, awkward and unarmed. One of the intruders had his arms locked behind his back in a few seconds, with only one grunt of protest as Zachary had tried to fight back. Zachary attempted to use the grip the man behind him had on him to kick out his legs and hurt the one now in front of him. But it didn't work like it did in the movies. The man behind him just ratcheted the hammerlock on his arms tighter and let his own weight pull down into his shoulders, so that he gasped in pain and couldn't even think of lifting his feet up to kick again.

"Stop fighting," the man holding him growled. "We don't want you."

Zachary tried to figure out what this meant while the man pulled out a pair of flex-cuffs and zipped them over Zachary's wrists. Then he shoved Zachary away, dumping him on the tiled kitchen floor. Zachary's tailbone hit the hard surface with an explosion of pain.

"Stay there, or I'll hogtie you too."

He ran thick fingers over Zachary's hips and backside and, for an instant, Zachary flashed back, sure he was going to be assaulted, but the man found his phone and slid it out, taking it with him so that Zachary had no way to call for help.

Sitting up straight was out of the question, given how much his tailbone was hurting, so Zachary let himself slump into lying on his side, partially curled up. He listened to them walking through the house.

Each of the bedroom doors was opened in turn. The master bedroom, the guest room, and then Kenzie's home office.

"In here!"

Zachary closed his eyes, concentrating. What did they want in the office? There was Kenzie's laptop, but they had walked past Zachary's laptop in the living room without comment, and it was newer than Kenzie's. She didn't store any valuables in the office, as far as he knew. There was no safe. Just office supplies, a bit of furniture, a few out-of-season clothes stored in the closet. They had walked by expensive furnishings and artwork on their way there.

Then he heard the sound of them going through the boxes.

The boxes of memorabilia stolen from Barnburners.

Was it Jennifer Brown and her boyfriend?

It couldn't be. It had definitely been two large men. Not a woman. Not Jennifer's slender boyfriend. But they could be hired thugs. They looked and acted like hired thugs. Quick and efficient, good at what they did. Not worried about hurting someone, but not there to do him physical harm, either. Zachary had just been an obstacle and could be disposed of however they saw best.

They weren't there for <u>him</u>.

They were there for the stolen memorabilia.

How had they tracked him? How did they know Zachary was the one who had come to their house and stolen the objects they had stolen?

Now they were stealing them back again. It was dizzying, wondering how many times the loot could be stolen.

It wouldn't have been hard to track Zachary. Jennifer knew that Zachary was investigating the burglary. He had introduced himself to her, given her his card, encouraged her to call him. There were not a lot of Zachary Goldmans in Vermont. His name wasn't registered to Kenzie's address anywhere, but they probably hadn't needed that. People knew him, knew that Walter Kirsch had hired him, could probably look up news articles online that linked him, Walter Kirsch, and Kenzie Kirsch. It wouldn't take long to figure out that he and Kenzie were a couple and that he would either be living with her or she would lead them to him.

Zachary let his head bump on the tile floor, frustrated with himself. He couldn't have left a much clearer trail for anyone who wanted to find him. They had told everyone that Walter Kirsch had hired him, trying to gain their trust.

The memorabilia Mason had been playing with had been thrown back in the boxes haphazardly, but it didn't take the thugs long to repack the boxes properly so that they could be closed and stacked. It didn't take them three trips to transport them like it had Zachary by himself. Between the two of them, they quickly carried all of the boxes out of the house and were gone.

CHAPTER 34

Hello? Anyone home?"

Zachary didn't know how long he had been lying there on the floor when he heard the voice. He should have figured out by then how to escape the flex-cuffs or have managed to get to his feet so that he could walk out of the house under his own power. But the ape had manhandled him more than he had realized. Between the pain in his shoulders and arms from being cuffed so tightly behind his back, the pain in his tailbone from landing on the floor, and the various other bruises and tender places, he couldn't do much more than kick himself around in circles on the kitchen floor.

"Help me!" he called out, projecting his voice toward the front door.

He heard a low voice, muttering, a radio squawk.

"Help?" he repeated. "I'm in here. In the kitchen. They're gone. It's just me."

It was still a few minutes before the heavy tread of footsteps entered the house, and Zachary strained to look up at his rescuer.

A uniformed cop. Zachary let his breath out in relief.

"Hey..." he greeted weakly.

"Zachary Goldman?"

"Yeah. That's me."

The cop got closer and crouched down. "It's me. Donaldson."

Zachary cricked his neck, trying to examine him from a better angle. "Oh, Donaldson." It seemed like the cop had come from another world. It had been a long time since he had worked on a case that Donaldson had been involved with, but he was a good cop. Not one of those who had a thing about private investigation as a matter of principle. Only if said private investigator got in the way and went places he shouldn't.

"What happened here? Your front door was hanging open."

"I... uh... a couple of intruders. Home invasion."

"You don't say." Donaldson looked around the kitchen. "You do live an interesting life, don't you?"

"Can you help me?" Zachary asked, irritated.

Donaldson hooked a hand under Zachary's armpit and lifted him to his feet. It was a hundred times better to be standing up instead of curled up on the floor in pain, but the movement hurt his shoulder. Donaldson examined the flex-cuffs and, in a minute, he had out a Leatherman tool and cut the plastic loops that held Zachary's wrists together. Zachary brought his arms back in front of him, his shoulders popping and grinding painfully. He rolled his shoulders and rubbed his hands together, trying to restore the circulation.

“Thank you.” Zachary blew out a long breath. “How did you know to come? Did one of the neighbors report it?”

“Nah. I’m not here because of this. I’m here to pick up some stolen property that you apparently recovered.”

“Oh.” Zachary looked in the direction of the bedrooms. “Well... that’s apparently what these guys were after too. I don’t know if they left anything behind.”

“You’re kidding me.” Donaldson shook his head in disbelief.

“No... I don’t know if it’s the guys who initially stole it, and they figured out that I was the one who... uh... recovered it from them.”

“You don’t know?”

“It wasn’t the same people, but these guys acted like hired thugs. Professionals.”

Donaldson glanced around the house, then nodded. “Nothing busted. Handcuffed you. No messy stuff. Just in and out.”

“Yeah.” Zachary nodded. “Five minutes. Let’s see if they left anything behind. But I doubt it...”

Donaldson nodded and walked down the hall after Zachary. Zachary minced along, hoping it wasn’t too obvious to Donaldson how much pain he was in. The doors to the bedrooms were open. Nothing appeared to have been touched. Zachary stopped at the office and looked in the door. All of the boxes and their contents were gone, as Zachary had known they would be. He gestured to the empty spot along the wall, where the boxes had left rectangular impressions in the carpet.

“This is where they were. These guys just walked in and took everything.”

Donaldson nodded and pulled out a notepad to make some notes. “Detective Shelly isn’t going to be happy about this.”

"No. But I promise you... this wasn't the way I had planned for things to happen..."

Donaldson walked into the room and looked around. There wasn't much to see. He bent down and picked up a USB drive that had been knocked to the floor and put it back on Kenzie's desk.

"Well, nothing for me to do here."

"Uh... what about the home invasion?"

Donaldson looked at him and sighed. "I suppose since I was first at the scene, I'll have to make a report. We'll need to call the robbery boys in to open a file and take your statement. That's not my department. I was just here doing a favor for a fellow officer." He rolled his eyes. "That's what I get for being a nice guy."

CHAPTER 35

There wasn't really much for Zachary to tell the detectives that showed up about the home invasion. He could give only a general description of the two masked men who had come into the house, accosted him, and reclaimed the stolen property. A look at the footprint evidence outside the house showed that there had been a third man outside, who would undoubtedly have snagged Zachary if he had managed to get out of the house through the garage. That made him feel a little bit better about not making it that far. Even if he had been faster, he wouldn't have gotten away.

The detective took pictures of the footprints, but just shook his head at the idea of making casts of them or even measuring them for shoe size.

"You said yourself, they were likely hired muscle. It isn't really going to help us to get their shoe sizes. Even if we were able to identify them, we still wouldn't know who had hired them, and that's the important question."

After looking once at the lack of memorabilia in the home office, the detective shrugged and made motions to leave. "You can drop your written statement off at the station any time. We'll be in contact if we have any questions or hear anything. But these guys were efficient. I think it's safe to say that we're not likely to find them."

"And you'll copy everything to Shelly in Montpelier? Since the stolen property relates to his case?"

"Yes, sir," the detective said tiredly, making Zachary realize that he'd already made this request several times. "I will make sure that Detective Shelly gets all of the details, sparse as they are."

"Maybe there will be something that is meaningful to him."

"Maybe, sir."

Zachary let the detective go, leaving him alone in the house once more. This time he made sure to lock the door and enable the exterior door and window alerts so that he would know if someone entered the house. He knew it was shutting the barn door after the horses were gone, but he felt more secure knowing that no one could sneak in again without his realizing it.

Unless, of course, he was so focused on his work that he didn't hear the alerts when a door or window was breached.

Zachary tried to sit down and resume the work he had been doing when the thugs had arrived, but it didn't make any sense to him and sitting was painful. He paced for a while, just trying to convince himself that he was safe and could get back to work. His brain and body were still on high alert, sure that he would be attacked again. He knew he should be grateful for his brain's hypervigilance; it was one of the things that had gotten him through the years of foster care and kept him safe from more than one abusive parent, sibling, or group home resident.

His impulsivity, on the other hand, had dumped him into more than one situation that he could have avoided if he'd been able to stop and think things through. His brain was both his protector and his enemy.

The ring of Zachary's phone made him jump, and he immediately whirled around to face the front door, sure that someone had again entered the house. He blew out his breath when he realized it was just the phone and picked it up. He wasn't in any mood to talk to a client.

But it was Kenzie's name on the screen so, after taking a few more breaths to calm himself down so that he wouldn't sound frantic when he answered the call, he swiped to answer it.

"Kenzie."

"Zachary," her voice was higher than usual. "I just heard about the break-in! Are you okay?"

"How did you hear about it?"

"I work in the basement of the police station. You and I both know plenty of the cops around here. Did you really think that I wouldn't hear?"

"I… no. I thought it would all be kept confidential. I didn't think of anyone telling you. Sorry… I would have called to give you a heads-up if I had known."

"Yeah. It's not exactly reassuring to hear from the cops that your house has been broken into."

"No." There was a pain in Zachary's chest, and he thought about Glen, in the hospital, going through his heart surgery. Zachary's pain, on the other hand, was not a cardiac event, but his guilt over Kenzie's house being violated and over her finding out from someone other than him. "I am sorry. They didn't act like it was a big deal, and I thought they would keep it private."

"I am the homeowner."

"Yeah. Didn't think of that."

"When were you going to tell me? Or were you?"

"When you got home. I didn't think there was any benefit to interrupting you at work. It would just distract you from your job."

Like Zachary was distracted from his. He couldn't seem to get refocused.

"Okay." Kenzie's tone had lowered slightly. Calming down a little bit. Realizing that everything was fine and that he had not been trying to keep the news of the break-in from her. "Okay, then. And nothing was broken? The door or a window?"

"No," Zachary admitted, disgusted with himself. "I left the front door unlocked and the alarm off when I got home. A lot of good they do when you don't use them."

"The detective said that it looked like a professional job. If they hadn't found the front door unlocked, they probably would have used a pry bar. They would have gotten in either way. At least leaving the door unlocked means that they didn't have to break in."

Zachary grunted an acknowledgment. He sighed. "Anyway... nothing broken, nothing to clean up. And you don't have to worry about tripping over the boxes in your office, since they have now been removed."

"Yeah. Not exactly the way you'd planned, though."

"No."

"And you're okay? You must be freaking out. Should I come home?"

"I'm... irritated and distracted. Mad at myself. Don't know that I'll get any more work done today. But I'll manage. You don't need to get off early unless you want to. I guess Dr. Wiltshire will understand if you tell him your house was broken into."

"Yes, I think he'd understand that."

“If you do come home early—and you don’t need to for me—just let me know, okay? Shoot me a text.”

“Okay...” Her tone was doubtful, inquiring.

“So I don’t have a heart attack when I hear the door.”

“Oh, yeah. Sure. Have you taken anything for the anxiety?”

“No.”

“Think about it.”

Zachary waited for more, but apparently, she wasn’t going to push it any further than that. “I will,” he agreed.

“All right. See you later.”

Zachary hung up and considered whether taking one of his anti-anxiety pills would help. He didn’t like to take them except when there was a clear need for one. And if he did, he would want to sleep. It wouldn’t help him get any more work done, and he didn't want to go to sleep when he should be vigilant about the door and whether the thugs would be back.

Of course they wouldn't. They had gotten what they were looking for. There was no need for them to return. But his brain wasn't ready to accept that. He needed to stay aware and alert, at least until Kenzie got home.

CHAPTER 36

Kenzie didn't get off work early, but she did leave work on time, which was early for Kenzie. She sent him a text, so he watched for her car, saw it enter the garage, and was in the kitchen when she entered through the connecting garage door. Zachary had already unlocked the door and disabled the door alert so that she wouldn't have to do anything other than walk in as usual. But once she was in, Kenzie deliberately locked all of the locks on the door and enabled the door and window alerts again before greeting him.

"Hey. You survived. How are you doing?"

Zachary hugged her briefly. His shoulders were still hurting from the way his arms had been wrenched around and handcuffed, but he didn't tell her that. "I'm good."

At her doubtful look, he reiterated. "I know I'm not supposed to say 'fine,' but I am. A bit freaked out over the whole thing, but it was minor. It was over fast. No permanent damage done." He made a motion indicating the rest of the house. “Have a look around. Nothing is broken or damaged.”

Kenzie walked around the house, then returned to his side in the living room and gave him a sideways hug. “You’re right. Everything looks fine. It even looks like you vacuumed.”

Zachary nodded. He had vacuumed the carpet once the wet footprints had dried to remove any traces of mud and dirt, erasing any sign of the intrusion.

“Thanks. That makes me feel better,” Kenzie said, looking around again.

Her mouth was tight, though, and her hug had felt rigid. He met her eyes.

“I’m mad,” Kenzie admitted. “Not at you. At them. I’ve always heard about how a robbery makes someone feel personally violated, but I never really understood how much... I’m just furious at them. The thugs and whoever sent them. I just want to kick the crap out of them. Coming into my house like that."

"I'm sorry—"

"Don't keep telling me you're sorry about it. I know it isn't your fault. It's theirs. And my father's."

Zachary looked at her, surprised. He hadn't even thought of being angry at Walter.

"Why are you mad at him?"

"Because he's the one that hired you for this case. This happened because of him. The last time he came here, he put a bug in my purse. This time, he set you on a case that ended up with my house being violated. I just feel like… I'm just furious at him. If he called me right now… he would regret it. Let's just say that."

Zachary nodded his agreement. He wouldn't want to be on the receiving end of Kenzie's temper at the moment. Walter had better watch his step with her.

"I told you that you would regret taking this case from him," Kenzie went on. "I warned you what he's like and that it wouldn't go like you expected."

"Yes, you did," Zachary admitted. "But I don't know if you can really put the blame for the robbery on him. He's not the one who ordered it. It has to be Jennifer and Michael, the original thieves."

"It's still his fault," Kenzie said bullishly. "One way or another. Why did he even want the robbery investigated in the first place? How does it benefit him?"

Zachary frowned and shook his head. "I don't think it does. I think he was just being generous, helping his friends who own the bar."

"That's not like him. He has his own interests at heart one way or another. He always does. If it seems like he's being generous, you can be sure you're not seeing the whole picture."

"I thought he was known for being a philanthropist."

"That's how he would like you to see him, sure. And Mom is. She'll throw money at an organization just because she thinks it sounds like a good cause. But with Dad, it's different. He gives money when he knows he'll get something back, whether it's to do with his reputation, or calling in a favor, or what. I used to just think he was generous. When I was young. But that is not the case."

"Oh. Well, that's too bad. He seems like a nice guy."

Kenzie's expression softened a little. "I do think he's a nice guy," she said. "To the people he loves. But he's also a shark, and you can't ever forget that."

It probably wasn't good for Kenzie to be dwelling on the negatives of finding out that her father was human, so Zachary looked for a way to change the subject.

"Did you want me to make something for supper? Order in?"

She leveled a look at him. "What would you make for supper? When have you ever made supper for the two of us in the time we've been together?"

"Well... I'm pretty sure I got out a tub of ice cream that one day..."

"A meal."

"That was a meal," he reminded her.

Kenzie cracked a grin. "Well, that's not going to cut it tonight. So have you got another idea, or are you just angling to order something in?"

"If you want to make something, that's fine with me. But I didn't want to suggest that you should. I know which side my bread is buttered on."

"So far, you don't even have bread, let alone butter." Kenzie finally let him off the hook. "Sure, why don't you order in? Whatever you're in the mood for, I don't have a preference."

Zachary walked over to the couch to sit down and pull the restaurant menus out of the drawer on the side table. An explosion of pain ran from his tailbone up his back, reminding him that he was going to have to be a lot more careful for the next little while. He tried to pull himself back into a standing position to relieve the pressure, but his knees were wobbly with the pain.

CHAPTER 37

Zachary!" Kenzie cried out in alarm and rushed forward. "What happened? Are you okay?"

He rocked a little, trying to get back up, but she pressed her hands against his chest and the pain prevented him from rising.

"It's just… it's nothing."

"It's not nothing. You're as white as a ghost. If you stand up, you're going to pass out, so just stay put."

Zachary shook his head. "I just bruised my tailbone."

"Bruised it, my foot! I've seen how you act when you're bruised. It's broken."

"Maybe. But there's not much they can do about that. I'll be fine. It will heal on its own. I just have to be more careful. I sat down too hard."

"How did you hurt it?"

"When..." Zachary tried to come up with the right words to explain that it had been the thugs who had broken into the house. Everything he thought of sounded too frightening. He didn't want to distress Kenzie any further. She would never forgive her father if she thought he was somehow responsible for injuring Zachary. "This afternoon..."

He was able to focus on her face, which was progress, because all he'd been able to see when the pain had overtaken him was a field of red.

"This afternoon." Kenzie sat down beside him and searched his face. "Tell me exactly what happened this afternoon."

"You already know."

"Well, I already know that there was a break-in. And that the thieves stole the memorabilia that you recovered. But somewhere in the middle there... you got hurt, and I don't know how."

Zachary cleared his throat. He tried to change his position again, and Kenzie didn't stop him, letting him squirm around until he found a position leaning over with his weight on his hip, which relieved the pressure on his tailbone.

"When they came in... I tried to run. They grabbed me. I tried to fight." He swallowed hard. "I landed on the floor."

"On your butt."

Zachary nodded, embarrassed. "Very graceful, I know. I'm not exactly the catlike ninja you might have thought."

She laughed. "I never thought that," she confessed. "Besides, you remember that shortly after we met, you had a spinal injury that severely curtailed any ninja-like moves."

"Well, before that, I'm sure I was much more catlike."

"You need to get it checked out."

"I've broken it before. It's one of those things they can't really do anything about. Just be careful how you sit. Get one of those donuts."

"Unless it needs surgery. The fact that you have had a spinal injury before makes this kind of thing dangerous. And if you've broken your coccyx before... you never told me that. How did it happen?"

"Similar," Zachary said curtly. "Fell on it."

She studied him. He didn't want to share any more of the experience with her and had lost interest in joking about it.

"I know you would prefer to just... sit it out..." Kenzie said, one corner of her mouth quirking up. "But I'm serious. You've had a spinal injury before. You've broken this bone before. There could be shock damage on up your spinal cord, compression of the spine from the way you fell, there could be bone chips that need to be cleaned up. You don't want sharp edges close to the spinal cord. So... you need to get it checked out. To keep me quiet, if nothing else."

Zachary sighed. He had hoped to just lie low for a few days and let it heal on its own. He knew it would take more than a few days, and he would have to be careful of how he sat down. But he had thought he could just do as he had done before and let it heal on its own.

"You don't really think it's dangerous, do you?" he asked. "I mean... it's my tailbone. Not my heart."

"Let's just go and get it checked out, and make sure."

"Can't you just look at it?"

"I don't have an x-ray machine."

"I don't really need an x-ray."

"You don't know that for sure. You hope that everything is fine, but you don't know."

"We could leave it tonight. Give it a few days to see how it does. It will probably heal on its own just fine."

Kenzie folded her arms across her chest. "I'm not budging."

Zachary rubbed his forehead. "Okay. Fine. Can we at least eat before we go to the hospital?"

"We can eat at the hospital cafeteria once we get you checked in. While we're waiting. At least we'll have something to do while we wait."

Zachary remembered the hard plastic chairs of the cafeteria. He was going to end up having to stand up all night. "I'd better get a cookie out of this."

"We'll get you a cookie."

* * *

Kenzie didn't have a donut pillow at home, but she had some other pillows that they tried to arrange in the car to make the bucket seats more tolerable. Kenzie drove slowly, wincing herself whenever they went over a bump or down into a pothole. Zachary realized partway to the hospital that he should have taken a painkiller before leaving the house. Maybe several painkillers. And maybe he should have put an ice pack on the tender spot.

“I’m so sorry,” Kenzie said. “There are so many bumps. They should fix these roads!”

“It’s okay. At least most of the potholes are filled with snow.”

Kenzie snorted. When they finally got to the hospital, Kenzie did her best to use her influence as a medical doctor to get Zachary seen to more quickly. But apparently, broken tailbones were not a high priority on the triage list, and being a doctor who dealt with corpses did not give Kenzie a lot of pull at the hospital. After confirming with the nurses that they were going down to the cafeteria to eat and would be paged if Zachary’s turn came up, they took the elevator down to the first basement level and walked slowly to the cafeteria. It was quiet, only a few people sitting at the tables eating, some of the food already being cleared away for the evening.

CHAPTER 38

Zachary was sitting awkwardly in the hard plastic chair, picking at his food and trying to stay balanced on one buttock and hip to keep the pressure off of his tailbone when his pocket started to vibrate. He pulled out his phone, hoping that it would be a message from the nurses upstairs that someone could see him. But it wasn't.

It was a number that he didn't know. Zachary looked at it for a moment, considering whether to answer it or just ignore it. He was at the hospital. He had a good excuse for not answering the phone if he needed one. But it was a Vermont number, not a toll-free or long-distance number, and therefore less likely to be a telemarketer or robocall. He let it go a couple more rings before finally deciding to answer. He put the phone to his ear.

"Goldman Investigations."

"Is this Zachary?"

Zachary froze. The voice was familiar. Slightly older and more gravelly than when he had first learned it, but still recognizable. Berk Goldman.

His father.

Kenzie had been telling him how much she disliked her father and her problems with him. She claimed to love her parents, though Zachary had difficulty reconciling her attitude toward her father with her claim of love.

But for Zachary, it was different. As a child, he had loved and longed to return to his mother for a long time after being put into foster care. But over the years, he had come to realize how toxic and abusive that relationship had been. And he remembered his father more as an angry drunk than anything else. He didn't remember ever wanting to go home because of him. Berk had been out of his life for decades. They'd had no contact since Zachary was ten. Until Zachary went looking for his missing brother and found Tyrrell drinking with Berk.

"This is Zachary," he acknowledged, voice tight.

Kenzie looked at him, her eyebrows going way up at his tone.

"Zachary. I'm looking for Tyrrell. Can't seem to reach him on his phone. I thought... you might know where he is. What's going on with him."

"I don't want you trying to contact him."

Berk chuckled. "Well, he's a grown man and you don't have any say over who he does or doesn't. And I'm still your father, so don't try telling me what to do."

"Stay away from him. He needs to stay sober. He can't do that if you're calling him and drinking with him."

"Oh, so you've decided what is best for him. How about you let the boy make his own decisions?"

"I thought you just said he was a grown man."

"And he is," Berk agreed. "You're the one who isn't treating him that way. You don't have any control over who he sees or spends time with. I've known him longer than you have, and if you think he's going to stop drinking or stop seeing me, you better think again."

"Leave him alone. Don't call again." Zachary lowered the phone and touched the red button to terminate the call. Back in the days before cell phones, he could have slammed the phone down with a satisfying crash to end the call, but cell phones required him to be more civilized. He felt like throwing it across the room to appease his temper.

Kenzie watched him with bright eyes, waiting to see what he would do. He didn't imagine she'd be very pleased if he gave in to his temper and threw the phone. She might think it was funny, but she wouldn't be happy about it. Zachary set it down on the table in front of him and straightened it. He grimaced at Kenzie.

"Bet you can't guess who."

Kenzie laughed. "I bet I can." She shook her head. "He has some gall calling you to get in touch with Tyrrell. He has to know that you have... er... negative feelings toward him."

"I think I made that pretty clear."

Kenzie nodded in agreement. She looked at the food left in front of Zachary. "You want another cookie?"

"Can't. Too full."

She nodded and accepted this. Zachary thought he'd done a pretty good job of eating compared with the period before Christmas and his med change. Especially considering the pain he was in, which was making him a little unsteady and lightheaded.

"Well, if you're done, we can head back up to the waiting room and see how long it is before they call your name."

Zachary pushed himself to his feet and held himself braced on the table for a few seconds, waiting until he was sure that he was steady. Kenzie eyed him.

“Are you sure you’re okay? Need a wheelchair?”

“I don’t need a wheelchair. It’s just a broken tailbone.”

“Are you experiencing weakness or numbness in your legs or back?”

“Just a little wobbly.”

“That sounds suspiciously like weakness or numbness.”

“It’s just the pain. It’s nothing.”

Every time she mentioned the spinal injury he had sustained in the car crash two years before or the possibility that he had reinjured it, he got more anxious and more adamant that he hadn’t. It had taken a long time to fully recover from the injury, and he still felt awkward running, walking backward, or any other ambulation than regular walking. Kenzie thought he had stopped his physio too soon and should have worked on those other movements more. But Zachary had just wanted to get on with life.

Kenzie looked at him for a minute, then turned away from him, pointing her body toward the elevators. “Let’s go up, then.”

Zachary hesitated. The more he thought about his gait and the possibility of facing more physio, the more stuck he felt. He didn’t want her watching him and, at the same time, was not sure he could move normally. It wouldn’t go over well with Kenzie if he took a step and fell flat on his face.

She was halfway to the elevator before she turned her head to see if he was following. Zachary swallowed and took a careful step toward her. Just a half step to be sure that his legs were strong enough to hold him and he wouldn’t collapse without the support of the table.

That was okay, so he took another step and then was shuffling toward Kenzie, more sure of his stability.

"Are you doing the zombie shuffle to be funny?" Kenzie asked. "Because you're worrying me."

"My foot is asleep, that's all."

"One of your feet? Which one?"

"It's just asleep from the way I was sitting. I shouldn't have been sitting that way."

He could tell she didn't believe it. In the elevator, Zachary held on to the rail and flexed and pointed his feet. They were fine. There wasn't anything wrong with them. In a few minutes, they were back in the waiting area of the emergency room. Kenzie told Zachary that she was going to find some coffee, and disappeared. He closed his eyes and waited, sinking into the throbbing pain.

It didn't seem like much time had passed when Zachary heard Kenzie's voice again and she was shaking him gently.

Zachary blinked and didn't catch the name of the doctor who was introducing himself with an East Indian accent. "Dr. Kirsch says that you may be experiencing some spinal injury symptoms," he stated. "Out of an abundance of caution, we want to check this out, and don't want you walking around. A nurse is bringing over a wheelchair and we are going to help you to move to it without putting extra stress on your spine. We don't want a lot of twisting and turning," the doctor advised, putting his gloved hand on Zachary's shoulder and gently keeping him from turning to look for the nurse.

"I've been okay. I fell down hours ago; wouldn't it be obvious by now if there was a spinal cord injury? After the car accident, it was obvious. I couldn't move."

"It can be tricky. It may swell or develop slowly over the next few days. A fall like that can cause some symptoms, but is not likely to be serious. Since you've had a previous injury, we want to look at your previous imaging and compare it to what we will do today. Then we will have a much better idea of what we are dealing with."

The wheelchair that a nurse eventually pushed over had a u-shaped cushion on the seat, which Zachary soon found was to take the pressure off of his tailbone and gave him much-needed relief.

"Fell on your bum, did you?" the nurse questioned loudly, drawing smiles and chuckles from the other waiting patients seated nearby. "Well, most of us have plenty of padding down there," she slapped her own ample padding, "but you certainly do not. We're going to have to get your girlfriend to fatten you up!"

"Actually, you might be interested to know that heavy patients are far more likely to break their tailbones," the East Indian doctor informed the nurse and Zachary. "An obese patient is far more likely to receive a tailbone injury than an underweight one." He smiled in Kenzie's direction. "But your girlfriend should still fatten you up."

Kenzie laughed, and Zachary grimaced, trying to laugh along with them. At least with the special pillow, he could sit and breathe without it hurting so much. The doctor would order a few x-rays, and everything would be fine.

CHAPTER 39

Kenzie had apparently made a good impression on the doctor, who saw that Zachary was given a small examination room to wait in rather than being in the curtained area where everyone else was being seen. When Zachary was changed, settled, and waiting for the x-rays, Kenzie joined him again. She looked over him, eyes critical.

"Hey. How are you doing?" she asked sympathetically.

"I should have just stayed home. There's nothing they can do for a broken tailbone. It probably isn't even broken. It's probably just bruised."

"Yeah, I know you're feeling anxious about it."

Zachary shifted, trying to find a comfortable position on his side. "I really want to just get out of here. Can't we go home and then come back if there are other symptoms? If it gets worse?"

"It's bad enough now. I don't want to risk it. If everything looks fine on the films, then we'll go home, and I won't be worried because I'll know it's been looked at properly."

The thought of being paralyzed again, even temporarily, terrified Zachary. He didn't want to have to go through all of that again. He hated to be helpless. He hated having to learn to walk properly again and to do physio for hours to build up the muscle memory and make things like walking, bending over, and reaching feel more natural again. He hated the way people looked down at him when he was in the hospital bed or wheelchair.

"This can't be happening. I just fell on the floor. That's all. It wasn't anything significant. It wasn't like the car crash."

"And hopefully, they'll tell me that I'm just worrying over nothing and send you straight home."

But he could tell that she didn't think so. Zachary breathed harder, trying to suck in more oxygen. What if even his breathing became paralyzed? It hadn't been after the car crash, but who was to say if there was new damage? He couldn't seem to draw in enough breath.

"Slow down," Kenzie advised. "Just take it easy."

"I can't breathe."

"You're panicking."

He tried to listen to her. Tried to slow his breathing, but it wasn't working.

"I think you need one of your pills."

"No. I'm okay. I can..." Zachary tried to do everything Dr. B had told him to help ward off a panic attack. All at the same time, which was confusing and chaotic. He worked on slowing down and breathing with his diaphragm, but that just made him more focused on the feeling of suffocation. He tried to anchor on things in the room. What he could see, what he could hear. He could hear Kenzie trying to walk him through the anchoring exercise, but he was already trying visualization instead. Picturing himself in a calm place. Somewhere he felt safe and secure. Home with Kenzie. In bed. He only had to revise a few things to picture them at home. But when someone started screaming down the hall, his muscles all tensed, and he gasped for breath.

"It's okay," Kenzie assured him. "If it's getting to be too much, take your meds. That's what they're for."

"I want to talk to her."

Kenzie frowned, her brow wrinkling.

"Dr. B. Do you think I could talk to her?"

The frown lifted, and Kenzie nodded. "Sure. She always says to call if you need to talk."

"She won't be in bed?"

"It's not that late."

Zachary motioned to the small locker that contained his clothes and personal belongings. Kenzie looked inside and retrieved his phone for him.

"It's okay to use the phone in here? I'm not going to get in trouble?" he asked.

"If there is trouble, I'll smooth it over."

Zachary fumbled with the phone, trying to find Dr. Boyle's number. Kenzie looked as if she wanted to jump in and help, but she didn't, letting him sort it out himself.

"Do you want me to stay with you, or do you want privacy?" she whispered as the call started to ring through.

Zachary extended the fingers of his other hand to her. She held his hand and stayed by his side as he waited for Dr. B to pick up. Eventually, his therapist did answer, right at the moment when he thought the call was going through to voicemail.

"Zachary. How are you?"

Zachary breathed out in relief. It still took him a few more gasping breaths to answer her, but just having her on the line seemed to help. “Doctor...” A shuddering breath out and another in. “I just... I don’t know what to do.”

“Okay. Let’s talk it through. What’s going on?”

“I... fell down. It wasn’t any big thing. Just falling on the floor. But Kenzie was worried, so...”

“How did you fall? Did you trip? Or were you dizzy or faint?”

“No... I was pushed. But... that’s not it.”

“Okay. Why is Kenzie worried?”

“I just bruised my tailbone, and she’s worried about... about spinal cord damage because of the accident. The car crash where I got hurt.”

"I remember talking about that, yes. So if Kenzie is worried about it, and she's a medical doctor, then you should probably listen to her concerns. Get it checked out."

"Yeah." Zachary licked his lips, but his mouth was dry. "I'm at the hospital."

"Good. Sounds like the right choice. What is it you're not sure about, then? You said you didn't know what to do, but it sounds like you're doing the right thing already."

Zachary cleared his throat, trying not to let his voice crack. There was a hot, hard lump in his throat and he didn't know if he could talk around it. It was silly to be calling his therapist. Stupid to be so worried when he was in the hospital where they could keep an eye on him and make sure that everything was okay.

"Just worried. What if there's damage? What if... I can't breathe?"

"You're breathing now. I think you'll be fine."

"It's hurting. I can't get enough air."

"What do you think you should do?"

"Kenzie said to take a pill."

"You can if you choose to. What do <u>you</u> think?"

"I just want… to breathe."

"You know taking your emergency meds will help with that."

"What if it's not anxiety? What if it's my spinal cord?"

"Then you'll be relaxed enough for the doctors to rule out anxiety and get to the real problem."

Zachary swallowed. He could see the logic of her response. Maybe she was right. Maybe they were both right. He just needed to take an anti-anxiety pill, and then all would be well.

"What if it makes me tired?"

"Yes, they often do, don't they? Why are you worried about that?"

"There's so much to do..."

"Your health comes first. Physical and mental. You can't do everything else if you're not well. You will be more productive overall if you're able to be calm and relaxed."

Zachary looked at Kenzie. She interpreted his look and reached again into the small locker to find the box of pills he kept in his pocket.

"Are you still there, Zachary?"

"I'll take one," he told Dr. B.

"Okay. Do you want me to stay on the phone? Or do you want to call me back if you need to talk more?"

"I'll call back."

"Sounds good. I'll be here if you need me. But I think you'll feel a lot better once you take your meds."

"Yeah."

"Good luck with your check-up. You let me know if you need anything."

"Thanks." Zachary did the best he could to muffle the sobs that were creeping up his throat. Sympathy could break him. He could stay strong in the face of anger or an attack, but give him compassion, and he melted into a puddle.

He hung up the phone and took the pill and the water that Kenzie offered him.

"Thank you."

He swallowed enough water to get the pill down, then closed his eyes, waiting for it to take effect.

“It’s going to be okay,” Kenzie assured him. “You’re in the right place. If there is anything wrong, we’ll get it dealt with. But like you say, it’s probably limited to your tailbone, and you’ll be able to go home in a couple of hours, once they’ve finished looking at the imaging.”

Zachary nodded, his eyes still closed. He tried to focus on his breathing, keeping an even rhythm in and out to stay in control. Kenzie stopped talking and let him be. She was probably wondering why he fought it so much. Why he fought having to take a rescue dose or taking all of the other meds every day. She didn’t know what it was like to be in his head. To need so much help just to get by and look normal. There were days when he felt like he could be normal, like anyone else, and it was so tempting to just go off all of the meds. But he knew how that had ended up in the past. And he knew, from experiences going on a med holiday to get a baseline or start building a new cocktail, or ending up without any meds like he did at the

Lodge, how quickly things would spiral out of control if he did that.

But that didn't mean he had to like it.

CHAPTER 40

Feeling better?" Kenzie asked.

Zachary realized that he was drifting, eyes still closed, and that the crushing anxiety had lifted. He could still think about the possibility of a spinal cord injury, could still worry about it, but the heart-racing panic over the thought of having done lasting neurological damage and not being able to breathe were gone. His breathing and his heart rate were settling down. The tight muscles in his stomach had relaxed.

"Yeah. Better."

"Good." She gave his shoulder a squeeze. "I hate to see you so anxious."

Zachary shifted, still not able to find any position that was really comfortable. But at least he wasn't sitting or lying directly on his tailbone. It was still sore and throbbing, but he relieved as much pressure as possible by lying on his side. They would probably give him a prescription painkiller before sending him home. Zachary wasn't sure he would take it. He always worried about conflicts between painkillers and his meds, having had problems after combining them in the past. And there was always the danger of addiction to the more powerful painkillers. Tyrrell and Berk were testaments to the fact that Zachary shouldn't be messing around with anything that he could get addicted to. Addiction was in their DNA.

"Where's my phone?"

"You just dropped it." Kenzie reached over and picked his phone up from the mattress. She handed it back to him. "Keep yourself entertained. Maybe message Rhys."

"I still have work to do," he reminded her.

Kenzie pursed her lips, looking at him. "I don't know if now is the best time for you to be working."

"I'm fine."

"Those are pretty powerful drugs."

Zachary nodded his agreement. That was why he didn't like to take them every day. But that didn't mean he had to put his life on pause whenever he took one. He scrolled through his contacts and found Detective Shelly.

He was fully expecting it to go to voicemail. Detectives were never there when he wanted them. But Shelly picked up after a couple of rings.

"Shelly."

"This is Zachary Goldman."

"I've been trying to reach you, Mr. Goldman. Where have you been?"

"Oh..." Zachary had noticed that there were missed call notifications on his screen, but hadn't taken the time to see who had been trying to reach him. "Sorry. I'm at the hospital."

Shelly was silent for a moment. “Visiting the McNichols?” he asked eventually. “I didn’t think he’d be having any visitors today.”

“No. I... I suppose you heard about the break-in at my house. Donaldson said that he was going to talk to you. And I filed a report here in Roxboro. I told them to copy you.”

“Yes,” the detective’s voice was somewhat snide. “I heard about your so-called break-in. Didn’t sound like there was any evidence to be collected.”

“It was pretty clean,” Zachary agreed. “We thought they were probably professionals. Hired help. Jennifer and her boyfriend must have tracked me down and hired someone to—”

“Yeah, I don’t believe that load. You think petty criminals would hire heavyweights to go back and steal their stuff back? No way. Not gonna happen. Those kids have cut and run. They’re not sticking around here to get caught.”

"I know they moved out of the house they were in, but with some work, we might be able to track them. Credit card receipts—"

"You think I'm that inept? Of course we're on top of credit card receipts. They're gone. Hit the road. They didn't stick around here long enough to steal their stuff back. Nice try."

Zachary was stumped. If they weren't the ones who had hired the thugs to retrieve the stolen property from his house, then who was?

"I don't think there was any break-in," Shelly said. "The loot just happened to get stolen before Donaldson got there to pick it up? A little too convenient for my tastes. This was a set-up. You returned the stolen goods to the McNichols."

"No! You can check with them. I didn't have anything to do with this."

"Yeah."

Zachary sputtered at the phone. He looked at Kenzie. “He thinks there was no break-in. That I did this myself.”

Kenzie took the phone from his hand. “This is the detective in Montpelier?”

Zachary nodded. He reached to take it back from her, but Kenzie kept it out of his reach, and he didn’t feel quick enough to grab it back. Everything had the loose, slippery quality that he associated with sleep or anxiety medication.

“This is Dr. Kenzie Kirsch,” she snapped into the phone. “What exactly is your problem, detective? How exactly do you think Zachary wound up in the hospital if there was no break-in?”

Zachary couldn’t hear Shelly’s response.

“Those thugs roughed him up, that’s how,” Kenzie snapped into the phone. “So don’t act like Zachary is making it all up.”

Another pause, while she listened to his protests.

"Well, maybe you should ask Donaldson why he didn't tell you all of the details. This is not made up. You call him and you get the scoop. Don't be a jerk and blame the guy who ended up in the hospital."

He said something back to her. Kenzie handed Zachary the phone back, her eyes bright with anger. Zachary took it uncertainly. Donaldson had, he thought, probably thought he was doing Zachary a favor, not exposing him to the humiliation of Shelly knowing that he had been handcuffed and thrown on the floor, helpless as a baby during the robbery. He hadn't anticipated Detective Shelly turning the blame on Zachary and the McNichols.

Zachary cleared his throat, grimaced at Kenzie, and put the phone back up to his ear. "Uh—hi. It's me again."

Shelly swore. His tone was definitely less confrontational. "You were injured in the robbery?"

"Yeah... maybe a broken bone or two, and they're checking for spinal cord injury... just waiting for x-ray now."

"And you're calling me for an update? Put your phone away and take care of yourself. And your girlfriend. She's a little firebrand, isn't she?"

Zachary glanced at Kenzie. "Yeah. I just wanted to make sure you knew about the robbery and the details that I know... which isn't really much. Just that I'm pretty sure they were hired muscle."

This time, Shelly didn't accuse him of making the whole thing up. "Do you have descriptions? I didn't get anything helpful from Donaldson."

"I asked the robbery detective to share with you, but I don't know if they've sent anything over yet. They were masked, so I can't tell you much except size... big goons like wrestlers or football players. No detectable accents. They took pictures of the boot prints, but… that won't tell you much other than that they were big dudes."

"Well, your original thieves didn't hire them. They wouldn't run before getting the merchandise back and, from the paper trail they have left, they ran last night. So not them. Which leaves… Janice and Glen Nichols."

Zachary shook his head. He closed his eyes, feeling drowsy. It took too much effort to open them again. "Not the Nichols," he disagreed. "Why would they do that? I would have gotten the stolen goods back to them or to you, and you would have released it to them. So why come after it here?"

"They couldn't wait. They had already arranged for the stuff to be sold at auction. They had already claimed it as stolen on their insurance. What you were doing threw a wrench in the works, so they had to get around you."

Zachary supposed that what Shelly said could be true, but it still didn't feel right to him. "They weren't the ones that set up the auction. That was Jennifer and her boyfriend."

"It could have been at McNichols's instruction. They might have all been working together."

A little extra money for Jennifer and her boyfriend. Her boyfriend was already in the business, so they were easy to rope into it. Or maybe it had been Jennifer who had suggested the fake robbery to the McNichols, showing them that they could make back more than what had been stolen if they handled it the right way. Maybe she knew that the bar was in financial trouble and went to Janice and Glen with the proposal.

"As an idea, that sounds fine," he admitted. "But... they don't strike me as the kind. And they were surprised to learn it was an inside job. Really upset about Jennifer being involved."

"Or they are good actors. Or what they were upset about was you finding it out. Maybe you weren't supposed to."

Zachary was about to say, “Then why did they hire me?” but stopped himself. Because they hadn’t hired him. It hadn’t been their idea to bring in a private investigator at all. It had been Walter’s idea. He had retained Zachary and given him a deposit before the McNichols knew what was happening. They couldn’t very well say at that point that they didn’t want a private investigator looking into it, free of charge to them.

“I can’t prove they weren’t involved,” Zachary admitted. “Maybe with a little more investigation, I could find something out. But I don’t know if Walter Kirsch will want me to go any farther. I’ve recovered the stolen property once; I’m not likely to be able to do it again. And he might not want to know if the McNichols were involved.”

There were a few beats of silence from Shelly. “Walter Kirsch?” he asked eventually. “That’s who hired you?”

Zachary suddenly wondered if he shouldn’t have revealed the fact. But it was too late to take it back now. “Well… yes. Barnburners is a favorite hangout…” He felt a little strange about saying it, knowing that Walter hadn't exactly been honest about that claim. "And he wanted to do something to help them out after the robbery."

"Walter Kirsch."

"You know him?"

"Know him? No. I'm too far down the social ladder for me to know him. But know of him? Of course. Everyone in the state knows about him. And everyone involved in politics in this corner of the country. He's a heavyweight. A different kind of heavyweight than the ones who broke into your house."

"Yeah. I guess he is. Kenzie said—"

"Wait a minute, did she say Dr. Kenzie Kirsch? She's Walter Kirsch's daughter?"

"Yeah. That's why he picked me for the investigation. How he knew I am a PI."

Shelly swore. Zachary had a feeling Shelly was reviewing everything he had done in the case, including his accusation that Zachary had reported a fake robbery to hide the fact that he had returned the stolen property to the McNichols. All of the things Shelly could be in trouble for.

“I’m going to go over this case with a fine-toothed comb,” he said finally. “If there’s anything else to be found, I’ll find it.”

“Walter is personal friends with the McNichols,” Zachary pointed out, knowing that he was stretching the truth slightly. “So you should be careful of any accusations you make against them. And Glen’s heart attack… I don’t imagine Walter would be too happy about that.”

In reality, Zachary doubted Walter would care about Glen’s heart attack. He might care if it meant that he didn’t get good service at Barnburners or that the bar had to shut down and he had to find a new hangout.

CHAPTER 41

While it seemed like it would take forever for the doctors to get the images they needed of Zachary's back and to review them and decide what was to be done with him, the doctor did eventually return to his bedside to report that there didn't appear to be any swelling around the spinal cord, no fractures to the vertebrae in his back other than his coccyx, and that he could go home and didn't need to spend the night at the hospital.

"There are still some concerns," the doctor told Kenzie, choosing to talk to her about it rather than to Zachary. Maybe because she was a doctor and he thought she would understand better or take him more seriously. Or maybe because Zachary couldn't keep his eyes open. "There could be some inflammation that is not showing up on the imaging. With Zachary experiencing some mild neurological symptoms, it is still advisable to take it very easy. Bed rest for a few days. Nothing strenuous for a couple of weeks. And a trip back to the hospital if either of you has any concerns about continuing or new symptoms."

Kenzie made noises of agreement. "Yes, I'll keep a close eye on him. He won't be doing any gymnastics for a while."

"Call or come back if you have any concerns at all."

"Thank you for your time, doctor."

Zachary was eventually released, taken to the curb in a wheelchair, then climbed into the car without assistance. Kenzie nodded her satisfaction and made sure he buckled in before pulling out.

Zachary watched out the window, his eyelids cracked open just enough to see the lights and shadows of the city at night.

"It's pretty," he breathed. "A long exposure to capture the movement of the lights..."

"Yeah?" Kenzie asked. "I bet that would be nice."

"It would." Zachary rubbed his forehead. "We're going home, right?"

"Yes."

"Back to your house, not the apartment."

"That's right. Why, did you need something at the apartment?"

"No. Maybe Tyrrell can stay there when he gets out."

Kenzie looked over at him. He could feel her eyes on him. "You haven't mentioned that before. Is that what you want to do?"

"Not using it anymore. He's going to need somewhere when he gets out."

"Yes. That might be a good solution. Lets him get back on his feet, but without us hovering over him, trying to direct everything."

"No hovering," Zachary agreed. "You don't hover."

"Well, sometimes I do." Zachary could hear the smile in her voice. "But I try not to."

"You're perfect," he told her. "I don't know how I could be with someone so perfect." He looked in her direction and attempted to put his hand on her leg, but missed. "Especially when I'm such a mess."

"You're not such a mess. You have some challenges." Kenzie shrugged. "But so does everyone. I prefer you."

"Doesn't make any sense." Zachary tried not to slur his words. He didn't want her thinking that he was drunk. "Choosing to be with someone like me? They say women pick men like their fathers. I'm not like Walter."

"No, you're not. I'm thankful for that. I knew I didn't want someone like him."

"But he's a good husband. A good provider. Makes good money, doesn't get mixed up in dangerous situations. Home every night."

"Zachary, you know nothing about my father. He's not a good husband. He and my mom have been divorced for years. And he was never home every night. He's always traveled away from home and stayed in Montpelier near the Capitol. Mom was home in Burlington, and he would be away a few days or a couple weeks at a time. Come home weekends and recesses. Make sure he was around for holidays. But he was never a father and husband who was there for the family. He lived a separate life."

"He's your father and he loves you," Zachary assured her.

Kenzie chuckled. "Sure, he does. Or so he tells me."

"He's like Gordon," Zachary suggested. He rubbed his eyes, thinking about Gordon and Bridget. "Gordon can give her everything she needs. Everything she ever wanted. He's all of the things that I could never be. She figured out what she didn't want while we were married. So she got together with Gordon because he's the opposite of me."

"I'm sure Gordon is no more perfect than Walter is." Kenzie drove for a few minutes in silence, thinking about it. "I don't know Gordon well, but there are definitely similarities. They both get what they want. If my dad puts his mind to something, he's going to get it, no matter what anyone else says. That's how he's always been. But you know what's wrong with someone like that?"

"What?"

"He doesn't really care about anyone else. I'm sure Gordon is devoted to Bridget, but probably only insofar as it suits him to have a wife like Bridget. He wants the beautiful socialite. The perfect children. Now he's a family man. That's the image he wants to project."

"He could have dumped her," Zachary pointed out. "When he found out she is sick."

"But it doesn't hurt him for her to be sick. It just means that people will feel sorry for him. They'll look at him and think he's an angel for sticking with her and taking care of her. But he'll just hire more staff to do the actual caregiving as she needs it."

Zachary remembered Gordon talking about everybody he had to take care of when Zachary was wrapping up the Lauren Barclay case. How he had to look after everyone at his investment banking firm, Drake Chase Gould, and Bridget, and the expected twins.

"How could you do that?" he mused aloud. "How could you be responsible for so many people? It would be paralyzing."

"Who? Are we still talking about Gordon? Do you mean Bridget and the twins?"

"And everyone else. All the people at Chase Gold. He has to take care of them, make sure that they aren't being forced to work too hard. Make sure the firm is not taking advantage of them."

"Well, yes, that would be a lot of people. But I doubt Gordon sees it the same way as you. To someone like Walter or Gordon, people are just... assets. You take care of your assets, but it isn't the same as you taking care of a person you care about. They don't spend any time worrying about whether people are happy or healthy. Not if it doesn't impact them."

Daniel, an employee at Chase Gold, had said that Gordon was a psychopath. Maybe he was right. Maybe everyone who ran a big company like that had to focus on himself and the company's bottom line, rather than the people employed there. Zachary had no idea how he would make a decision that would affect hundreds or thousands of people, knowing that every choice he made would be bad for a certain portion of them. People would be hurt, fired, or have their feelings ignored. But Gordon could make choices without getting bogged down by the minutia. He didn't need to know how it would affect everyone.

"I'm not perfect," Zachary told Kenzie as they drove into the garage. "I'm never going to be like him."

"Good. I don't expect you to be. I wouldn't want to be married to Gordon. Or to Walter. They are egomaniacs. You have more compassion in your little finger than both of them put together."

"And that's good?" Zachary looked at his little finger and thought of all of the times he'd been paralyzed by a choice, worried that whatever he chose, it was going to hurt someone.

"Yes," Kenzie agreed. "That's good. Are you going to remember any of this in the morning?"

"Don't know," Zachary murmured. "We'll just have to wait and see."

CHAPTER 42

Zachary slept in late in the morning due to having taken the additional anti-anxiety meds the evening before. He was also very sore after the manhandling by the thieves. Not only his tailbone, but all over. Like he'd been beaten up or hit by a truck. He didn't think that he'd been roughed up so badly when they had caught him, but maybe he hadn't realized at the time how hard he had fought or how many times he had been hit.

He waited until the early morning hours before taking a painkiller, wanting to be absolutely sure that he wasn't mixing it with the anti-anxiety meds. He was extra careful not to mix painkillers with other meds after an incident when he'd been staying overnight with Mr. Peterson, his old foster father. He groaned and struggled to get out of bed to go take something, waking Kenzie.

"Hey, are you okay? What's up?"

"Just need a painkiller."

"For your tailbone?"

"For my everything."

"Oh, poor Zachary. You stay put; let me get it for you."

Zachary settled back into place on the bed. He wasn't going to argue this time. It wasn't about being a gentleman and letting her sleep. She had offered, and he would take her up on it for once.

Kenzie got up and went to the en suite bathroom. Zachary listened to her going through the medicine cabinet and eventually picking what she deemed to be the right painkiller. She returned with a glass of water and a couple of white pills. "This should help."

He didn't bother asking what they were and just swallowed them with the water. "Thanks."

"Do you want anything else? Ice pack? Heating pad?"

“No. I’ll just sleep it off.”

“Okay.” Kenzie leaned in to give him a peck on the cheek and settled back into bed herself. She ran her warm hand over his back, rubbing it in soothing circles for a couple of minutes. Then she stopped and he could tell from her long, even breathing that she had fallen back asleep.

And then sleep had overcome him, and he had slept fitfully until late morning, unable to do anything else. He eventually managed to drag himself out of bed and to the bathroom down the hall. When he opened the door, Kenzie was there waiting for him. She smiled.

“How are you feeling this morning? Like crap, if needing a painkiller during the night is any indication.”

“Yeah. Sore. And hungover from the pills.” Zachary rubbed his face, trying to wake up properly and focus on Kenzie and his surroundings. But he felt like he was in a dark room and could only just make out the things right in front of his eyes.

Concentrating on anything more than a foot or two away seemed impossible.

"Well, back to bed with you. You know the doctor said he wanted you on bed rest."

"I can sit on the couch."

"Nope. Bed. If you want, I'll bring your computer in when you've had enough sleep. But bed rest means bed. Not doing anything to aggravate your back."

Zachary wobbled slightly. She took him by the arm and escorted him back to the bedroom and helped get him settled again. He was sore from sleeping on his side for the past few hours, but he couldn't lie flat on his back or sit up.

"I'll get you some cushions to make it easier to sit later on," Kenzie promised. "For now, try the other side." She helped arrange pillows and blankets to stabilize his position and make him more comfortable. "You need anything else? Hungry?"

"Does this mean I get breakfast in bed?" Zachary teased, his voice still rough and gravelly with sleep. Kenzie did not approve of any practice that would result in crumbs between the sheets.

"Only while you're on prescribed bed rest. This is not going to carry through to weekends," Kenzie responded in a mock-severe voice. It wasn't like Zachary ever slept in or demanded to be served breakfast in bed. She was the one who usually had to coax him to eat.

"Aww," Zachary pretended to be disappointed. He closed his eyes. "Not ready to eat anything yet."

"Okay. I'll check again later. Do you mind if I vacuum? Will that bother you?"

Zachary shook his head. "No. Won't bother me. I don't think I'm going to go back to sleep."

But he was asleep again before he heard the noise of the vacuum cleaner.

* * *

When he next awoke, Zachary thought by the angle of the sun through the window that it was around noon. He rubbed his eyes. He never slept that late, even sick. But knowing that he wouldn't be allowed to get up to sit in the living room, there wasn't exactly any point in trying to get up.

"Hey, Zach. Ready for something to eat?" Kenzie asked, coming in to check on him after a while and finding him awake.

"I guess. Don't really feel like anything, though."

"Maybe not, but you're already late taking your morning meds, and some of them need to be taken with food."

Zachary grunted his acknowledgment. He was used to having to plan mealtimes around his med schedule.

"Granola bar?" Kenzie suggested, since it was Zachary's usual go-to choice for breakfast.

“No.” Zachary was strangely turned off by the thought of anything sweet. He considered, trying to think of something that would be appetizing but didn’t require Kenzie to do any preparation. He wasn’t likely to eat more than a few bites. It wasn’t worthwhile for her to spend an hour preparing something.

“Maybe… those cheese strings?”

“Sure. You probably want something other than just cheese, though. Yogurt? Cereal?”

“No…” He tried to decide what else he could get down. “Toast?”

Kenzie nodded. “I assume you don’t want marmalade on it. Some strawberry jam?”

Zachary had learned in foster care to eat whatever was on offer. But he had to admit that marmalade was not something he had ever developed a taste for. The bitterness of the peels made him wince.

“Just plain. Margarine.”

“You’re sure?”

He could understand her confusion over his not going with his usual breakfast choices. “Just... nothing sweet right now. Can’t stomach it.”

“Okay. No problem. Cheese string and buttered toast it is. Be back in a few minutes. Oh—and I found this in my office.”

Kenzie handed him a USB drive.

Zachary held it in his palm and looked at it for a minute, trying to remember where he had seen it before.

“Where was this?”

“In my office. It was on my desk, but it’s not mine, so I assume it’s yours.”

Zachary frowned. “No. I… I remember seeing it there. But I thought it was yours. Who else’s would it be?”

Kenzie raised her brows and shook her head. “You’re the detective. You figure it out.”

She obviously thought it was his, even if he didn’t remember. And he couldn’t blame her. He was easily distracted, lost things without realizing it, or had to spend an hour looking for something he had misplaced because he had left his phone in the fridge or some other weird place. It wouldn’t be out of the realm of possibility for him to forget that he’d bought or been given a USB drive for something. He had a vague recollection of Donaldson picking it up off the floor in Kenzie’s office. It could have been there for months without either of them seeing it. Partially hidden by the furniture, or left on the desk or another surface and forgotten about.

Kenzie left to prepare his breakfast/lunch, and Zachary moved around restlessly, trying to find a position that didn't aggravate his tailbone or another bruise or pulled muscle.

"Will you bring me my laptop?" he asked when Kenzie returned with a lunch plate bearing one unwrapped cheese string and one slice of buttered toast. She set it on the side table along with a small plastic box filled with his daytime meds. There was still a glass of water on the table, lukewarm from the night before.

"Don't eat over your keyboard."

"I won't. Want to see what's on this drive." He tapped the USB stick against his palm. He could not remember what he might have used it for or who he might have been given it by, but still hadn't managed to dredge up anything from his unwilling brain. If he knew where it had come from, that knowledge was currently lost in fog.

Kenzie ducked out to the living room and returned with his laptop and charge cord. “Food first,” she advised. “So you can take your pills. Then you can play on the computer.” She smiled teasingly to let him know that she was only pretending to act like she was his mother instead of his partner. But she still wanted him to be sure to eat and take his meds.

Zachary left his computer on the bed beside him, unopened, and reached for his plate. He took a couple of bites of the toast and then washed his pills down with warm water. He peeled a long string off of the cheese and stuffed it into his mouth. He knew that the enjoyment he got from playing with his cheese was juvenile, but what was the harm in a little ritual that encouraged him to eat when he had little appetite?

“Need anything else?” Kenzie asked. “I didn’t get you another painkiller. How is your pain level?”

Zachary shrugged with one shoulder. “Tolerable.”

"Let me know if you need anything. I'll probably go out this afternoon to get a couple of cushions for you."

"Thanks." As it was, Zachary was going to have to lounge on his side to use the computer placed on the mattress beside him. It would be a lot more dignified and bother his shoulders and back less if he could sit upright.

Kenzie walked back out to continue with her housekeeping chores, Zachary assumed. Or to have her own lunch or take a break before going out to do the shopping.

Zachary turned the laptop around and opened the lid. He logged in to get past the lock screen and then put the USB stick into one of the ports.

Gerry, his computer guy, would undoubtedly not approve of him putting an unknown USB drive into his computer. But they had set his computer up not to autoplay anything that was plugged into it. He could at least examine the file system before deciding what he wanted to do with it. And the USB drive wasn't really unknown. It was his or Kenzie's; he just didn't know which. One of them had been given it and then forgotten about it. People did that all the time, sharing music, pictures, or other files.

It could be a drive with some of Mr. Peterson's photography on it, and Zachary had just forgotten about it.

Or not.

CHAPTER 43

Zachary's laptop brought up a file listing for the contents of the USB drive.

Zachary and Mr. Peterson had traded digital pictures plenty of times, and he knew that the list of files was nothing to do with photography. There were several image files, but the names were not formatted incrementally or like anything Zachary had ever gotten from his friend before. And there were too many other types of files mixed in with the images. Word processing and spreadsheet files. Various log or system files. A number of large PDFs. Nothing meant to launch when the USB was put into a drive. He didn't see anything executable.

There were several layers of folders, and he clicked through them, just looking at the file and folder names to start with. Projects, dates, maybe some company names. Nothing that sounded familiar, either from cases that he had worked on or anything that Kenzie had mentioned. He wasn't sure how her files would be named. Still, nothing in the filenames sounded even vaguely medical, and he didn't see any x-rays or colored scans on the thumbnails of the graphic files.

Zachary drilled down another level in what seemed to be a project folder and stopped, staring at the name on a subfolder.

Bieberstein

He gazed at it for a few minutes, frozen, while his brain tried to process its significance.

He had met a Blair Bieberstein on the Lauren Barclay case. A case that he had taken for Gordon Drake. The same Gordon Drake as he had just been talking to Kenzie about the night before. Bridget's new partner, the father of her children. CEO or managing partner of Drake Chase Gould, a new and very successful investment banking company.

Of course, if there was one Bieberstein in Vermont, there must be others. Blair's parents, siblings, cousins. Just because Zachary had never run into the name anywhere before or since, that didn't mean that Blair Bieberstein was the only person in

Vermont who bore that name. It was just a coincidence. He had seen other names as he went through the USB drive, and if he hadn't actually known a Bieberstein, it wouldn't have ever attracted his attention. There were other surnames or corporate names on other files and folders, and none of them had meant anything to Zachary. Common names like Brown and Jones. Old Vermont family names. And names that meant nothing to him because he didn't have any experiences to attach to them.

Eventually, Zachary started to click through other folders in the file structure. He still didn't actually open any of the files. Those with graphic thumbnails he studied for a second or two longer, but he didn't have any experience in investment banking or whatever finance documents were in the folders, and the images didn't mean anything to him.

He looked for the names of other employees that he had met at Chase Gold, as the firm was affectionately called, and eventually changed his approach and put several names into the search field in turn. Drake, Chase, and Gould all brought up hundreds of hits. It could be research on the firm. Someone might be looking at a financing or buyout and had compiled stacks of research on them. They could be internal files from Chase Gold that someone had taken home to work on. But even if the files had been copied for a legitimate purpose, how had they ended up in Kenzie's office?

Perhaps one of the thugs had dropped it. It would have been easy for a USB drive to drop out of one of the men's pockets as he bent over to pick up the boxes. If he hadn't noticed, he might have inadvertently left it behind.

But what would a hired thug be doing with hundreds of files of research on Chase Gold?

It seemed very unlikely that a criminal for hire would be carrying financial documents on a USB drive. Unless he'd picked them up at the last office he'd hit. Maybe someone had hired him to retrieve the USB drive, the same way as he had been hired to retrieve the boxes of memorabilia from Zachary.

Zachary tried searching the names of other people he had met at Chase Gold. There were hits, but far fewer. He tried Bieberstein, and the list of files containing his name was lengthy. Zachary tried "Blair Bieberstein," putting the name in quotes, figuring that would foil the search. If the Bieberstein named on the folder he had seen was for another Bieberstein, then "Blair Bieberstein" would not have any hits. But there were hits. A lot of them.

Zachary turned it over in his mind. He could open the files and start reading through them. But he didn't like the idea that they might be password protected or that they might somehow leave footprints on his system or send out a beacon when he opened one that would alert someone at Chase Gold about a breach of their security protocols and lead them straight back to Zachary. He'd already dealt with one homicidal maniac at Chase Gold and didn't relish another. Especially not when he was already sore from the previous day's encounter. Whether he had any spinal cord inflammation or not, he didn't need to risk a physical altercation with anyone.

* * *

"Bieberstein," Blair answered his phone briskly. "Who's this?"

"Oh, hi. It's Zachary Goldman. I don't know if you remember me from—"

"Sure, I remember who you are. What do you want?"

Zachary smiled at the brusque question. He knew that Bieberstein didn't intend to be offensive by skipping over the usual small talk and progression up to what he had called about. He was just being efficient. Cutting away all of what he saw as unnecessary deadwood and going straight to the heart of the matter. Zachary wasn't exactly a social acquaintance, so why had he called? He must want something.

“I have come into possession of a USB drive,” Zachary explained. “It seems to be filled with documents about Chase Gold.”

“Came into it how?” Bieberstein asked. “What kind of files?”

“I haven’t opened them in case they are sensitive or set off some kind of alarm. There are lots of documents. Hundreds. Whole tree structures, from what I can see. There is a subfolder named Bieberstein. When I search Blair Bieberstein in quotes, I get a lot of hits.”

“You’re saying that it is a USB drive filled with files about me?”

“No, it obviously isn’t just about you. I thought maybe it was research documents that someone had compiled about the company. Maybe they are planning to buy it. If it’s not that... then I think it might be documents pulled from your server.”

Bieberstein swore. One short, staccato syllable.

"Take a picture of it with your phone," he instructed. "Text it to me right now."

Zachary obeyed, taking a shot of the screen that was currently up on his laptop. He texted it to Bieberstein and then put the phone back to his ear.

"I sent it."

"Hold on."

Zachary waited while Bieberstein checked out the file. Zachary could hear rapid key clicks before Bieberstein said anything. Then another oath.

"Where are you?" Bieberstein demanded when he resumed the call. "I'll come to you."

Zachary hesitated for just an instant before giving Bieberstein Kenzie's house address. He couldn't exactly go to Bieberstein. Not when he was supposed to be on bed rest. Kenzie would kill him if she came home to discover that he had gone out. And that was ignoring the fact that he could aggravate the injury to his spinal cord, which was a risk he was not willing to take.

“Got it,” Bieberstein snapped. “I’ll be right over.”

“Hey, uh, Blair...” Zachary was awkward calling him by his first name. But he didn’t want to just address him by his surname and, though he knew that the employees at Chase Gold frequently referred to him as “Biebs,” he didn’t know whether they did so to his face or how he would feel about Zachary taking this liberty.

“Yes?”

“Listen, I’m on bed rest from an injury. I’ll get up and unlock the door for you and disarm the security alarm, but then I’ll be back in bed. Just come in and find me. And... be sure to lock it once you’re in.”

“Roger,” Bieberstein agreed, without bothering to ask Zachary how he had been injured. He hung up.

Zachary looked at the time and tried to estimate how long it would take Bieberstein to drive there. He didn't want to leave the house unlocked and unsecured for too long. He didn't want to leave it unsecured at all. The very thought ramped up his anxiety, and he didn't want to have to take another rescue dose of anti-anxiety meds. Not two days in a row. If the house were only unlocked for ten minutes, that wouldn't be a risk. No one was going to know that it was unlocked and no one would try to break in during those ten minutes.

Still, he tried to plan it as closely as he could, doing a quick Google Maps search to see what the predicted driving time was from Chase Gold to the house, then trimming it by a couple of minutes, anticipating that Bieberstein would have a lead foot, wanting to get there as quickly as possible.

He watched the clock closely, then eased himself out of bed and walked slowly and carefully to the front door, trying to keep his back straight and to use the best possible posture, like a model walking with a book on top of her head. He disarmed the alarm, unlocked the locks on the front door, then walked back to the bedroom without looking out the window to see if Bieberstein was driving up yet. If he gave in to the compulsion to check once, he would be checking every thirty seconds until Bieberstein actually arrived. He slipped back into bed, turning the opposite direction from what he had been facing before and moved his computer to the edge of the bed. It took a little shuffling around to get the blankets and pillows into the configuration that eased the pain the best. He continued to click through the file tree structure, looking for any other indications as to what kind of information was on the drive.

There was a rapid knock on the door, followed by the sound of the door opening, closing, and the locks being turned. Zachary breathed out, relieved.

“Blair? I’m in here.”

Bieberstein was at the bedroom door a moment later. His eyes swept the room briefly. He grabbed the chair from Kenzie’s dressing table and dragged it over to the side of the bed.

Zachary had previously compared him to a hyperactive squirrel. Not aloud; just in his mind. Bieberstein was a small man, always moving, some kind of math and finance genius that no one could compare to.

“Is that it?” He nodded to the drive sticking out from the side of Zachary’s computer.

Zachary nodded. Bieberstein reached over and pulled it out.

CHAPTER 44

Zachary's computer beeped and issued an error warning for not ejecting the USB drive before pulling it out. He clicked the error and then closed the computer lid. Bieberstein sat down on the chair and pulled his own laptop out of his bag. He opened it up, inserted the USB drive, and touched the laptop's biometric sensor to unlock it. His eyes drilled into the screen as he clicked and typed, moving quickly through the contents of the USB drive, exploring what Zachary had already seen. As Bieberstein faced Zachary, his screen was not visible, so Zachary didn't know if he was opening files or just viewing the names and thumbnails.

Bieberstein ran his fingers through his hair. He continued to look at the contents of the drive. He stood up, set the computer down on the chair, and started to pace back and forth. Bieberstein had said that he thought better on his feet. Zachary waited to see what he came up with.

"This is not good," Bieberstein said. "I thought that maybe if they had files on me, they were just headhunters. Trying to see if they could hire me to work for another firm. I get offers sometimes."

Zachary nodded, not surprised. Bieberstein had locked up one of the positions at Chase Gold before anyone else had even been considered, leaving the rest of the interns to fight over the last remaining position. Bieberstein had shot ahead of them with his employment assured. No one wanted him to go anywhere else.

"But this is not a headhunter file." Bieberstein stared up at the ceiling as he strode back and forth, thinking about it. "This is industrial espionage."

Zachary had been afraid of that. "How bad is it?"

"Really bad. This is privileged information that no one outside the firm should have. Or even see. Did you look at these files?"

"I only looked at the names and the thumbnails. I didn't want to open anything and risk infecting my system or setting off an alarm."

Bieberstein nodded his understanding. He muttered to himself, too low for Zachary to understand. It sounded like he was running through scenarios in rapid-fire, looking for the best possible outcome.

"Where did you get this?" he asked. "Can you tell me that?"

"I would if I could... but I really don't know. The house was broken into yesterday. The thieves took several boxes of stuff. That was in the room that the boxes were stolen from. I don't know... maybe one of them dropped it."

"Who were they?"

"They were masked. I think they were hired thugs. Professionals that someone paid to come in here and take those things."

"What did they steal?"

"Sports memorabilia. Some... mementos and valuables that had been stolen from a sports bar a couple of weeks ago. They didn't have a high intrinsic value. I was hired to see what I could do. I recovered them from the people who had stolen them, brought them back here, and then I guess... someone stole them from me."

Bieberstein rubbed his hands together rapidly like he was trying to warm them up. He gazed up at the ceiling, stopping close to Zachary.

"What made them so valuable? Why did they hire you?"

"The memorabilia? Nothing. Some of them had been sold to private buyers already, and some were going to be sold at auction. I didn't look at everything in the boxes, but I didn't see... certificates of authenticity or anything like that. Some stuff was signed. Baseballs, hockey pucks, posters, pictures..."

"Sounds like junk," Bieberstein said with a jerk of his head that might have been a shake or a tic.

"Well... for anyone who wasn't into the teams, I guess that's exactly what it is. I have an inventory list..." Zachary thought about it before opening his computer. Was that classified? Was he sharing private client information if he showed Bieberstein what had been stolen? He didn't think it was secret. And they were each helping the other, trying to sort out a crime that involved both of the companies they were working for. He lifted the lid on his laptop. "You'll keep this confidential?"

Bieberstein widened his eyes. He made a motion toward the USB drive. "This is the sensitive information. Not your inventory of stolen property. I'm the one who should be asking you for confidentiality."

"Well then, I guess we both agree to keep each other's information confidential."

Bieberstein nodded his agreement. Zachary took a couple of minutes to find the inventory list. He then displayed it on the screen and turned it toward Bieberstein. Blair looked it over, reading parts of the list out loud very quickly, muttering in between some of the items. He started pacing again, still repeating inventory items aloud. He started reciting the memorabilia by team, with all items for one team in a list. The list on Zachary's screen was haphazard. Bieberstein had, Zachary realized, memorized the list and was now breaking it down and resorting it, looking for patterns. It was no wonder that he was so valuable to the firm.

After repeating the items by team, Bieberstein repeated them again, grouping them together by like item. All posters together, all balls or pucks, all signed photographs, all scale replicas.

"Wait..." Zachary held his hand up.

Bieberstein stopped pacing and looked at him.

"The car. The Montreal Canadiens car. My nephew was here playing. He ended up playing in that room and taking a bunch of the memorabilia out of the boxes. He wasn't supposed to, so that got him in trouble. He was trying to show me the little station wagon. He'd been playing with it on the floor. I just wanted him to pack everything back away so that nothing would get lost or broken."

Bieberstein's head was bobbing up and down, eyes bright as he followed Zachary's narrative.

"He was trying to show me that the doors open and shut. It had little doors on the side and in the back. It was a replica station wagon, so there was space inside for cargo. A rectangular space, about this big." Zachary held his fingers up.

Bieberstein rocked back and forth on his heels, thinking about it. "Just the right size to put a USB drive inside."

Zachary laughed. Was that where the USB drive had come from? Mason had taken it out or dropped it when he had opened the doors to the little car? Then he had left it on the floor when he had packed everything back up. Maybe in plain sight, maybe behind one of the boxes hidden from view until the boxes were removed. But the thugs picking up the boxes would have no idea that it was part of the loot they were supposed to be collecting.

“That’s where it came from,” Bieberstein said, “but how did it get into the car in the first place?”

CHAPTER 45

Then it all started to click into place. Zachary looked at Bieberstein.

"Oh, no."

"What?" Bieberstein asked. He paced across the room. "You know who did this? You know who is trying to bring down Chase Gold?"

"Do you think that's the goal? To ruin the company? Couldn't it be... for a takeover or something like that? Maybe they want to buy Chase Gold."

"Maybe they do. If so, you can get the best price by devaluing the company first. Put it into bankruptcy, buy it as a going concern, then bring it back to life under new management. You get all of the assets at bargain-basement prices, can strip out what you don't want, then build it up again."

Zachary tried to imagine how that scenario might fit. He wasn't a finance guy, but he didn't see how that would work. There had been some other plan.

"Whoever is leaking this information, they have to be stopped," Bieberstein said. "I can try to trace the breach from our end, get a look at security logs and who would have had access to copy this off the system. But I don't know where you were in the chain. Why would someone put a USB drive in a toy car? Were they hiding it?"

"I have an idea," Zachary told him. "But I'm going to need some time to sort it out."

Bieberstein nodded. "More important to stop the leak on my end. If nothing can get out, then whoever your man is, wherever he is in the process, he can't get the information."

"So... you'll take that to Gordon Drake? And talk to the IT guys?"

Bieberstein nodded. “Yeah. He’s probably the guy to talk to. Mr. Drake has kind of... kept in touch since the whole thing with Lauren. Much more involved than he used to be. With me, anyway.”

“I don’t want you to tell him that this came from me.”

Bieberstein twirled on his heel and looked at Zachary. “Why not? You’re friends with him. He’s hired you before. He would be happy that you found this and turned it over to me. He’d be grateful to you.”

“I know. It isn’t because we don’t get along.” Though there had been a distinct chill from Gordon since the day Zachary had protected the twins from coming to harm. Zachary wasn’t quite sure why. Was it because Gordon thought he should be their protector? Did he feel inadequate or embarrassed that it had been Zachary who had seen the danger before anyone else? Zachary didn’t quite understand the change in attitude from someone who had always been warm and pleasant to him in the past. Too warm and pleasant, in fact. Something seemed to have reset Gordon's attitude. But that wasn't why Zachary didn't want Gordon to know of his involvement with the USB drive. "I have my own reasons for keeping this quiet. Do you think you could just tell him that some geek friend of yours came across this and realized that it was sensitive information about Chase Gold? But he's paranoid and doesn't want to be identified?"

Bieberstein smiled. "Are you paranoid?"

"Let's say I am. I don't really qualify as a geek, but... if you could sell that...?"

"Yeah, no problem. And for the record..."

"Yes?"

"You're a lot more of a geek than you think."

Zachary laughed. He might like his electronic toys, but he had never been smart like the kids at school. And never been obsessed or a collector of any of the popular TV or computer worlds. As a foster kid, his concerns had been elsewhere and he'd never had money or the ability to hang on to anything but his most priceless possession. He didn't think that he qualified as a geek. But he took it as a compliment from Bieberstein.

"Thanks. And I appreciate you coming right over here. I don't suppose your bosses at Chase Gold like you taking off and disappearing in the middle of the workday."

Bieberstein waved this concern aside. "I'm not an intern anymore. And they know I practically live there. HR is always telling me that I need to take care of my health and not put in too many hours."

"Better health, better wealth." Zachary remembered the tagline from when he had been investigating Drake Chase Gould.

Bieberstein nodded sagely.

"Still running on the treadmill?" Zachary asked him.

"Yeah. But I use the safety strap now."

“Good idea.”

Bieberstein sat down with his computer on his lap once more. He clicked a few times before taking the USB drive out of the port and slipping it into his pocket. He put his laptop back in his shoulder bag.

“Thanks for the information.”

“Yeah, you bet.”

“You want me to lock up or reset the alarm for you?”

Zachary shook his head. He wasn’t going to give the security codes to anyone, especially anyone involved in corporate espionage in any capacity. He knew corporate spy craft was a nasty business, and he didn’t want to get caught in the middle of it.

Except he already was.

* * *

Zachary didn't want to make the next call. He knew he had to for several reasons. But he was stuck. He couldn't see any other way out of it.

It took quite a few rings before the other party picked up.

"Zachary. I was hoping to hear from you."

"I wonder if you would come to meet with me."

"Well... that would be nice, I'm sure, but I'm sort of tied up today. We can just make it a phone call this time."

"I really need to see you face to face. This is too sensitive to deal with over the phone."

"I'm sure someone in your profession has already checked for bugs," he said dryly. "This line is secure."

"It needs to be face to face."

“I can’t just drop everything.” A definite note of irritation had crept into his voice. “I have had a very busy day and still have several meetings ahead of me.”

“Reschedule them.”

“Really, Zachary—”

“This is more important. Trust me.”

There was silence on the line while the other party considered this assertion. He sighed in exasperation. “This had better be good.”

“Get here as soon as you can.”

“Where?”

“Same place we saw each other last.”

Zachary hung up.

CHAPTER 46

Zachary didn't know how long it would take. He couldn't look up the amount of time it would take him to drive there, as he had with Bieberstein, since he wasn't sure of the starting point. But it would probably be an hour, more or less.

He was still feeling somewhat hungover from the anti-anxiety meds and painkillers. Zachary wasn't normally one for taking naps, but he felt like he needed one. He was tired enough that he could have closed his eyes and drifted off for half an hour or an hour and would probably feel much better when he woke up. But he couldn't sleep knowing that the front door was unlocked and unsecured.

Instead, he lay there, listening to every creak and groan of the house. Listening for a car to pull up in front of the house and for footsteps to walk up to the door. The turning of the doorknob, and then footsteps down the hall...

He was on edge, his whole body coiled for action even though there was nothing to do. It wasn't the same as the anxiety he had felt the night before, wondering whether he was going to end up paralyzed by a spinal cord injury. It wasn't the same as when he worried about Bridget or the twins. It was more raw. Vigilance. The anticipation of danger. Masked men had broken into the house once when he had left the door unlocked. It could happen again.

* * *

It was an hour before he heard a car pull up. He couldn't see it, but he heard the door slam shut and footsteps up to the house.

There was a knock at the door. Zachary had forgotten to tell him to let himself in. He shifted his position and contemplated getting up. Standing was not as painful as sitting; he could get up, answer the door, and just stay on his feet for the meeting.

Getting out of bed without sitting on the side was more like falling out of bed onto his hands and knees and then finding his way to his feet afterward. He made his way stiffly down the hall and to the front door.

The door opened just as he was getting there.

“Zachary? Are you there?” Walter looked around the door. Zachary stopped where he was, one hand on the wall to support himself.

“Come in. Sorry, I forgot to tell you to just let yourself in.”

“The door was open...”

“I know.”

Walter was frowning, studying him. “Is something wrong? Are you sick?”

Zachary didn’t bother to answer. “Come on into the living room.”

Walter obeyed, settling himself on the couch. Zachary remained on his feet. Not only was it better for his tailbone, but it gave him the advantage of being higher than Walter. A position of power. He could really use the edge since Walter had just about every other advantage over Zachary. Zachary leaned against a bookcase.

"You weren't honest with me about the break-in."

Walter looked surprised. "I wasn't honest with you? What are you talking about? I understand now that it was an inside job, but I didn't know that at the time."

"You weren't in on it?"

"Why would I be in on it? You found the stolen goods, so you know that I didn't get anything out of it. It was nothing to do with me."

"Then it was just bad luck?"

Walter blinked at him. The long, slow blink of a snake, focusing on an enemy. "What are you talking about?"

“I’m talking about the car.”

“What car? I’m afraid you’ve gotten yourself all mixed up over this. I don’t know what you mean.”

“The replica Habs station wagon.”

Walter’s eyebrows went up. “I’m not sure I know what you’re talking about,” he said politely.

“One of the waitresses said that she’s seen you fiddling with it, so there’s no point in pretending. A little car just the right size to hide a USB drive in.”

Walter shrugged. “Just because I may have touched it, that doesn’t mean that it is something I would remember. I’m sure you’ve seen things at restaurants or other people’s homes that you don’t remember again later.”

“If you weren’t involved in the theft, then I guess you must have been pretty shocked by it. Not only that there would be a smash and grab at your 'favorite' sports bar, but that it would happen when it did and that the car would be taken."

Walter said nothing, still sitting there looking at Zachary as if he had no idea what he was talking about.

"You never thought that your dead drop would get stolen."

"Dead drop." Walter's face remained blankly impassive. But Zachary could see his jaw clench and a tendon stand out on his neck.

"Everybody wondered why you were so interested in the bar and in the robbery. Why you were interested in finding out who had committed the robbery and recovering the merchandise. Everybody wondered why you even went to the bar in the first place. You were out of place. You weren't interested in any of the sports. You weren't attached to any of the teams. You just went there, had a drink or a snack, and left again."

"Everybody relaxes their own way. I enjoyed the ambiance of the place."

"You needed a place where you could exchange information. I don't know if you were the one leaving the information or the one picking it up. Or did it go both ways?"

"What information?"

"The information on Drake Chase Gould."

Walter stared at him. He gave up on pretending not to know what Zachary was talking about. "Where is it?"

"It's not here."

"It wasn't in the boxes." Walter's eyes scanned the room. Did he think that Zachary would hide it there?

"I think it's time to give up on recovering it. It was a long shot from the start. You must be looking at other ways of recompiling it or getting another copy."

"It can take months to put together a package like that. Replicating it..." Walter shook his head. "That's not as easy as it sounds. People lose trust. In a game like this, you have to have trust. Or the flow of information dries up."

"Is that how you see it? A game?"

"Call it what you like. The stakes are high. Higher than you could ever realize."

CHAPTER 47

You want to take Drake Chase Gould down."

Walter's shoulders lifted and fell. He rubbed the back of his neck. "Unless you work in the circles that I do, you don't know the impact that a company like that has nationally and internationally. How many pieces of the political puzzle and the outcomes of bills and sessions depend on what is happening in the financial world. We live in a capitalist society. Everything hinges on money."

"What would bringing Drake Chase Gould down accomplish for you? Are you saying it's still political? Nothing to do with lining your own pocket?"

Walter made a face. "I have all of the money I need. Some things are far more important to me. I am someone who makes things happen. I don't know if someone like you can understand that."

Zachary nodded slowly. He understood that he and Walter operated in two completely different worlds. Their paths had crossed with each other, but they didn't really inhabit the same realms. From the beginning of his life, Zachary had struggled simply for survival. He had enough money now that putting a roof over his head and food on the table was no longer a problem, but he still saw the world through that lens. And it was a world that Walter had never inhabited. He had been born with money, as much of it as he needed.

Zachary had glimpsed that world for a short time while married to Bridget. She hadn't been that wealthy herself, but she intended to be. She had wealthy and powerful friends, and she used them to improve her circumstances. She was well-spoken and beautiful; people liked her right from the start. Zachary wasn't sure why she had married him in the first place. She must have thought that she could mold him into what she wanted her husband to be. She had placed opportunities before him and encouraged him to talk to influential people and get involved in the political games, but that had never been for him. In his mind, he would always be fighting for survival.

That had been Zachary's first glimpse of Walter's world. He had seen more of it when Gordon had come into the picture. Not just to give Bridget everything she had ever dreamed of, but also showing Zachary the mercenary way he ran his business, how he used people as pawns, all while smiling and acting like a benevolent father. Daniel had said that Gordon was a psychopath and Zachary couldn't decide whether this was true or not. Gordon seemed like a nice guy, as did Walter, but were they just wolves in sheep's clothing? Men who had learned how to present themselves to others but who didn't really care about those around them?

Zachary was concerned with self-preservation, but he couldn't imagine not being concerned about the people around him. Bridget and Kenzie had both said it before, but in very different tones of voice. Zachary had to help people. He had to rescue them. He just didn't know how else to be.

"Do you even care?" Zachary mused, then realized that he'd said it out loud.

"Do I care about what?" Walter asked, shaking his head slightly.

"Do you care about anyone else? Do you care anything about what happens to the people around you? Or just about yourself?"

"I care very much for certain people in my life. And I want to make the world a better place for them. If I have influence, why shouldn't I use it?"

"And people who aren't in your little circle of friends and family, what about them? You don't care what happens to them?"

"I try to do the right thing," Walter said deliberately. "And I believe that if I do the right thing, aimed at helping those in my life, that the rest will fall into place. I can't be responsible for everybody. They will… take care of each other."

"When you sent two thugs here to get the stolen merchandise so that you could retrieve your USB drive, did you care what happened to me? How Kenzie would feel about having someone break into her house? How she would feel if I got hurt or killed in the process?"

Walter chuckled. "You hire professionals to do the job they were trained to do. And then you trust them to do it."

"So, no. You didn't care."

Walter motioned to Zachary. "You seem to have survived the incident. To be honest, I didn't think you would be here. I assumed the house would be empty during the day." He shook his head. "I guess I had in my mind that you had an office somewhere that you operated from. Not just... this."

Walter rolled his eyes. Arrogant. Lowering his opinion of Zachary on learning that he just lounged around all day in Walter's daughter's house. Not a true professional, just a hanger-on.

"I heard that you were here when it happened, but they said that they hadn't had any trouble taking care of you. I would never authorize the use of violence or killing someone to get them out of the way. There are always other choices. I have made my living in finding ways to leverage people. Finding ways to change the world one step at a time, to make it a better place for my wife and daughter."

There was no hint of an "s" at the end of daughter. No hint that he had also been thinking of Amanda as he had been working at changing the world.

Walter studied Zachary. "What happened? You don't look good. But then... you don't usually."

"The way they threw me down and restrained me may have caused some spinal cord damage. I'm supposed to be in bed."

"Well, at least sit down," Walter looked slightly alarmed. "I don't want you collapsing on me."

"Sitting is worse than standing."

"I never intended anything to happen to you. I gave you the case, didn't I? Why would I turn on you and try to hurt you? It was supposed to be a simple operation. In and out. Grab the boxes and get out. Faster than the original burglary. Things always go better when you use professionals." He raised an eyebrow, looking at Zachary. "Almost always."

Zachary wasn't sure whether he was referring to the thugs who had injured him or the fact that Zachary hadn't produced the hoped-for results.

"And Kenzie? You didn't think of how she would feel having her house broken into? Scared? Violated? You didn't care about any of that?"

"It was more important to get that information back. More important than some fleeting emotions." Walter held up his hand to stop Zachary from interjecting. "I know my daughter.

She may react emotionally to begin with, but she gets over it quickly. She will find a way to move on."

"What about when she knows it was you?"

Walter gazed at Zachary. He pressed his fingertips together in a steeple shape. "I was not planning on her finding out that it had anything to do with me."

He didn't ask Zachary not to tell her. He was used to making things happen, so maybe he already had a plan in mind to keep Kenzie from finding out. And now that Zachary knew... maybe Walter had a new plan for him too.

"I don't want Kenzie to find out," Zachary told him. "I want her to be happy. To have a relationship with you that isn't so... negative. She deserves to have good family relationships."

"Yes. She does."

"Do you know anything about Gordon Drake, the man who owns Drake Chase Gould?"

“Of course. I made it my business to know about him.”

“I mean personally. Do you know what kind of a person he is? Or about his family commitments?”

Walter shook his head. “Why would I? It isn’t his family life that concerns me.”

“He’s a family man. Has a wife with Huntington’s disease and newborn twin girls. Premature, so they have health issues. And also the Huntington’s gene.”

Something flickered in Walter’s eyes. “That’s too bad. That’s a tough situation.”

“Tough. I don’t think you know how tough it is to have a wife who is dying.”

“No?” Walter looked at him. “That’s so different from having a daughter who is dying?”

Zachary considered. “I don’t know. Maybe it isn’t. How would you have felt about someone who came gunning for your business while Amanda was sick?”

CHAPTER 48

This isn't personal. I told you that. Drake Chase Gould is not good for business in Vermont. Having a big investment banking firm here—it's not what we do. He thinks that he can just pay off anyone in the state. Anything he wants, he can just throw money at it, and it will go away. Take it to the big city. Why isn't he operating on Wall Street like everyone else? Vermont is community minded. Small towns, small businesses, families."

"Maybe because he has a wife and children to take care of. Maybe he doesn't want them in New York and doesn't want to be away from them while he operates from there."

"He needs to take care of his own. That's not my responsibility."

"His wife is my ex," Zachary told Walter. "She <u>is</u> family."

Walter rubbed his brow line, scowling. "Why would she be with someone like him after being with you? You and Gordon Drake are nothing alike."

“I know,” Zachary agreed. He braced himself against the wall, his legs getting tired and his tailbone throbbing. Were his legs weak just because of the pain in his tailbone? Or was it the neurological damage that Kenzie and the doctor at the hospital had feared?

“You’re supposed to be lying down,” Walter told him.

“Yeah.”

“Where do you want to lie down? The couch? The bed?”

“Bed.” Zachary already knew how uncomfortable sleeping on the couch was. And it would be that much worse with his injured tailbone.

Walter got up and took Zachary by the arm. He held him firmly and guided him down the hallway back to the bedroom. He helped Zachary to get over to the bed, and Zachary tried to climb in without aggravating his tailbone, back, or any other part of his body that was bruised or sore, which was basically impossible.

"This is from the robbery?" Walter demanded. "The guys who stole the mementos from you?"

"Yeah. They didn't give you any details?" Zachary thought it was best not to indicate that his most painful injury was his tailbone. That would make it sound like a joke.

Anything could have happened in the robbery that Walter had set up, knowing that he was sending professional criminals to his daughter's house, where they could run into either Zachary or Kenzie. He didn't know their schedules or anything about them. Those goons could have pulled knives or guns when they encountered Zachary in the house. If they hadn't been wearing masks, they would have been faced with the dilemma of whether to kill Zachary in case he could identify them. They could be murderers, rapists, terrorists. Walter had known they were bad news, and he'd sent them into his daughter's house.

"I didn't ask for details," Walter admitted. "I got the report that you had been here at the house but that they had dealt with you. I didn't think I needed to know any more than that."

"They invaded my house. They tackled me, handcuffed me, left me that way. I could have been knocked over the head and ended up with a fractured skull. Had my throat slit. I could have had a heart attack. You didn't care?"

"I didn't say I didn't care. I said I didn't want details."

Zachary heard the garage door motor. Walter stood there looking at him. It was early for Kenzie to be getting home. Walter had probably thought that she was at work and had been counting on the fact that she would be gone until the early evening. He didn't know that she had just been out running errands.

They listened to the kitchen door opening and Kenzie hanging up her winter gear and then coming down the hall. She didn't call out, but looked around the doorway first to see if Zachary was asleep. She saw her father standing there and her jaw dropped open. No words came out.

"Hi, sweetie," Walter greeted, stepping toward her and giving her a hug and a kiss on the cheek. "I'm so glad you're home. I didn't know how long you would be out."

"Just a couple of hours," Kenzie said, her voice heavy with suspicion. "Just running some errands. Picking up a few things for Zachary."

Walter motioned to the bed. "I was just helping Zachary to get settled again. Came over to discuss the case and any progress he had made."

Kenzie looked at him, eyes narrowed. "I thought the case was finished. Zachary identified who stole the memorabilia and recovered the stolen property. That's the end of it, isn't it? It isn't his fault that they were stolen again from here, and I don't want him wasting his time chasing after them again. Especially not while he's still recovering. I'd say the case is done and you owe him the rest of the agreed-upon price, wouldn't you say?"

Walter nodded. "Yes. I just wanted to get a few more details from Zachary. I will send him the money to wrap this up right away." He smiled at her. "I'm not trying to rip him off."

"No renegotiating. You just give him what you said you would, and no more investigating. The case is done."

"Yes, MacKenzie," Walter agreed in a smooth, soothing voice. "I'm not here to ask Zachary to do anything else. In fact," he turned and met Zachary's eyes. "I want to make sure he doesn't try to pursue any more action in this case. Not after being injured. Leave the police to clean up any loose ends. I don't think there is any point in trying to trace the stolen articles any farther. It isn't like they were that valuable. I was just hoping to do something for a friend."

Kenzie nodded. "Good." She looked past him to Zachary. "And you're not going to pursue it any further on your own, are you?

This case has already been enough of a pain. Whoever has those things now, let them keep them."

"It's too bad we weren't able to return them to the McNichols," Zachary said slowly, staring at Walter. "They've really had some bad luck with all of this. The memorabilia wasn't valuable enough to claim it on their insurance. The police detective thinks that they were involved. Glen had a heart attack and is convalescing. I hope they get a lot of donations to replace what they lost and success with their fundraising for anything else. They <u>deserve</u> that."

Walter nodded. "Yes, of course. They are good friends. I wouldn't want any lasting harm to come to them because of this."

"I hope things turn out for them too," Kenzie agreed. "It's been quite a run of bad luck."

Zachary rested his head and closed his eyes. Maybe now he would be able to sleep. It had been quite the afternoon. But he thought that, even with being on painkillers, he had done a good job of sorting things out to correct as much of the damage as he could. Drake Chase Gould had back the data that had been stolen, so it couldn't be used against them. He and Walter agreed that nothing more would be done to harm any of the people involved. And hopefully, Walter would make the McNichols whole, donating memorabilia or cash back to them. It would be like none of it had ever happened.

"You should invite your dad for supper," he suggested to Kenzie. "You didn't have any plans, did you? We can just order something in."

"I don't know if I want to have a dinner party when you're not able to participate," Kenzie pointed out. Being forced to make small talk over dinner with her father without Zachary being there to act as a buffer was probably not what she would have planned if they had talked about it ahead of time.

"You haven't visited with your dad for a long time. You don't have anything else you have to do, do you, Walter?"

Of course Walter had said that he had the rest of the day booked up, all kinds of things to get done. But he had made the time to come see Zachary. And he said that he wanted the opportunity to connect with his daughter. They were both going to have to make some adjustments if they wanted to have a good relationship. Kenzie had been doing couples therapy with Zachary, so she should have some good tools in her communications toolkit for finding common ground and being cordial to her father. So that maybe it could develop into something more in the future.

"No, of course I can make time," Walter said. "It doesn't have to be anything fancy. I can drive to the sandwich shop and pick something up, if you like. Do you still like tuna salad?"

Kenzie snorted. "You know I don't like tuna!"

Walter gave a smile, enjoying her reaction. He had obviously intended to provoke her.

“How about you, Zachary? Sandwich shop? Or do you want something hot?”

“You and Kenzie could go out to a restaurant if you wanted to. I’m not really hungry.”

“No. I’m not leaving you alone the rest of the night,” Kenzie interjected. “Here. Let me help you get more comfortable, and then we can decide what we’re ordering.”

CHAPTER 49

Kenzie had spent longer having dinner and visiting with Walter than Zachary had expected. Zachary had spent most of the time sleeping, his body exhausted by the combination of pain, medications, and the visits with Walter and Bieberstein. He didn't talk much to Kenzie after Walter left. She came in and cuddled with him as best she could with his injury, rubbed his sore muscles for a while, and both of them drifted off to sleep. So it wasn't until the following day that they really talked about how her evening with Walter had gone.

"It actually wasn't a bad visit," Kenzie said, smiling and lifting her eyebrows to express her surprise over the fact. "Usually, when I see him, he wants something. Or even if it is just for a visit, it's on his own terms. He has his own agenda and plan, like it's a business lunch. But last night, there was no agenda. He was just here. And he didn't have a bunch of other meetings to run off to like usual. It was like... being at home again."

Zachary nodded. He was sitting at the table, which made him feel more human and less of an invalid. He could get reasonably comfortable with one of the coccyx-cradling pillows that Kenzie had purchased for him. His tailbone was still sore, but he could sit up for a while. He also found that his back was a lot sorer than he had expected it to be. Kenzie had talked about the possibility of a compression injury to his spine, and he felt like everything had been bruised or pulled. The muscles in his back felt like he had overdone it lifting weights at the gym.

Or what he assumed it would feel like if he had overdone it at the gym, since he wasn't actually one for lifting weights.

He unwrapped his granola bar slowly, trying to minimize the amount of crinkling noise the wrapper made, which he found extra irritating all of a sudden. "I'm glad you had a good visit with him. It's been a long time, hasn't it?"

Kenzie looked thoughtful. "Yeah. I don't know if we've really had a good sit down and just talked about life, what we're doing, and our interests since Amanda died. We've talked, sure, on the phone and the occasional face-to-face, usually at some fundraising event that Mother has roped us both into. You can't actually talk at something like that. Not like last night."

"What did you talk about?"

She shrugged and spread marmalade on her toast. "Just... stuff. Movies, weather, holidays, work. Anything and everything. I've never really listened to him talk about his lobbying. I kind of shut that off, decided that he was dishonest and that I didn't want to hear anything about it. Especially back then, when he was lobbying so much for changes in the transplant system. I was really angry with him for what happened to Amanda."

"But that was a long time ago now."

She nodded. "Sometimes it seems like it was just yesterday. But that was before I even decided to go into medicine. I'd done some college, but then I just drifted. Mom told me that I would figure out what I wanted to do sooner or later, but I wasn't passionate about anything. She had all of her causes and taking care of Amanda, and I just messed around, wasting my time. I wish I had decided to go into medicine earlier, but..." She shrugged. "I guess she was right. I just needed time to figure out what I wanted out of life."

"And you've changed your mind about Walter's lobbying?" Zachary asked, circling back to what she had said.

"I don't know. Like I said, I didn't really give him a chance before. You know, when we were little, I always knew that he was a white hat. One of the good guys. Lobbying for reforms that would benefit society. Not one of the lobbyists who hire themselves out to the big gun corporations and try to pave the way for them to make more money or a bigger piece of the pie. Then I kind of changed my mind. Not a black hat, maybe, but it was a lot darker gray than they had told me as a kid."

"Is anyone really all white hat or black hat?"

"No, I guess not. But I enjoyed hearing him talk last night about what he is doing to help people. Some of the initiatives he is working on sound really worthwhile."

"And did you tell him all about your work with the medical examiner?"

Kenzie grinned. She took a big bite of her toast and chewed it while she considered her answer. "He's not as squeamish as I thought he would be. I guess he's gotten used to the fact that I work with dead bodies. Braced himself for it. I wouldn't discuss the state of the bodies I see or the results of the tests run on tissue and fluid sample over dinner with him like I can with you, but he held up pretty well."

Zachary chuckled. If Walter talked too much about his lobbying or about a cause where Kenzie wasn't on the same side as he was, Kenzie could easily change the subject to the details of her own work. Then they could choose a less controversial topic, like movies or the weather, that they could both agree on.

"I guess maybe he isn't quite the villain I thought he was," Kenzie admitted. "I may have judged him too harshly. Or... maybe he is just mellowing more with age. People do tend to get a little less... intense over time. He hasn't let go of his ideals, but... maybe it was just last night. He just seemed more open. Less opinionated or zealous. Something like that."

Zachary thought back to Walter's comments about Drake Chase Gould. He hadn't seemed very mellow when he talked about the danger that a corporate giant like Chase Gold could be to a small state like Vermont. Maybe he was just learning to hold back his opinions when talking to his daughter. Set aside the agenda for the night and just enjoy being with her for once.

"I'm glad you had a nice time with him."

"Me too."

* * *

It was Sunday, so probably not the best day to call Blair Bieberstein back to see whether he'd been able to get anywhere on his analysis of the server logs and tracking back who had leaked the information on the USB drive. But Zachary knew from past experience that the employees at Chase Gold worked long hours, both weekdays and weekends. He decided to give it a try anyway. Kenzie was in her office catching up on some personal emails. Maybe emailing Lisa, her mother, about the visit with Walter.

Zachary tapped the number on his phone. He was expecting to have to wait a number of rings before Bieberstein got around to answering his phone. He would be distracted by whatever job he was working on. He might even completely ignore his phone and Zachary would have to leave a message or call back later. But he'd only heard one ring before Bieberstein picked it up.

“Goldman!” he greeted.

Zachary wasn't used to being addressed that way, but shrugged it off. “Hey. I was just wondering whether you had been able to get anywhere on the data on the USB drive. I know these things probably take a lot more time and analysis, but…"

"Right, right. The USB drive." Bieberstein sounded even more hyper than usual, if that was possible. Maybe he'd just polished off a couple of energy drinks. Caffeine was definitely one of his vices. Zachary still wasn't sure if he went for the harder stuff. They'd discussed meth at one point, but Bieberstein hadn't admitted to being a user himself. "Did some analysis on the servers…" He went off into a long, technical spiel about what he had done to backtrack where the data had come from and who'd had access to it over the previous few weeks. Zachary was quickly lost in the jargon.

"So, where did that get you?" he interrupted when he heard Bieberstein stop for breath and maybe another gulp of his high-octane drink. "Did that get you any closer to figuring out who it was that stole or leaked the information?"

"I'm telling you, man," Bieberstein assured him.

"Okay..."

Bieberstein went through some more of the procedures he had gone through. "But then I got a call from Mr. Drake. He wanted to know what was going on, why I was into the security files. So I explained to him about the leak. I didn't tell him where I got the USB drive," he assured Zachary. "Don't worry. I remembered not to mention your name, just my geeky friend who didn't want to be brought into anything."

"What did Gordon say about it?"

"He's a good guy, Mr. Drake. You remember that he helped me out when I got out of the hospital. Made sure that I was somewhere safe until all of that stuff blew over."

"Yes. I remember. He seems like a good guy." Zachary didn't want to say more than that. Whether Gordon was really a good guy, deep down, or just a psychopath who put on a good show of caring for people. Zachary didn't know and didn't want to speculate.

"Anyway. He pulled me off of it. Told me to get back to my regular work, that he would put the cybersecurity guys on it. We've got a contract with this high-priced IT team. Very good at what they do. I probably should have talked to them in the beginning anyway, rather than diving into it myself. But I thought I would be able to identify who it was that had copied the files initially..."

"You didn't find out who it was?"

"No."

Zachary rolled his eyes. Bieberstein could just have said that to begin with, instead of going through the long narrative of what he had done to try to track the culprits down.

"Will you find out what these cybersecurity guys discover? Will Gordon let you know who it was?"

"No. Not my area, so I highly doubt it. Mr. Drake likes people to stay in their own lane. Security isn't my forte, so he probably won't get back to me on any of it. I'm good at it, mind you.

Whoever stole those files did a really good job hiding their footprints. But I get why he wants me to stick to my job. I already bounce between departments and different projects, depending on where my expertise is needed. He has to put some kind of limits on where I am and what I'm doing."

It sounded more like that was what Bieberstein had been told than that he agreed with it.

Zachary sighed. So his one avenue of exploration into Drake Chase Gould had been closed off. He could call Gordon and ask him about what they found out, but since it was really none of Zachary's business and Gordon's attitude toward him had cooled lately, he figured the chances Gordon would tell him anything about it were pretty slim.

CHAPTER 50

Zachary was taking a walk around the block when Janice called. He was getting a bit of cabin fever, mainly staying indoors, as it was still too painful to go for a drive in the car, even with one of the special pillows. The bumps and potholes were just too much for him. Kenzie said that he should be starting to feel better before too long and, in the meantime, if he couldn't drive, he could at least go for a walk. Get out, get some fresh air and sunshine, and he would feel a lot better than if he just stayed home staring at the computer screen all day. Just don't slip on the ice and fall on his coccyx.

It was good advice, except that Zachary was now paranoid about slipping on a stray patch of ice and landing again on his broken tailbone. Who knew if it would ever heal properly if he did that. Most of the neighbors kept their sidewalks well-shoveled, so there really wasn't anything to worry about. Still, one or two places had not been properly shoveled throughout the winter and were covered in ice and packed-down snow.

They were shiny and slick in the sunlight. Zachary strayed off the sidewalk and into front yards to avoid the super-slick surfaces.

His phone ringing made him jump, which made him panic about slipping and falling. But in a second or two, he had regained his equilibrium and worked his phone out of his pocket, taking off his glove to answer it.

“Goldman Investigations.”

“It’s Janice McNichol, Zachary.”

“Oh!” Zachary smiled. It felt like a long time since he’d talked to her. Ages ago.

“You know, I never did thank you for the work that you did on our burglary—on the theft of the memorabilia from our bar. I know that I wasn’t the one who hired you and I was kind of resistant at first, but I’m glad that Mr. Kirsch was able to get you on the case. I feel a lot better knowing that it wasn’t just a random burglary. That probably doesn’t make sense because you would think I would be more worried about it being random than planned… but I'm not. I feel a lot better knowing that it was someone who had the inside track and that she isn't here anymore. I don't have to worry about it happening again."

"You can have background checks run on people before you hire them. Or in the probationary period after you hire them. If you want to be more sure of this not happening again."

"But Jenn wasn't a new hire. She'd been there for a few years. It was that new boyfriend of hers. And I don't think we can get background checks run on every new boyfriend or girlfriend that our employees hook up with. Jenn passed all of the pre-screening that we did. I don't think you can stop people from meeting someone else who influences them three years later."

"No," Zachary admitted. "You're right about that. You couldn't have known what would happen."

"Yeah. And I don't think the odds are very high of it ever happening again. And Glen is getting some cameras installed inside and outside the bar so that people know they're being watched. If they're being watched, I don't think they'd do anything like that."

"It's a good deterrent. Just make sure it's not the only thing you are relying on. You know how they were able to get in to go through the charade of a smash and grab, so you need to fortify the windows and doors a little better. And be aware of what's going on, anything that seems out of place. I don't know if there was ever any sign that Jennifer was having financial issues or any problems with her boyfriend, or if everything just seemed perfectly normal up until the end..."

"Well..." Janice drew the word out. "Hard to put your finger on anything. But she had changed. She wasn't as happy. Got in late for her shift some days, which she had never done before. But nothing that would have predicted what she was going to do."

"No. But maybe if you knew something was wrong, you might have talked to her, and she might have done or said something to clue you in that everything wasn't right with her. Or not;

there's no point in what-ifs. You did the best you could, and now you know a few more things you can do to improve security some more. Maybe you prevent a bigger theft in the future."

"That's right!" Janice agreed, sounding happy and relaxed about it. Zachary was glad. He hadn't wanted to make her feel guilty for not knowing what Jennifer had been about to do before she did it. No one could predict the future. "And we might have more that we need to protect in the future."

"Oh? Your fundraising has gone well?"

"It's been amazing. You wouldn't believe it. We got a couple of large donations from anonymous donors. Corporate donations, I would guess, because they're too big for patrons. And we've had a lot of memorabilia donated as well. We published a list of what we had lost on our social media networks. Some of the things that have been donated to replace them are almost identical to the originals. It's amazing."

“That’s great.” Zachary chuckled to himself, glad to hear that Walter had gone ahead with helping Barnburners get back to where they had been before the robbery. Some of that “almost identical” memorabilia were probably the exact same items as had been stolen from them in the first place. “How about that little die-cast Habs car? Did you get one of those?”

“No. Not yet, at least. They were a limited run. Those things always are because it increases their value. I’d love to get another one, but I don’t know if we’ll be able to find one. Maybe some time.”

Zachary frowned and wondered what Walter had done with the Habs car. Kept it as a trophy? As a reminder of what he had done to get back into his daughter’s good graces? Maybe he kept trophies of all of his wins. Or perhaps it had attracted the eye of one of the goons and he had pocketed it before giving the rest of the merchandise to Walter.

Whatever had happened to it, the bar wouldn’t miss that one little item. They had been more than compensated for their loss. Though Walter couldn't do much to make up for the cloud of suspicion they had been under or for Glen's heart attack.

"How is Glen doing? Is he still in the hospital?"

"No, they don't keep them for very long. Snake out the pipes and send them home. He's doing pretty good, to tell the truth. Better than I thought he would be. The doctors say it's lucky he found out now about his arteries before they were totally blocked. He's young enough that if he takes care of himself—stops eating fried food and staying up late at the bar, maybe gets out for a walk now and then—that he can probably live a long and happy life. With some young guys, the first time anyone knows they have heart disease is when they have a massive coronary and drop dead."

"Well, good thing that didn't happen to him."

"I guess if you're going to have a heart attack, a police station is a good place to do it. Full of trained first responders. One of those AEDs right there. If he'd been at the bar late at night or out on the highway... he could be dead now."

CHAPTER 51

Lindsey dropped Mason and Alisha at the house, stopping for a moment on the doorstep to thank Zachary and Kenzie.

"I appreciate you taking them to see him. I didn't want to visit Tyrrell myself, but what else was I going to do, sit in the lobby while they visited with him in a family visit room? That would be pretty awkward. And driving all the way out there just to sit and wait for the kids... this is so much nicer."

"We were going to see him anyway," Zachary said with a shrug. "I knew he'd like to see the kids, so I figured they might as well come along if it worked for you."

She nodded. "It's really nice of you. I know that it's not always easy to deal with kids who aren't your own, especially when they are..." She looked significantly at Mason and made a face, not putting it into words in case Mason overheard her.

"I get to be the uncle who spoils them," Zachary said. "You're the one who gets to deal with them afterward."

"Well, don't give them too much sugar!" She smiled again in appreciation. "Goodbye, guys. You be good for your Uncle Zachary, you hear me?"

"We will, Mom," Alisha assured her.

Mason, of course, was distracted and didn't answer. He was looking closely at the burglar alarm panel.

"I bet I could figure out your password," he told Zachary.

"Mason," Lindsey said in a firm mom voice.

He glanced over at her but decided she wasn't serious enough for him to pay attention to her yet. "Do you think I could?" he persisted. "I can see which buttons you push most often. It would be like solving a code."

"Mason, your mom is talking to you," Zachary pointed out.

Mason heaved a sigh and looked at her. “What?” he demanded, as if she were the child and was getting on his nerves with her constant questions.

“You be good for Uncle Zachary and Auntie Kenzie.”

“I will!” Mason gave another exasperated sigh. “I was just talking to him. You were interrupting.”

Lindsey shook her head at Zachary and stepped back. “Have a nice visit. I’ll see you guys in a few hours.”

Both of the children said goodbye.

“We’re going in Zachary’s car,” Kenzie told them after Lindsey left. “He’ll go get it warmed up, and you come with me and tell me what you want to bring for a snack.”

She led them into the kitchen to look into the cupboard that Kenzie kept stocked with snacks that Zachary liked, to encourage him to consume more calories and get his weight back up to normal. Zachary went out to his car, started the heater, and scraped frost off the windows. By the time they got out to the car with their snacks in hand, the inside was comfortable.

They were good for the trip out to the detox center, playing on their phones or electronic games and munching on snacks. Zachary enjoyed the highway drive and the fact that he could sit comfortably in the car again, even without the special cushions. Though he was using one since they would be in the car for longer than he was used to, and he didn't want to take the chance that the weight on his tailbone would cause the injury to flare up again, even if it were only temporarily.

He liked highway driving, though with Kenzie and the kids in the car, he had to watch the speedometer and not go too much over the speed limit. Any time he caught the turning of Kenzie's head to look at the gauge, he lifted his foot off the gas to slow it down.

Zachary felt like it had been a year since he had seen Tyrrell. It wasn't as bad as when he had been missing, of course. Finding him while he was out on a drunken binge had been such a huge relief when Tyrrell had been missing for weeks and Zachary hadn't even known for sure whether he was alive.

This time, he knew he wouldn't be facing a sloppy hug and Tyrrell's sorrowful ramblings about what an awful father he was to his kids and that he could never go back to them again. Zachary wouldn't have to face his father. This time, Tyrrell would be clean and sober, and he would have a better outlook on his future. Plans for how to get back on his feet again and be a part of the children's lives.

After checking in at the reception desk, a young man in scrubs met their little group and escorted them around to a family visit room. There was comfortable, worn furniture, some toys and books on shelves, a checkers/chess game set, and a few other things to help keep families occupied during visits.

They waited there, Mason bouncing on the couch and chairs to test them out and rifling through the shelves to see if he could find anything interesting. Knowing how attached he was to his electronic games, Zachary didn't expect him to find anything there that would keep his interest for long. Would things have been better or worse for Zachary if there had been handheld games around when he was a kid battling with ADHD? Being forced to play outside was a common strategy foster parents used. It was probably better to get hyperactive kids out in the fresh air doing physical activities than letting them hyperfocus on electronic games.

Then Tyrrell arrived. Mason squealed and launched himself at Tyrrell, giving him a tight hug and immediately launching into a long-winded explanation of everything he had done since he last saw Tyrrell. Tyrrell reached for Alisha to pull her into a hug as well, kissing her on top of the head and whispering something in her ear that made her smile.

Zachary and Kenzie waited until the kids had taken a little time to get reacquainted with Tyrrell and had settled down into their chosen seats before also greeting Tyrrell and giving him hugs and congratulations for being able to stick with the program for six weeks.

He looked good. Happy and clean and strong. The Tyrrell that Zachary had been used to seeing before he had fallen off the wagon. But this time, Zachary knew that it was partly an illusion. Yes, Tyrrell was getting better, but he wasn't "cured." He hadn't left alcoholism behind years ago, as Zachary had first assumed when Tyrrell had told him he'd had problems with alcohol. It was still very present in his life and something the rest of them would always have to be mindful of.

"How's it going, bro?" Tyrrell asked happily, thumping Zachary on the back as they hugged. "You're looking a lot better than the last time I saw you."

A testament to Kenzie's efforts to get him into better physical shape, eating better, getting a little exercise, and trying to get into a routine that would allow him to get more sleep at night, though that one seemed to be an elusive goal.

"You are, too," Zachary told him.

"Hell, I hope so!" Tyrrell laughed. "Considering the shape I was in before I got here!"

"Daddy!" Alisha exclaimed, horrified. "You swore!"

Tyrrell chuckled. "I'll put a quarter in your mother's swear jar the next time I'm there," he promised. Which wasn't much of a promise, considering that he would probably never be in Lindsey's house again. Maybe to step in the door while he waited for the kids to get ready, but more likely, he'd wait in the car while she got them dressed and packed and then sent them out.

Tyrrell gave Kenzie a quick hug and kiss on the cheek after releasing Zachary. "And thank you for getting me into this program," he told her. He looked like he would say something more but then thought better of it. Maybe he'd realized that Kenzie hadn't just used her medical connections to get him into the program, but had paid for his stay as well. If he acknowledged that he knew she had spent money for him to get into the program, it would mean that he was accountable to her if he ever fell off the wagon again. And, of course, he would probably fall off of the wagon again. Sobriety was not a journey in a straight line.

They sat down and asked Tyrrell all about the program and his progress and plans for the future. He'd had plenty of therapy and career counseling. The facility was associated with several outpatient placement programs, so maybe they would be able to find him a job when he was ready to venture into the world again. Somewhere like K&L Construction, where he'd been given a chance despite their knowing that he was a recovering alcoholic? Or would they help him find a career placement that was more suited to him? Zachary hadn't thought that casual labor and construction were a good fit for Tyrrell. But of course, he took what he could get. Someone with his history didn't get a lot of opportunities.

Mason was playing with a car, getting louder and louder with the engine noises he was making with his mouth. Tyrrell tried to quiet him a couple of times, and they all rolled their eyes at each other, knowing that he wouldn't quiet down for long, but would soon be back to the same volume as he had been.

Zachary looked over at Mason, watching him for a minute. He had been wrong about Mason choosing his electronic games over something more physical. He must have found a toy car that he liked on the shelves of toys in the room.

He was looking at the car in Mason's hand for a minute before he realized that it was not one he had found on the shelves of the visitor's room. It was a little die-cast station wagon with the red horseshoe shape of the Montreal Canadiens logo on the side.

Kenzie had been saying something to Tyrrell about the different therapies offered in the program but stopped speaking, looking at Zachary questioningly.

“You okay?” she asked tentatively.

Zachary stared at the car in Mason’s hand, trying to think of the right response to the question.

“Zachary?”

“Where did you get that car, Mason?” Zachary asked.

Mason looked at him, mouth open to answer, and then closed it abruptly. He tried to shove the car back into his coat pocket. “From a friend,” he mumbled.

“Mason, come over here.”

Mason reluctantly approached his uncle. Zachary put his hands on Mason’s shoulders, looking him in the eye. “That looks like the car that you were playing with at my house.”

“It’s Auntie Kenzie’s house,” Mason pointed out.

"Yes, it's Auntie Kenzie's house. Isn't this the car that I told you was not yours? That you were supposed to put back in the boxes with the rest of those things?"

Mason's eyes were wide. He looked around the room guiltily, searching for an acceptable answer. Tyrrell's face was red, but he didn't interrupt to reprimand Mason.

"You took it with you instead of putting it back in the boxes, didn't you?" Zachary prompted.

"No. It's like that one, but this one is from a friend." Mason displayed the car. "The one that was at Auntie Kenzie's house didn't have this on it," he told Zachary, pointing to a long scratch along the side.

"Can I look at it for a minute?" Zachary asked.

Mason handed it over reluctantly. "It isn't yours," he insisted.

Zachary looked the car over, then tried opening the side doors and the back door where he knew the USB drive must have been hidden.

The side doors opened out, as Mason had been trying to show him at the time.

But the back door did not. There was no way anyone could have wedged a USB drive into the car.

CHAPTER 52

Zachary was watching the TV casually while typing a message to Rhys. Not paying a lot of attention to the TV, but watching it in the breaks where he waited for Rhys to message him back. Rhys hadn't had a lot to say to Zachary since their argument. Zachary hoped that enough time had passed for Rhys to let go of whatever anger and resentment he had and be on the way back to being friends again.

Relationships were a tricky thing. Especially when they involved teenagers, with all of their volatility.

He looked up at the TV screen when the next news story came up. In surprise, Zachary looked at the man on the screen and called out to Kenzie.

"Hey, your dad is on TV."

"What?" Kenzie was down the hall. Zachary hadn't been paying any attention to whether she had been doing work in her office, cleaning the bathroom, or doing something else. He'd been focused on his own thing. "Walter's on TV?"

She walked into the living room and stood slightly to the side, so she wasn't obstructing Zachary's view line, and looked at the screen. To begin with, it was just a still photograph of Walter with a few words about his work on the bottom of the screen and the newsreader announcing the new story about a bill being passed. Then there was a video of Walter talking about the reasons for the bill being passed and the benefits that it would have to the people of Vermont.

"Turn it up."

Zachary thumbed the remote, turning the volume up for Kenzie. Then there was a video of Walter shaking hands with another man. The two of them smiled and posed for the camera, arms around each other's shoulders.

The other man was Gordon Drake.

Zachary stared at the screen, jaw dropping. He looked at Kenzie and then back at the screen in disbelief. “That’s Gordon.”

“Oh, yeah,” Kenzie nodded. She had only seen Gordon in person once or twice. “I didn’t know that they knew each other, did you?”

Zachary remembered his confrontation with Walter after the theft of the memorabilia from the house. Walter railing about how bad Drake Chase Gould was for Vermont. The dangers of having such a huge corporate entity making decisions that affected everyone because of their impact on the local economy. Walter had made it clear that Drake Chase Gould was an evil Vermont had to be rid of.

And now he and Gordon Drake were standing arm in arm as it was announced that the bill Chase Gold had sponsored had gone through the senate.

Zachary tried to reconcile the two opposing pictures.

His first thought was that Walter had used the private data from Chase Gold to blackmail or pressure Gordon into sponsoring the bill. That was why he had been gathering information. Not to take Chase Gold down or to take them over, but to be able to pressure and manipulate them into sponsoring the initiative he was lobbying for.

Walter had always seen himself as a white hat, Kenzie had told Zachary. But that didn't mean that he couldn't use a corporate sponsor to push through a law that he saw as beneficial.

But Walter had never seen that data that had been left for him at the bar. Zachary had found the USB drive and returned it to Chase Gold before it had reached its intended destination. Walter had done everything he could to get it back, including hiring Zachary and then arranging to steal the recovered goods back from him. But he hadn't been successful. He hadn't ever laid eyes on those files.

That didn't mean that he couldn't get it from somewhere else. Maybe the person who had leaked it had made an extra copy of the data for safekeeping. Or Walter had gotten more data from another source. Walter could still have the information Zachary thought he had protected.

Looking at Gordon's and Walter's smiling faces and their arms around each other, Zachary had a sick feeling in his stomach.

What if the whole thing had been a setup, from start to finish? What if there had never been any actual corporate espionage? What if it had all been a sham? Walter got one of the thugs to drop the USB drive in Kenzie's office when they stole the boxes of recovered memorabilia. Zachary found it, reviewed the contents, and discovered what appeared to be private information about Chase Gold.

Why hadn't the drive been password protected?

What were the chances that the stolen data would just happen to be about a company that Zachary had been involved with before and had contacts at?

Had Zachary unmasked Walter? Or had Walter set up an

elaborate scheme that had placed Zachary in a place of apparent power over him, establishing this secret between them that bonded them together. Something that they both kept from Kenzie.

It was that secret and the injury that had sidelined Zachary that had paved the way for Kenzie and Walter to spend a pleasant dinner and evening together, beginning to heal the rift that had been between them ever since Amanda's death.

Zachary had always been amazed at chess players and how the masters could see so many moves ahead and determined the outcome of the game before it had been played out. Was that what Walter had done? Arranged the chessboard so that there was only one possible outcome of the game?

"We should have Walter over for dinner again sometime," Kenzie said, still watching her father's image on the screen. "This time, with you back on your feet again, you can join in."

Zachary nodded slowly. "Yeah," he agreed. "You should see your dad again."

Did you enjoy this book? Reviews and recommendations are vital to making a book successful.

Please leave a review at your favorite book store or review site and share it with your friends.

ABOUT THE AUTHOR

Award-winning and USA Today bestselling author P.D. (Pamela) Workman writes riveting mystery/suspense and young adult books dealing with mental illness, addiction, abuse, and other real-life issues. For as long as she can remember, the blank page has held an incredible allure and from a very young age she was trying to write her own books.

Workman wrote her first complete novel at the age of twelve and continued to write as a hobby for many years. She started publishing in 2013. She has won several literary awards from Library Services for Youth in Custody for her young adult fiction. She currently has over 80 published titles and can be found at pdworkman.com.

Born and raised in Alberta, Workman has been married for over 25 years and has one son.

* * *

Please visit P.D. Workman at pdworkman.com to see what else

she is working on, to join her mailing list, and to link to her social networks.

* * *

If you enjoyed this book, please take the time to recommend it to other purchasers with a review or star rating and share it with your friends!

www.ingramcontent.com/pod-product-compliance
Lightning Source LLC
Chambersburg PA
CBHW081141300726
48982CB00006B/1027

* 9 7 8 1 7 7 4 6 8 2 5 9 3 *